RHAPSODY

by

KG MacGregor

Bella
BOOKS

2012

RHAPSODY

by

KG MacGregor

Bella
BOOKS

2012

Bella Books, Inc.
P.O. Box 10543
Tallahassee, FL 32302

Printed in the United States of America on acid-free paper

First Bella Books Edition 2012

Editor: Katherine V. Forrest
Cover designer: Judith Fellows

ISBN-13: 978-1-59493-293-9

Other Bella Books by KG MacGregor

Aftershock
House on Sandstone
Just This Once
Malicious Pursuit
Mother Load
Mulligan
Out of Love
Photographs of Claudia
Sea Legs
Secrets So Deep
Small Packages
Sumter Point
Without Warning
Worth Every Step

Acknowledgments

Most editors hold that the first page of the book is its most important. Readers may argue that it's the last. I think it's this one, the only chance I have to thank everyone who helped make this a better book.

Katherine V. Forrest worked her usual magic as editor, and you can thank her for richer characters, more vivid descriptions and an extra twist here and there. It's always a great privilege to work with her, since I learn something from her on nearly every page.

My love to Jenny, who, for over a year, listened patiently to each iteration of the story as it evolved. She gives me technical advice, encouragement and all the support I could ever need.

Special thanks to Karen Appleby for cleaning up the typos, Judith Fellows for another captivating cover, and all the Bella staff for all their work behind the scenes.

About the Author

A former teacher and market research consultant, KG MacGregor holds a PhD in journalism from UNC-Chapel Hill. Infatuation with *Xena: Warrior Princess* fan fiction prompted her to try her own hand at storytelling in 2002. In 2005, she signed with Bella Books, which published the Golden Crown finalist *Just This Once*. Her sixth Bella novel, *Out of Love*, won the Lambda Literary Award for Women's Romance and the Golden Crown Award in Lesbian Romance. She picked up Goldies also for *Without Warning*, *Worth Every Step* and *Photographs of Claudia* (Contemporary Romance), and *Secrets So Deep* (Romantic Suspense).

Other honors include the Lifetime Achievement Award from the Royal Academy of Bards, the Alice B. Readers Appreciation Medal, and several Readers Choice Awards.

An avid supporter of queer literature, KG currently serves on the Board of Trustees for the Lambda Literary Foundation. She divides her time between Palm Springs and her native North Carolina mountains.

Please visit her at www.kgmacgregor.com.

Prologue

First runner-up…that means you lost.

Ashley Giraud parked her rental car, a conspicuous Victory Red Chevrolet Impala, in the long line by the curb and turned off her headlights. Before she could move, her car door was opened by Donald Weber, a classmate from twenty-four years ago at Adams County High School and the current mayor of tiny Maple Ridge, Missouri, population 2,833. She had tried all day to shake Donald, but he seemed determined to serve as her escort.

Gallantly removing his suede fedora, he extended an arm. "Miss Muldoon would have been pleased at such a beautiful day, don't you reckon? They say she never stepped foot out of her house when it rained or snowed."

"A lovely day for sure, Donald."

Cool, crisp autumns were one thing—perhaps the only thing—Ashley missed about Missouri. Tampa had weather like this, but only for a few days in January and never with the color that was sprinkled throughout the trees of Maple Ridge. Donald was right. Cassandra certainly would have come out on a day like this.

With her arm hooked through Donald's elbow, she leaned forward slightly so the heels of her pumps wouldn't sink into the soft ground as she walked among the headstones to the canvas tent erected by Taylor and Sons Funeral Home.

Cassandra's cherry casket sat before two rows of folding chairs that held her family, including her elderly father, who had to be well into his nineties. More than a hundred townspeople had followed from the church to say their final farewell at the cemetery. No one had expected to bury Maple Ridge's most illustrious citizen at only sixty-seven years old.

"And Jesus said…"

The Muldoons were Baptists, and it was their pastor who led the service. Cassandra herself had never been much for church, since her reluctance to get out in bad weather precluded perfect attendance. The only thing worse than not going to church at all, she said, was going only sometimes because people would notice your lapses. In fact, Cassandra didn't do much of anything if she couldn't do it perfectly.

Better to be forgotten than remembered for your deficiencies.

"…and we deliver our sister Cassandra unto you…"

From the sunny periphery, Ashley stared at the elegant casket's fine grain and brass handles, trying to imagine the lining inside, probably satin. Cassandra would have preferred cotton sateen, since she abhorred polyester. At least she would have been glad for the closed cover, even had her death not come in a horrid fire that swept through her house in the night. The idea of someone else applying her makeup might have brought her back from the dead.

Two-thirds of the people in attendance were women of various ages. Judging by their posture, makeup and elegant dress, many had been students at the Muldoon Pageant Class, Cassandra's afternoon program to train young ladies for potential careers on the beauty pageant circuit. Ashley recognized a few who won the title of Miss Adams County, but only she had equaled Cassandra's feat of winning the Miss Missouri crown. Ashley then bested her with third runner-up in the Miss America contest, earning a scholarship to the University of Missouri in Columbia, where she had majored in broadcast journalism.

Noticeably absent from the mourners was Lori Spearman, who had left Maple Ridge not long after Ashley to marry Matt Hodges, the slugging third baseman for the Kansas City Royals. Lori was two years older than she and had always been one of Cassandra's favorites.

With a final prayer the service came to an end, and the somber crowd seemed to heave a collective sigh of closure. Ashley stepped under the tent as the family filed out, determined to say her own private goodbye.

It wasn't to be. Donald turned up at her side again like a bad penny. "Such a tragedy. They say she died right there in her bed, like she never even knew the house was on fire." Lowering his voice, he added, "Not that I'm gossiping or anything, but her sister said she got so she sipped the sherry a little too much, if you know what I mean. Arthritis and all…the poor woman."

Not that he was gossiping or anything. Ashley remembered how Cassandra would take a single cordial into her parlor each night after dinner.

A proper lady never drinks more than one.

"Now that Miss Muldoon is gone, that makes you our most prominent citizen…you and Lori Spearman, that is. She comes back to Maple Ridge to see her folks every now and then, and people get all excited about seeing her ballplayer husband. Any chance you'll settle back here one day? Maybe start up the Pageant Class again?"

She'd rather get rabies from a rat.

"I'm afraid I don't keep up with the pageants anymore, Donald. My life is in Tampa now."

Today was Ashley's first return to Maple Ridge since high school. Her departure had been a turning point in her life, when she inventoried all she had learned, and chose what to remember and what to try to forget.

"You don't miss our town even a little bit?"

She smiled wistfully and let her eyes wander the vividly painted tree line. "I have to admit it's pretty here, especially in the fall." When it became clear Donald wasn't leaving her side, she took his arm again and started the deliberate walk back to her rental car.

"We'll miss Cassandra, but at least we have her legacy with all these graceful ladies from her school, present company included." He shuffled ahead to open her car door. "The church put together a potluck for everybody in their fellowship hall. You'll join us, won't you?"

"I wish I could." Far from it. She had been in Maple Ridge for only two hours and was already itching to leave. "As it is, I have just enough time to get back to Kansas City for my flight, but thank you so much for the invitation."

Driving past fields of newly-sprouted cover crops, Ashley considered Donald's observation that Cassandra had left a legacy in the women she trained. There was no denying she wouldn't have become the person she was today had it not been for her time in Cassandra's Pageant Class, and it nagged her that after traveling so far for the funeral she had left things unsaid at the gravesite.

She turned around and drove back to the cemetery, only to find the burial crew already at work on their final task. Resigned to watching the proceedings from afar, she parked by the gate and turned off the ignition.

"So much I wanted to say, Cassandra."

She wondered if any of the women in attendance today still heard Cassandra's voice the way she did, the recitation of her austere rules and humbling derisions. It was doubtful any of them had been impacted the way she was.

You're the special one, Ashley. I'm going to open all the doors for you.

Not a day went by when Ashley didn't look back on her life and gauge the influence of Cassandra's hand. Everything she was—and wasn't—she owed to this once-glorious champion of beauty and grace, now marred for eternity by the fire that had claimed her life.

"I can't imagine your horror…burning to death in your bed."

The Bobcat dozer scooted forward and back, packing the dirt so it was even with the surrounding grass. The other crewman smoothed the surface with a rake.

She started the car again, never taking her eyes from the distant scene. "Now I can only hope you're burning in hell."

Chapter One

"No wonder you call yourself a pig."

"It's HOG, not pig. Say it with me—Harley Owners Group."

"Whatever." Julia Whitethorn tucked the smartphone under her chin as she gathered her hair coloring supplies from the cabinet. She didn't have time for Teddie's false indignation. "I found it in that bag of trash you shoved under my passenger seat. Thanks a lot. Damn thing scared the crap out of me when it rang. I thought it was the rapture or something."

"I sort of doubt you'll get that announcement," Teddie mumbled, her voice groggy from sleep.

"Are you still in bed? It's almost ten o'clock."

"Christ, I've got to go to work. Just leave it by the back door."

"That's why I called, numbskull. I'm already at the shop. You forgot that I do Ashley Giraud first Monday of the month."

"I'd like to do Ashley Giraud."

"I was right the first time. You're a pig." Julia ended the call and set Teddie's wayward phone on the counter, walking her thoughts backward to recall what she had come to the kitchen to get. "Towels!"

The pantry held a supply of white towels, meticulously folded and stacked, at least what was left over following their busy Saturday. The linen service picked up on Tuesdays and Fridays, but Julia had opened the salon this morning just for her special client, the local news anchor on TV4. In return for making Ashley Giraud look like a million dollars once a month she got a tagline at the end of each six o'clock newscast, *Ashley's Hair by Rhapsody.* Truth be told, the shop had just about all the business it could stand, but she had to admit she liked the added prestige of having a local celebrity as a client.

In fact, business had grown steadily since the move three years ago to Old Hyde Park, Tampa's toniest neighborhood. The slumping real estate market had allowed her to grab this office condo at a bargain-basement price, and now she had a full kitchen, two stylist stations with sinks, a waiting area and two rooms upstairs that she rented out for manicures and body waxing.

Rhapsody was a whirlwind of activity Tuesday through Saturday, but her regular hours hadn't meshed with Ashley's schedule. According to her assistant producer, Sergio Flores, who made all the arrangements, she filmed promos and interstitials on Monday afternoon and didn't want to change her hair in the middle of the week. He spelled it all out for Julia in a formal contract—once a month for color and cut, and no style changes without prior written approval, even if Ashley insisted. She and Ashley had bent those rules last month on their very first appointment but not so Sergio would notice.

Her own mop of wavy brown hair was behaving itself today thanks to a trim she'd gotten Saturday from Suzy, the salon's other stylist. Despite her profession, Julia had never attempted to hide the few gray hairs that highlighted the top and sides. She liked to call it premature, but Teddie insisted gray wasn't premature for someone of her advanced age, which was all of thirty-six. She had worn her hair the same way for the last ten years, collar-length and off her face. The only variable was where it would decide to part itself each day, if it parted itself at all.

Though it was officially her day off, Julia had dressed in her usual black pants and white shirt. The quasi-uniform wasn't elaborate, but having a consistent look for the whole staff gave Rhapsody a more professional image.

She looked around with pride at her shop, which had been scrubbed top to bottom by the Sunday cleaning crew. The floors and cabinets were light oak, with black granite countertops, style stations and sinks. Suzy O'Neal, who worked the chair closest to the back door, tended several plants that accented the room, but Julia couldn't name a single one. All she knew was that she wasn't to touch them—ever.

The ambience at Rhapsody was a far cry from the avant-garde salons downtown with their white porcelain floors, gauzy linen drapes, and a hostess delivering flutes of champagne as she took appointments on her Bluetooth. That was arguably the most expensive champagne in town whether you drank it or not because the average haircut in one of those places was at least a hundred bucks. Julia charged half that, and she'd match her styling skills to anyone's.

She had eight minutes before her appointment, enough time to dash next door to Larry's Java Bar for a caramel latte, and she grabbed an extra thinking Ashley might appreciate the gesture.

As she returned through the back door, she saw Ashley stepping out of her dark red sedan, dressed apparently for work in a chocolate brown pantsuit with several thick strands of amber beads plunging to her cleavage. It wasn't hard to see why Teddie wanted to do Ashley Giraud. Every aspect of her appearance was faultless down to the last detail—her perfectly lined green eyes and long lashes, light peach-colored lipstick, French manicure and glossy shoulder-length dark hair. She wasn't the usual TV waif either—at least a size fourteen by Julia's guess—and she carried herself elegantly.

"I think you're the only person I know who does her hair before coming here," Julia said as she held the door.

"Force of habit," Ashley replied, shrugging sheepishly. "I never know when my phone's going to ring with some producer telling me I have to be on the air in three minutes."

"Sounds like you need a break."

"Easy for you to say. You don't have a perky twenty-something lurking over your shoulder, just waiting for that one time you're out of position so she can slide into your chair."

"I always thought that was a cliché."

"Jane Pauley would disagree."

Julia chuckled as she held out the paper cup. "Caramel latte, skim milk."

"Yum!"

She stowed Ashley's handbag—a black Botegga Veneta worth more than Julia made in a week—and helped her into a shimmery, wraparound bronze robe. "So how did we do last time? Was your producer okay with the color and cut?"

"It was great, and as you can see"—she fluffed the ends around her shoulders—"it held up for the whole month. Did Sergio not call you?"

"Yeah, but his opinion doesn't matter as much to me as yours."

"I loved it, and you were right. He didn't even notice the color change."

They had conspired last month to go with walnut, a slightly lighter shade closer to Ashley's natural hair. A gradual lightening over the next couple of years would make it easier to manage once she started to go gray. From what Julia could see of the roots, that day was closer than Ashley probably wanted to hear.

Julia adjusted the chair and twirled it toward the mirror. Tugging gently at the shoulder-length strands, she checked how her last cut had held up. "So we color again and trim it up, right?"

"Sounds good to me." Ashley rested her iPhone on her lap and settled back. "You're sure you don't mind me having this on?"

A placard between Julia's station and Suzy's politely asked customers to limit their cell phone conversations.

"We only put that sign up because one of Suzy's regulars used to talk incessantly the whole time she was in the chair. She'd call one person after another just to jabber about how she was getting her hair cut and what color nail polish she should get. It was either put up that sign or drown her in the sink. I was leaning toward drowning if you want to know the truth."

Getting to know a new client was a lot like dating. The last thing Julia wanted in her shop was awkward silence, but it took a while to sort out what to talk about and how deep to go. Some clients were all business, most were casual acquaintances and a few were genuine friends. She hoped Ashley would eventually become one of the latter, especially since they had a mutual friend in Robyn Maguire. So far the anchorwoman was proving hard to read, barely saying anything beyond superficial niceties and hair chat. Her serious demeanor had Julia worried after their first appointment, until Robyn explained that Ashley may have been upset at the time, since she had just returned from a funeral in Missouri.

"Have you talked to Robyn lately?" she asked.

"If you count last Thursday when I found her rummaging through my desk. She came by to check on one of her interns and needed a paperclip for something."

Julia laughed at the mental image of Robyn getting caught pilfering at the TV station. She was a broadcast journalism professor at the University of Tampa, and the one who had steered Ashley to Rhapsody when her former stylist sold her business. In their small circle of lesbian friends, Robyn was the most neurotic, and such a scene for her would have caused as much angst as the discovery of a sex tape.

"I can only imagine the look on her face."

"She was mortified. I tried to act furious but I couldn't keep a straight face. You two have been friends a long time, right?"

"Let's see, I was twenty-four when we met, so that's been twelve years. She and Elaine weren't part of the party crowd, and that's what I liked about them. All these other women around here…there's just too much drinking, too many drugs and *way* too much drama. I don't have to deal with that from Robyn and Elaine."

"Yeah, it's just the petty larceny you have to worry about."

It was nice to glimpse this playful side of Ashley. On her

nightly newscasts, she came across as polished and professional, just what you wanted in a local news anchor. Comments about her being a lesbian came up from time to time among the customers at Rhapsody, since the wall-mounted TV was always tuned to TV4 and she appeared throughout the day in promos. Some treated the tidbit as gossip or curiosity, but the more common attitude at the shop was pride in her success. They all knew where Julia stood, and if they didn't like lesbians they could get their hair styled somewhere else. Ashley's only public comment on the subject had come several years ago when she politely confirmed the fact to a reporter at the *St. Petersburg Times* before lamenting that she preferred to *report* the news, not *be* the news.

According to Robyn and her partner, Elaine Vandenbosch, Ashley was single and not much for socializing beyond occasionally meeting them somewhere for dinner after her six o'clock newscast. Stalker problems, she had explained, and that always sent Robyn's protective streak into overdrive. Julia had promised not only discretion at Rhapsody, but total privacy for Ashley's visits.

Total except for Teddie, who burst through the back door. "You'd think a smartphone would know better than to get thrown out with the trash."

Julia was gently tracing Ashley's hairline and ears with Vaseline to prevent staining from the hair dye, and barely flinched from her work. "It's on the counter. Get it out of here before it rings again." Lowering her voice, she directed her remarks to Ashley. "Her phone. It doesn't just ring…it roars like a motorcycle."

"You make it sound so ordinary," Teddie whined, tapping her phone to reproduce the distinct ringtone. "It's a 1999 Harley Electra Glide."

"It's obnoxious." Julia assembled her supplies on a rolling cart and turned back to her client. "Would you like a magazine to read while I mix this color?"

"No, thank you." Ashley tipped her head slightly as if trying to check out Teddie in the mirror.

"My friend, Crystal Teddrick." Julia counted under her breath for how long it would take Teddie to make her usual unforgettable impression. She was hard to miss with her nose and ear piercings, bold tattoos on both forearms and, today, a lime green Mohawk. At twenty-three, she was barely bigger than the average ten-year-old. And she absolutely hated the name Crystal.

"Teddie Teddrick, at your service," she said to Ashley, bowing gallantly. "And you are the beautiful Ashley Giraud. I am enchanted to make your acquaintance."

"Oh, please," Julia said. "I'm sure Robyn and Elaine have told her all about you already."

"Right…my sordid past. But anyone can turn her life around with the right motivation," Teddie answered flirtatiously, never taking her gaze from Ashley's.

"Pleased to meet you," Ashley said formally, her tentative smile nowhere near as dazzling as the one she flashed each night at sign-off.

Teddie stepped close enough to jab Julia in the ribs. "You're getting a better class of customer these days."

"And you're late for work."

"I bet you drive a beautiful car, Miss Giraud," Teddie added, puffing out her chest beneath a black tank top that showed off her muscular shoulders. "Bring it by Sterling Wheels on Kennedy for an eco-friendly hand wash. Ask for me and I'll give you a shine you'll never forget."

Julia sighed deeply as the door closed behind her presumptuous friend. "Sorry about that. She left her phone in my car yesterday. I thought she'd be here and gone before you got here."

"It's no problem. Robyn and Elaine have mentioned her. They say she's…high energy."

"Thanks to a fixed diet of Red Bull." She finished her mixture and pulled on a pair of clear plastic gloves that covered her wrists. One row at a time, she painted Ashley's hair a deep, rich brown. Working so close let her notice the smallest of details, like her meticulous makeup, sculpted eyebrows and faint, sweet perfume. It was as though Ashley had followed a rule book for perfection. She probably had, since she was a former Miss Missouri. "I hate to think what Teddie must have done for you to hear about her from Robyn and Elaine."

"Nothing really. I had dinner with them the day after she talked Elaine into going for a ride on her motorcycle. The poor woman's knuckles were still white."

"I'm not surprised. Teddie said she had claw marks on her stomach."

Ashley shuddered visibly. "I'd have done the same thing. The only way you'd ever get me on the back of a motorcycle would be with half a dozen Valium and a mile of duct tape."

"I'd like a picture of that if it ever happens."

"You and everyone else. That's a big game at the station, getting hold of pictures and video of the others doing silly stuff. They did a beach story last year and Melitta got one of the interns to track down a picture of me in the swimsuit competition at the Miss Missouri pageant when I was seventeen years old. I was humiliated."

"I remember that!" Julia had thought it odd at the time that someone as smart and dignified as Ashley had begun her path to fame on a stage like that. Beauty contests were for shallow airheads. "What was humiliating about it? You were gorgeous."

"Please. No one wants to invite those comparisons. None of us will ever be seventeen again."

"Sometimes I think Teddie will always be seventeen…or twelve even. At least she's careful on that bike of hers. My mom puts the fear of God into her every day."

"Your mom?"

"Yeah, Teddie lives with her." Julia finished painting all the strands and tucked them into a shower cap so the dye could do its work. "She's a juvenile probation officer, and she picked up Teddie's case after she got nailed for shoplifting and truancy. Turned out she was living in a junked car because her father had thrown her out when he found out she was gay. Mom had a little experience with that"—she framed her face with her hands and pasted on an innocent smile—"so she took her in. That was, what…seven years ago. Little rat never left."

"Do you have any other brothers or sisters?"

"Nope, just me." It was pleasantly surprising to hear Ashley ask about her family since Elaine had described her as not very social. "What about you?"

"One brother, Dixon, a year and a half older. He's a basketball coach at Brunswick College in Georgia. I'll see him in a few weeks in Atlanta. His team always plays in the Battle of Georgia Tournament over Thanksgiving."

Julia settled into the other salon chair and checked the clock. Twenty minutes should do it on the color. "You grew up in Missouri, right?"

"Mmm…it's the prettiest place, especially in the fall." The sour look that accompanied her description persuaded Julia to move the subject of Missouri to the "Do Not Discuss" list.

They drank their lattes and passed the dyeing time talking about the TV news interns Robyn placed at the station, and how Ashley had allowed herself to get roped into visiting Robyn's class as a guest speaker each semester.

"It's actually kind of fun to talk to all those fresh faces, but don't tell Robyn. I always want her to feel like she owes me a million favors so she'll send me the best interns."

When Ashley settled her neck into the groove of the sink and closed her eyes, gravity erased her tiny crow's feet, and with them a few years off her beautiful face. But to Julia, her finest feature was her hair, thick and silky in the warm stream of water from the corrugated hose. Most women who came to Rhapsody would kill to have hair like that.

Julia went to work intently on cutting and styling, replicating the simple look Ashley had worn for years, curled under gently at the top of her shoulders with feathered bangs. Movement caught her eye, and she noticed Ashley's elegant fingers dancing on the arm of the chair as if playing the piano in accompaniment to the tune she had begun to hum. "Song in your head?"

Ashley stopped abruptly. "I didn't even realize I was doing that. I get that ear worm every time I come in here."

"What ear worm?"

"You didn't recognize it? I guess my humming must be just as bad as my singing. It was Gershwin, *Rhapsody in Blue*."

"Oh, right. Now that you mention it…I'm not much for classical music but that one I remember because of the name."

"I played an adaptation of that for the talent competition in my old beauty pageant days. It's still on my very small repertoire after all these years." Ashley made an odd face, not exactly a frown but close. "If I hadn't spent thousands of hours learning that one little piece, I might still be stuck in Maple Ridge."

It was the second time she had disparaged her Missouri home, and Julia wondered if her recent visit for the funeral had dredged up bad memories. "Then on behalf of Tampa Bay, let me say thanks. And now I bet it gets stuck in my head too."

"So how did your hair salon end up with a name like Rhapsody?"

"My mom's idea. When I first opened about ten years ago, I rented some space on South Dale Mabry in what used to be a music store. We had the tackiest wallpaper you ever saw—gigantic sheet music—but the landlord wouldn't let us touch it. Mom suggested we just go with it, and she's the one who came up with the name. I don't think she had Gershwin in mind, though. She kept singing one of those falsetto songs from the sixties…sounded like a bunch of cats in heat."

"Now that would make a nice ringtone. You might consider downloading that on a certain someone's phone one of these days when she isn't looking." She covered her mouth as if the words had slipped out. "Sorry, I've been corrupted by the practical jokers I work with."

"And I'm sorry I didn't think of it first," Julia answered, sharing an evil grin in the mirror as she put the finishing touches on Ashley's hairdo. "That should do it. Just fluff your bangs a little and give it a light spritz right before you go on the air. They'll look like they were just cut."

"I'll be sure to pass that on to makeup." Ashley pulled a twenty-dollar bill from her purse and offered it to Julia.

"Oh, no! We went through this last time. It's all covered in the contract." And besides, she never took tips from her friends, and she wouldn't mind at all hanging out with Ashley Giraud. "Look, I'm sure Robyn and Elaine have told you all about our little gang. Like I said, we're not big partiers but we're up for just about anything…movies, dinner, goofing off mostly. Teddie never says no to anything. Love to have you join us whenever you can."

Ashley's smile flickered, replaced by a distinct look of uneasiness. "I appreciate that but I…I work such weird hours. I hardly even get to see Robyn except at the station."

Sensing she had overstepped, Julia quickly walked back her invitation. Ashley's friends were probably elite professionals like herself, the Who's Who of Tampa. "Yeah, I know what you mean. I work weird hours too. Not till midnight like you, but I'm usually up half the night anyway because I don't start my day until about eleven. It's hard sometimes to get in sync with normal people."

"That's exactly what I mean. And even when I do try to get out, it's like the station knows it and they call right in the middle of whatever I'm doing. I just hate to impose that on people. It's no way to treat friends."

"It's okay, I understand." She presented her with a complimentary bottle of conditioner and walked her to the door. "Just if you ever get time and want something to do with us, you're always welcome."

All in all it had been a good second appointment, even though it had ended with Ashley in retreat. It seemed she was open and relaxed as long she was the one in control of the conversation, but her guard had gone up the instant she felt her privacy threatened. She was the same in person as on the news… that is, she wanted to ask the questions, not answer them.

Chapter Two

"…with the Lightning working out two free agents at goalie—Ontario's Mark Langman and Latvia's"—Keith Capuzzo's head tilted as he sounded out the name one butchered syllable after the other—"Alex…sejs…Ignat…jevs." He straightened up and grinned at the camera. "And that's all for sports. Back to you, Ashley and Rod."

Ashley turned to co-anchor Rod Gilchrist and said, "Let's hope for Puze's sake they go with Langman."

"For all our sakes," Rod added with a chuckle. "That'll do it for us. Stay tuned for *Your World Now* with David Hunt."

"Have a great evening, and we'll see you back here at eleven." Ashley held her smile until the producer yelled that they were clear, and then abruptly gathered the notes she used to review her segments while the camera was elsewhere. Another day she might have found Puze's gaffe endearing but it irked her that he had behaved so silly on the air. At this rate they'd fritter away their reputation for intelligent news coverage, which was all that kept them competitive with Tampa's news leader, the sensationalist Channel 20. Fires, gunshots and car wrecks always drew more eyeballs than political, business and health news that actually affected people's lives.

"Someone is working his way toward an unemployment check," a booming voice announced. News director Norman Jarvis walked onto the set and shook hands down the line with his news team—Ashley, Rod, weather reporter Melitta Thorpe, and with a mock scowl, Puze. Still in the throes of his mid-life crisis, Jarvis—no one dared call him Norman—wore his thinning hair in a short ponytail that complemented his finely tapered goatee. "That's another one in the can. I'm sending a crew out to cover a hit-and-run in Plant City. It's all we're working for tonight, so I'll see you back here at ten thirty."

Already, Rod had stripped his lapel mic and stepped off the platform. As usual, he would be the first one out the door, rushing home to have dinner with his wife and kids. Ashley admired that he took his family duties seriously, though it generally meant he left the real work of gathering and editing the late news to others. She had known when he came on board four years ago that he'd been hired only as a talking head, but at least he did that marginally well. What mattered most to management was that viewers liked him, and he made sure of that by talking regularly about his kids.

Ashley stopped at the vanity to wipe off the extra makeup Sergio had applied just before the show. It looked natural on the air, but clownish in normal light. She was joined by Melitta, a statuesque African-American and former fashion model whom Jarvis had plucked from the talent pool seven years ago and groomed as the station's meteorologist. Ashley had bristled at her hiring because Jarvis clearly went with looks over credentials, but Melitta's dedication and intellect had helped her grow into the job quickly. More important, she had become Ashley's sounding board and Ashley hers.

"What in the world got into Puze?" Ashley groused. "The hard part should be gathering the news, not reading it."

"Viewers probably got a kick out of it. Jarvis…not so much."

"Great show, ladies!" Reporter Mallory Foster, wearing a tight black skirt and four-inch stiletto heels, bustled between them and reached into a drawer. "Don't tell Sergio but I'm stealing this lipliner. The other one he gave me isn't sharp enough for when we shoot after dark." She was their newest hire, an attractive blonde who had performed so well in her internship last year that she already was vaulting over more experienced reporters for air time.

Melitta cocked her head. "You're covering the hit-and run? I thought Plant City was Scott's beat."

"Jarvis said he didn't answer his page." Mallory hastily applied the liner and fresh lipstick, and then dashed off with the waiting camera crew.

"If I were you, I'd keep an eye on that one," Melitta mumbled under her breath.

"Mallory? No kidding. Once that kid gets some experience under her belt, the sky's the limit. I won't be surprised if one of the networks snatches her up." Ashley appreciated Mallory's skill and work ethic, both of which she chalked up to a first-class education in Robyn's program at the University of Tampa.

Melitta reached out to stroke Ashley's hair. "By the way, I've been meaning to tell you I like your new color."

"Shhh! Sergio doesn't know we changed it. It's just a teensy shade lighter."

The woman's voice dropped to a comical baritone. "Sergio may not know, but I can spot a color job all the way from Pasco County. This new girl you got...she does good work."

"I'll be sure to tell her you said so." Ashley admired her look under the Hollywood lights. Julia had been right about the spritz making her bangs look freshly cut.

Julia...

The only certain way to correct a mistake is not to make it.

She could hear the words as crisply as if Cassandra were there to admonish her in person.

Thoughts of Julia Whitethorn had bothered her all day. If she had it to do over again, she would have shopped around for a new stylist instead of jumping into the arrangement with Rhapsody on Robyn's recommendation alone. Now she was committed for a year, and even then a decision to switch to someone else might cause hard feelings between her and Robyn.

The problem wasn't her hair—it looked and felt fantastic. Nor was it the setting. The shop was comfortable and conveniently located between her home and the station. And Julia had been more than accommodating in scheduling private appointments on her day off.

The problem was Julia.

No, that wasn't fair. Ashley herself was the problem, with all her eccentricities and phobias. Stumbling upon Robyn at work had been a gift, a chance to connect with a career-oriented woman who understood, at least in theory, that newspeople lived their lives in the public eye. She relished the idea of having lesbian friends, as long as they were already in relationships and not on the prowl. But now both Robyn and Julia were trying to draw her into more, and with people who didn't recognize how the wrong kind of association could reflect badly on her image. Fending off social invitations from her stylist wasn't supposed to be part of the bargain.

Julia was actually a very nice person. It was hard to imagine they had enough in common to be real friends, but she deserved better than the lame, transparent excuse of weird work hours that had tumbled out of Ashley's mouth on the spur of the moment. Her main reservations at the time had to do with Teddie, who was far too outrageous for her taste in friends. It wasn't that Teddie wasn't nice too—she probably was—but her shocking appearance seemed to shout "Look at me!" and Ashley didn't care to draw that kind of attention when she was out in public. She had cultivated an image to correspond with the one she projected on TV—professional, affable, well-dressed, low-key and refined. A single deviation could leave a lasting impression, and with social media all the rage, anything that someone found funny or potentially scandalous would be broadcast all over the Tampa Bay market in a matter of minutes. She had become adept at controlling her social environs, always conscious of leaving a way out in case a situation became uncomfortable.

The company you keep is who you are.

And then there was the vibe, not a real one in Julia's case but a potential one. An invitation to "goof off" together wasn't exactly flirting, yet the romantic angle always seemed to be lurking under the surface whenever she spent time with single people. Men hit on her way too often, probably because they'd heard the stories of her relationship with network news star Valerie Reynolds and wanted to prove she just hadn't met the right man yet. But nothing compared to the anxiety she felt around women who showed an interest in her, which had happened recently at a dinner party given by Jarvis and his wife, and again at a benefit for the Literacy Foundation. The idea of getting involved with someone romantically had been off the table for so long that it was second nature to shut down even the hint of it before it could take root. In hindsight, it seemed Julia was just being friendly, and that's why Ashley felt bad about blowing her off. Maybe she could work in a quick call tomorrow to say she had gotten compliments on her hair. It would give her a chance to affirm that theirs was a business arrangement.

Before she could get out of her office, she was cornered by Jarvis, who guided her back in and closed the door ominously.

"What?"

"We're friends. Right, Ash?"

He had a maddening way of making that sound like the kiss of death. Jarvis was, in fact, her oldest and dearest friend, an old-school newsman who had hired her at the network fresh from the Kansas City affiliate. From her first day in Washington, she made him as a womanizer, and set him back on his heels when she told him she wasn't interested in men. The revelation actually seemed to pave the way for their friendship, and after Valerie outed her in a magazine interview that got picked up on all the wires, she saw the writing on the wall for her national news career. Diversity was fine, but only one lesbian per network, please. When Jarvis got the offer to be news director at TV4, she jumped at the chance to follow him to Tampa as co-anchor of the local news.

"I took a look at that story idea you gave me." His grim expression said it all, but he spelled it out just the same. "I like the one about tracking donor organs...but I don't have the budget for it."

"It's worth it, Jarvis. We can get a whole week of interviews out of it, and just think how rewarding it would be for people to see—"

"No budget," he repeated firmly. "You said it yourself in your pitch. Some of these organs could end up as far away as Seattle, and I can't afford to fly you and a production team all over the country for interviews. Great idea, though."

One she'd have to file under It's the Thought that Counts. Her prospects for landing a big story in time for this year's Emmy nominations were fading fast. Exposés and in-depth features usually took months to develop, and the one that had gotten most of her energy this year—contamination at the desalinization plant—had been scooped by the *St. Petersburg Times* after nearly four months of investigative work. There was still time to put together a poignant series on someone battling disease or facing mortgage foreclosure, but Ashley hated the idea of exploiting people for their news value.

She also hated the idea of competing with her peers for awards, having gotten her fill of contests years ago with the pageants, but they mattered in this business. Her five-year contract was up in April and a fresh nomination would go a long way toward bolstering her bargaining position with Carl Terzian, the station's general manager.

"I'll think about it some more," she said. "Maybe there's a way we could do it with local recipients." She picked up her purse to indicate that she needed to run, but Jarvis held his ground.

"One other thing. I've noticed...you've picked up a few pounds." He said it gently, an obvious effort not to hurt her feelings. "Carl mentioned it too, so I told him I'd check to make sure everything was okay."

Ten pounds, all since her trip to Missouri nearly seven weeks ago. A few days off the treadmill had become a few weeks, now going on two months. Any excuse not to exercise was good enough for Ashley. Add that to her habit of taking comfort food to the extreme when she was upset—hot apple pie with ice cream for dinner, cashews by the pound and chocolate in every drawer—and the picture of her crumbling discipline was complete. Nothing was harder than keeping her weight under control, and she had completely let go of her efforts as she prioritized getting her head back on straight.

"I guess I need to have my thyroid checked again," she said, sighing dejectedly. She had trotted out the inactive thyroid excuse four years ago after she had crept up two sizes in as many years. Her doctor had found her metabolic function only slightly diminished, not enough to prescribe medication, and suggested she walk more and stick to a diet of fresh foods. A miracle fat-burning pill would have been more to her liking.

"Let's hope it's okay." He probably knew the thyroid excuse was a crock, but he was kind enough not to call her on it. "I know it's hard, Ashley. This has nothing to do with your work. You're the best newswoman in town, but you know how Carl can be."

Carl would have her in a size two, as long as she kept her boobs. "I'll get some blood work done and see if it's flaring up again."

He nodded enthusiastically and grinned. "Good, good. And I thought maybe you might want to book a couple of weeks over the holidays at that resort in Cancun. It'll be better if Carl knows we're already on it."

Back to the fat farm, she thought miserably. So much for spending Christmas with Dixon and his wife. "Fine!"

"I'm sorry." He came around her desk and enveloped her in a bear hug. "I hate this part of our job, but it's a reality we have to deal with."

"I know. It's not your fault. I should have gotten a handle on it sooner."

She hurried through the parking lot in a light drizzle, intent on getting out before Jarvis could invite her to dinner, where he would tempt her with a juicy ribeye and crème brûlée, oblivious to the irony. If her current weight struggle was on Carl's radar already, this was serious business. She needed to look her best for contract negotiations.

Only four blocks from the station, she pulled into the parking garage of a downtown office center. The garage was largely deserted but for a cluster of cars parked near the glass entrance of the well-lit second-floor lobby. With a silent nod to a security guard behind a high granite counter, she stepped aboard the elevator and took it to the fourteenth floor. These were her terms—she would visit Dr. Friedman only in the evenings when her other patients were gone, and when the building wasn't full of gawkers who might observe her walking into a psychiatrist's office.

When you are beautiful, people look more intently for your flaws.

The trip to Missouri hadn't brought the closure she and her doctor had hoped for. On the contrary, it had triggered a rise in her old feelings of self-recrimination and isolation, another frustrating twist on what was shaping up to be a lifelong journey. At forty-one, she had come to grips with the likelihood that she would spend her life alone. What she couldn't handle was the reawakened bitterness about it, and the envy she felt for those who had what she lacked—Rod and his family dinners, Robyn and her loving partner Elaine, and even Jarvis, who was now on his third wife. If it took another agonizing round of therapy with Dr. Friedman to get back to stasis, she had little choice but to see it through.

Carole Friedman answered her knock and quickly ushered her inside. She was a petite woman in her mid-fifties with dark hair and eyes, a self-described Reform Jew who believed in practical, real-world solutions. "Ashley, I'm glad you decided to keep our appointment."

"I just do what the voices tell me," she said dryly. "Just kidding."

Unfazed by the jibe, Carole hooked elbows with her and guided her past the vacant receptionist's station to the office. A table lamp softly lit the corner where a love seat and armchair created a cozy area for discussion. "Unfortunately depression can be cyclical, but many people develop skills and strategies that help them rebound quickly from periods of emotional complexity. Tell me what you're feeling now."

It was good to know this spiraling crash was only emotional complexity. "The usual. Can't sleep, can't concentrate, can't stay out of the refrigerator. Little things irritate me, like people at work goofing off. I even got mad at Puze tonight...over nothing."

"What do you think might be behind this?"

"Isn't it obvious?" It irked her that they seemed to start over from the beginning at each appointment, but then everything about seeing a psychiatrist left her feeling frustrated. She'd been coming here off and on for seven years in an effort to learn whether she controlled her own destiny or if it was already scripted by circumstances she couldn't change without turning back the clock. It hadn't helped to discover that it probably was both, but at least Dr. Friedman was able to guide her through the difficult task of identifying those areas where she could chart her own course. The way Ashley saw it, her life boiled down to being TV4 news anchor Ashley Giraud. Prior to coming to Tampa, she had been KBC news correspondent Ashley Giraud, and before that, Miss Missouri Ashley Giraud. Building her life around her public identity had not only simplified the process. It had allowed her to operate at the surface level of what people could actually see, which meant she didn't have to dig deeply into things that made her uncomfortable...except for these last few months, when Dr. Friedman had urged her to begin the daunting process of moving past her old issues.

"So you feel certain it was going back to Missouri."

"I'm certain that it started the minute I got word Cassandra had died. I'm certain that going to her funeral made it worse instead of better. I'm certain that she pops into my head all the time, no matter what I'm doing."

"How would you describe your feelings, Ashley?" The question hung in the air for several seconds before Dr. Friedman followed up. "Were you sad about Cassandra's death?"

"What kind of person would I be if I didn't feel at least a little bit of sadness because someone died? I was sorry for her family, and for all the people who thought her dying was a great loss. But I sincerely doubt those people knew her the way I did. If anything, I feel guilty for watching them grieve and not being able to share it."

Again Dr. Friedman was maddeningly silent for nearly half a minute, no doubt to provoke her into answering her own question. Finally she relented and asked Ashley, "Is it possible you have it backward? That, in fact, you really are feeling a loss, even though you don't want to?"

No, it wasn't possible.

"Feelings like these can cause a great deal of conflict, Ashley. We're conditioned to feel sad when someone dies, but it's also human nature to start forgiving the shortcomings of those who are no longer with us. Problems then arise when our real emotions no longer match the attitudes we've trained ourselves to hold. As we shed long-held beliefs and opinions, it can feel like a betrayal to our intrinsic values."

How many times did she have to say this? "I'm not shedding anything. I wish I were. Going there was supposed to be the end of it, and instead it feels even worse than it did before."

"Why do you think that is?"

"Because now I'm starting to worry that my problems don't have anything to do with Cassandra. Maybe I've been screwed up all along...and this is never going away." Her voice shook as she struggled not to cry. Crying made an awful mess of her makeup.

"It will, Ashley. You still have a lot of growing—and healing—left to do. If you're willing to work at it, a rich, full life is waiting for you."

A rich, full life through therapy would take years if it happened at all. What Ashley needed was a way to manage the crisis du jour before she packed on ten more pounds to carry into her contract negotiations, or screwed up on the air because her head was somewhere else.

"I hear her voice all the time." She realized at once how alarming that must sound to a psychiatrist. "I don't mean I hear her actual voice. It's just that I'm constantly remembering all of her rules and sayings. They bombard me out of nowhere. I feel like I did twenty-some years ago when I was afraid to do anything without her approval."

"Is her approval still important to you?"

"Of course not," she insisted, frustrated that she kept using the wrong words. It made her sound like she was under a spell or something. "She used to say that by putting ourselves on display we invited others to judge us. So what do I do? I choose a career that means I have to live in a fishbowl. The only time I'm not on display is when I'm alone in my house with the doors locked."

"You've always liked your solitude, Ashley. Are you feeling more isolated than usual?"

"No, but I used to feel like it was a choice. Now I'm not so sure. I shut down everyone I meet without even thinking about it." Over the years, solitude had become a defense mechanism, something she cultivated in place of relationships, even convincing herself it was what she wanted. So why was she annoyed with herself over turning down Julia's invitation?

"Maybe because you're afraid there are others out there like Valerie. You're worried that if you open up someone will betray you the way she did."

"It was never Valerie that I was worried about." After their disastrous fling twelve years ago, Ashley admitted to herself she simply wasn't wired for romance. Breaking things off abruptly had left Valerie hurt and frustrated, and thinking Ashley had dropped her out of paranoia about being in the closet, she had lashed out by going public about their affair in a magazine interview. The worst of it for Ashley, however, was the sudden call to the station from Missouri—the first and only time she had spoken to Cassandra since leaving Maple Ridge at age eighteen. The woman had been lurking all those years, watching for Ashley to break one of her precious rules, and had taken spiteful pleasure in the damage it had done to her career.

Secrets don't keep themselves.

"She won't ever call you again, Ashley."

"I know," she said quietly. Since coming to Tampa she had lived an impeccable life, combining professional excellence with commendable community service. Her personal life—which was close to nil—she had kept entirely off the grid, so there was nothing on that front for anyone to scrutinize. "How am I going to stop feeling like she will?"

Dr. Friedman clasped her hands to lean forward and rest her elbows on her knees. Ashley recognized it as her persuasive posture, the one she adopted when trying to steer the results toward something she knew Ashley would resist. "There are a couple of approaches we can take. An anti-depressant might—"

"No medication," she said adamantly. It made her feel weird and she didn't trust herself to hold up on the air.

"Then that limits our options. The last time you felt you were sinking into this hole, we thought it would be a good idea for you to get out more with friends. I believe you had gotten to know someone from work, a woman and her partner. How did that work out?"

"Robyn and Elaine…very nice people. We've been getting together about once a month for dinner, but I haven't seen them since I got back from the funeral."

Dr. Friedman had picked up early on her penchant to plan all her social engagements around dinner during the week. It had nothing to do with a desire to share culinary interests or break bread as a cultural ritual. She liked it because there was only a three-hour window between newscasts. Meet, eat and retreat.

"Robyn set me up with her friend to have my hair cut. She—"

"It looks very nice, by the way. I like your new color."

"Thank you," she said, cringing at the mention of her change. How could Sergio not notice when everyone else did? "Anyway, I was about to tell you that Julia—that's her name—invited me to join them when they got together, but…these are all lesbians."

"And you have a problem with that because…?"

"Because if I start socializing with a bunch of women like that, eventually someone's going to get interested in more. Then it just gets uncomfortable for everybody."

Dr. Friedman began to nod then changed directions to shake her head, her way of saying she understood but she didn't agree. "That's it in a nutshell, isn't it, Ashley? You don't want to meet anyone because you're convinced you'd rather be alone than risk personal failure. Am I right?"

Ashley nodded slightly. More than personal failure, she feared hurting someone else if—or rather when—she reached the limit on how close she would allow them to be.

"What about all the things you're missing out on in between? Movies, cookouts, art galleries. There is so much you could be doing."

Goofing off with friends, as Julia had suggested, was exactly the sort of activity Dr. Friedman had encouraged for years, but even now her defenses were kicking in. "Look, I work hard five days a week. My weekends are for unwinding, not worrying about whether or not my mascara is clumped or if my belt buckle matches my jewelry. Isn't that what you say I need to do...just relax and be myself?"

"Yes, but you've conveniently left out the part about being yourself with other people," the doctor said, the corner of her mouth turned upward in a chastising smirk. "You're falling back into that vicious cycle again. Withdrawing leads to introspection...which fuels your anxiety about being judged. You become depressed and..."

"...withdraw even more."

"Feelings are the hardest to change, Ashley. That's why we try to lead with behavior. The only way to break this cycle is to turn your focus outward. Pick some activities you enjoy and get yourself out there. Open up. Throw a big party for everyone you know and ask them to bring their friends."

She tried to envision what such a collection of people would look like. There would be Jarvis and Connie's socialite friends, Melitta's hip-hoppers and Puze's jock sniffers. Add to that Robyn's circle, which included a hair stylist and a tattooed shoplifter with green hair. She'd probably need the medication after all.

Chapter Three

Julia rested against her broom as the TV4 news team signed off for the night. In the next chair, Suzy was finishing her last client of the day, a woman of about sixty-five with gorgeous silver hair.

"Watch, Arlene. Here it comes." Suzy twirled the chair just in time for her customer to catch the promo script across the bottom of the screen. "See? I told you we were famous."

Arlene looked at Julia in disbelief. "I thought you were kidding. She really comes here?"

"Once a month, right there in that chair." She and Suzy got a kick out of their customers' reactions when they realized Ashley Giraud had her hair done at Rhapsody.

"I really like her," Arlene said. "She always seems so...I don't know, real. I feel like she could just come in and sit down in my living room and feel right at home."

"I'm sure she could." Julia didn't have the heart to disagree, but there was nothing about the Ashley she knew that suggested she would be comfortable in a stranger's living room. "She's a very nice lady. And she has great hair."

"Oh, it's gorgeous," the woman said. "I can ait to tell the girls at my church that we get our hair done at t e same place."

The door closed behind her and Suzy slapped her hand in a high five. "You just made Arlene's day. She'll be on the phone all night calling everyone she knows."

Fifty-one-year-old Suzy had worked by Julia's side for sixteen years, since her first job at the busy mall salon. She had eagerly followed when Julia opened her own shop but wanted no part of ownership, opting instead to rent her chair. Work was where she came to relax, she said, and she didn't need anything extra to worry about. With three grown children and a late-in-life toddler, it was easy to see why.

Julia swiped her broom underneath Suzy's chair. "I'll clean up if you want to head on home. I've got a late appointment with Robyn, and Elaine's bringing dinner."

Suzy shook her scissors menacingly. "She better not stink up this place with all that garlic again. Tell her I'll cut off that braid of hers and stick it in her pocket." Elaine's last dinner had been so pungent it took them days to get rid of the smell.

"Believe me, she got the message. It'll probably be tofu something we can't even taste."

"Tofu's good for you," a voice called from the stairwell. Jasmine Copley, resident flower child and Rhapsody's waxing specialist. Like Suzy, she rented a station upstairs, which she decorated in soft warm colors with candles, incense and sounds of nature. Waxing at Rhapsody was a private and sensuous experience, and also popular, judging from the steady traffic up and down the stairs.

Julia liked the look and feel of a bikini wax but saw no point in putting herself through the trauma of more than that. Maybe if she were seeing someone who found the Brazilian sexy…no, probably not even then.

"My six thirty canceled so I'm heading out, Jules," Jasmine said. "Just two more days and I'm off to Belize."

"That's it. Keep rubbing it in." Julia swatted at her with the broom. "Why can't you stay here and stuff yourself with turkey like everyone else? Aren't you thankful?"

"I'm thankful I won't get all that bad karma from eating dead animals."

"I'll be sure to save you a sprout or something."

The slow thumping on the steps signaled the end of the day for Inez Villanueva, the third-generation Cuban-American manicurist who occupied the second room upstairs. At the eight month mark of her pregnancy, every step was arduous. "If I thought there was anything to that myth about castor oil inducing labor, I'd drink a gallon of it tonight."

"He'll get here soon enough, kiddo," Suzy said. "And mark my word, you'll be saying, 'God, if I just could have had one more night of sleep.'"

Thanksgiving was shaping up to be a quiet week at Rhapsody with Jasmine on vacation and Inez going on twelve weeks' maternity leave. Even Suzy was planning to take a four-day weekend. Julia liked the idea of having the shop all to herself for a couple of days. Rhapsody was her domain even more so than her small cottage. It was why she hadn't minded when Ashley Giraud's producer had insisted on Mondays, and why she encouraged friends like Robyn, Elaine and Teddie to come in after everyone else was gone.

It was almost fifteen minutes later when Robyn stumbled through the door, her figure a blur as she yanked off her suit jacket and kicked both pumps across the floor. "God, I've been looking forward to this all day!"

"Getting your hair cut?"

"No, just sitting down and turning off my brain. It's ridiculous how much there is to do at the end of the semester. It's bad enough I have a pile of research papers to grade. I had to do site visits for all of my interns, so I spent half the day in traffic."

Julia smiled at her recollection of Ashley's story. "I heard you got caught ransacking someone's desk on one of your site visits."

"Oh, my God! That was so embarrassing." Robyn's mass of freckles faded under a deep blush as Julia brushed out her wiry red hair. "If that had been anyone but Ashley, I probably would have been arrested."

Robyn and Elaine had been fixtures in her life since their meeting at a Tampa Bay Pride event twelve years ago. They were new to the area then, moving from Wisconsin where Robyn had completed her PhD in journalism. Julia had been with Rachel in those days, and to this day Elaine never missed an opportunity to say she had known they were wrong for each other from the moment they met. For some reason, everyone on earth had realized that before Julia, who took nine years to figure it out.

As Julia washed Robyn's hair in preparation for her cut, Elaine stumbled through the back door, her arms wrapped around a massive Crock-Pot, its cord dangling to the floor.

"Mediterranean stew," she announced, leaning down to give her partner a peck on the lips. In contrast to Robyn, she was clad in jeans and a tie-dyed T-shirt, her usual attire for work at home as a technical writer. "And before you ask, I left out the garlic."

"Suzy will be glad to hear it. I won't tell you what she threatened, but it involved scissors."

Elaine wore her ash blond hair in a single braid all the way to her waist, and she let Julia trim it only once a year just to keep the ends healthy. She served herself a bowl of stew and took a seat in Suzy's style chair. "That woman has some serious anger issues. I guess I would too if I had a two-year-old at her age."

Robyn sat up from the sink and dabbed her face with a towel. "Ashley told Julia about catching me in her desk. Do you think she tells everybody? They probably think I'm a kleptomaniac."

"Just because you steal stuff?" Elaine asked drolly. "I hate to tell you this but they've probably sent a memo around the station with a warning."

"For what it's worth, I think Ashley thought it was hilarious," Julia said. "I got the feeling you guys might be the only people she actually likes." She related the story of how Ashley had tap-danced her way out of an invitation to join them at get-togethers like these. "She acted all uptight with the idea of anybody getting in her space. I was just trying to be nice."

Robyn shook her head. "I don't know, Jules. She's never been anything but sweet to us, but I always get the impression she has to be in control…like she has one foot out the door already. I wouldn't take it personally."

"You need to keep your head still or you'll be looking like Teddie," Julia said, waving her scissors under Robyn's nose. She felt bad pumping her friends for information on Ashley Giraud, but it actually bothered her that Ashley had blown her off like a stalker. "Are you sure she's even gay?"

"She says she is, but I know for a fact she doesn't date anybody."

"Then what's the point of even having a sexual orientation?"

With her mouth full, Elaine managed to mumble, "So says the woman who hasn't had a date in three years."

Julia stuck out her tongue. "That was a low blow. Wait till I get you in my chair."

"We invited her last year to come down to Boca Grande when we rented the villa," she went on. "I thought she was going to say yes until Robyn told her we always tried to have our friends down while we were there. I think she got worried there'd be a lot of people."

"She's very conscious of her public image," Robyn explained. "She talked to my class about it last year, how she's very careful to choose which causes to support or which events to attend. From where she stands, it's all about reputation and integrity. You remember what happened to the sports reporter from TBZ who showed up in the birthday party picture that Bucs linebacker posted on Twitter?"

It was quite the scandal, Julia recalled. Drug paraphernalia had been plainly visible in the background in close proximity to the reporter. Poor guy had lost his job, all the while proclaiming he hadn't known it was there. "She's afraid we're a bunch of drug addicts? She ought to know you wouldn't hang out with people like that."

A sputtering motorcycle announced the arrival of Teddie, who soon came in and tossed her helmet onto the faux-leather couch in the waiting area. "People are assholes."

Julia smirked. "People in general or just the ones who don't tip?"

"Jordan's bitchy queen asshole girlfriend says she can't handle it anymore and she's going back to Virginia. I'd like to help her get there on the toe of my boot."

Elaine got up and set her bowl on the kitchen counter. "You mean your friend with cancer?"

"Yeah, like she doesn't have enough to worry about. Now her girlfriend leaves."

Julia stopped cutting long enough to give Teddie a sympathetic hug. It was tough on Teddie to have her close friend dealing with such a gloomy prognosis. "I know it's no consolation, but if Jordan's girlfriend says she can't handle it, she probably can't. Does Jordan have anybody else who can help out?"

"Her cousin's coming down from Ohio to stay with her."

"Let us know what we can do," Elaine offered. "Get yourself some stew."

Teddie stirred the pot and examined the contents. "Where's the beef?"

Julia and Robyn chuckled softly as they waited for Elaine's response. The very same conversation was repeated almost verbatim every time they got together for one of her vegetarian meals.

"That beef you ate three days ago is probably still in your intestine."

"I figure my ancestors didn't fight their way to the top of the food chain so I could be a vegetarian." The stew dripped down Teddie's chin as she took her first bite. "But this ain't half bad."

"You say that like you're surprised."

"See, this is the perfect example of how we are when we're just hanging out," Julia groused. "Nothing fancy…just a bunch of friends talking about stuff they care about. What's so threatening about that?"

Teddie flopped into the chair Elaine had vacated and stared at Julia with her head cocked. "What's she going on about, Doc?" It was her pet name for Robyn.

"She's pissed off because Ashley Giraud won't give her the time of day."

"I'm not pissed off." She stopped cutting and glared at Robyn. "I can't believe you just told her that."

"What? You got the hots for Ashley Giraud? Get in line. She's a babe."

"You think Ashley's a babe?" Elaine asked, and then huffed with disbelief.

"Sure, why not?"

"Because she's like twenty years older than you and probably never wore leather in her life."

"I think she found me interesting. Didn't she, Jules?"

"Frightening and interesting aren't the same." She couldn't leave Teddie thinking she was interested in Ashley or there would be no mercy. "And no, I don't have the hots for Ashley, but I thought she was nice and I asked her to hang out with us. She blew me off."

"Maybe she's just shy."

"How can she be shy? She goes on TV every night in front of hundreds of thousands of people!"

"No, I bet Teddie's right," Elaine said, directing her remarks to Robyn. "You guys knew each other a whole year before you ever brought me along for dinner."

"And before we ever talked about anything besides work," Robyn agreed. "She's a pretty tough nut to crack. She once told Elaine and me that she appreciated how we were such good friends, but I swear we barely know her. If we're what she considers good friends, she's probably not all that close to anybody."

"Never even been to her house," Elaine added. "You know what I'm going to do? I'm going to invite her to Robyn's birthday dinner and not tell her anyone else is coming."

"Don't do that," Julia said. "She'll feel like she's being ambushed. If she doesn't want to get together with us, we shouldn't trick her."

"Fine, but I'm still going to ask her. Maybe she'll come now that she knows we don't bite."

Teddie arched her eyebrows lasciviously and grinned. "Says who?"

Ashley smiled and greeted her fellow shoppers as their faces lit up, thanking those who said they watched her on TV. Being recognized as a local celebrity was good if you needed a table at Bern's Steakhouse, but not for a stop-off at the pharmacy. It was unnerving to have strangers pay attention to what she put in her basket, right down to her choice of feminine products.

She was next in line at checkout when the clerk barked rudely at the customer in front of her, a woman of about thirty wearing khaki chinos and a blue cotton sweater that had lost its shape from one too many tumbles in the dryer. "Unless you have another four dollars and fifteen cents, you'll have to put something back."

"But this coupon says these diapers are supposed to be on sale."

"We're sold out of that size. I can give you a rain check, but I can't substitute."

Ashley noted the woman's small pile of goods, which along with the diapers included children's cough medicine, Vicks VapoRub and baby formula. Imagining the worry the young mother must be feeling, she fished a five-dollar bill from her wallet. "Here, I can help."

The woman smiled with recognition. "Oh, my goodness. You're Ashley Giraud."

She felt herself redden as others began to look on and whisper. "Looks like you have your hands full at home," she said, gesturing at the items on the counter.

"I sure do. The last thing we needed in our house was the flu." She looked longingly at the cash in Ashley's hand. "But I shouldn't take your money. I get paid tomorrow, and I can just pick out a smaller package to hold me over till then."

"It's okay. Just get on back to your kids and make them feel better. That's what matters."

"Thank you. You are so sweet." She handed Ashley the loose change from the clerk, started for the door and stopped. "My husband and I watch you every single night."

Ashley curbed her attitude as she checked out with the rude clerk, remembering every single interaction mattered in the public sphere. Then she slipped out with her purchases, glad the ordeal was over for another month.

She headed south on MacDill Avenue to her Ballast Point home, situated on a side street three blocks from the waters of Hillsborough Bay. It was an eclectic neighborhood with both modern and historic homes of all sizes. Hers was a single-story Mediterranean built in the late 1930s and expanded by the succession of subsequent owners. She had made a few changes of her own to the exterior, enclosing the entire front yard inside an electric gate. Dixon had insisted on that after one of her more ardent fans had followed her home.

As the gate closed behind her, she mentally went down her checklist of things to do before heading back to the station in only two hours. Most nights her mindset between newscasts was that she was still at work. It wasn't as if she could shrug out of her dress and stockings and truly relax. She typically used this time to digest the local papers, not so much for the news as to see what stories the papers were playing with front page coverage, sidebars and editorial commentary. It was always good to keep a finger on the pulse of the competition.

The garage led through the laundry room to the kitchen, with its brown granite island and deep red cabinets. It was an elaborate kitchen for someone who rarely cooked. As far as she was concerned, it was silly to spend hours in the kitchen to do something Whole Foods could do better. She could count on one hand the number of times in eleven years she'd had guests over for dinner, and all but one of the meals had been catered.

The living area, which included the master suite, and guest bedroom and bath, were on the opposite side of the house across a wide living room dominated by a rarely used grand piano. She spent most of her waking hours in the den off the kitchen, either at her cluttered desk, in her beloved reading chair or on her detested treadmill.

Tonight she never made it as far as the den. Instead she popped a frozen gourmet dinner into the microwave and spread the *Tampa Bay Guardian* out on her counter. The

Guardian was a twice-weekly alternative newspaper, a small independent outfit that focused on local business, media and politics. Ashley grudgingly admired them for their adversarial take on practically every issue of the day, especially the work of its star reporter Lamar Davidson, whose two favorite topics were city politics and the awfulness of Channel 20 news. The mainstream press had cut back so much on their resources that they rarely engaged in prolonged investigation and analysis, but the *Guardian* thrived on stirring up its readers.

Lamar was usually complimentary of TV4's news coverage. In fact, he even called her from time to time begging for an interview, but Ashley granted those only when the station forced her into it for publicity reasons, and they hadn't done that for the *Guardian*. There was no greater torture than having to field questions about herself. She enjoyed her phone chats with Lamar though, since he sometimes shared tidbits of what he was working on in hopes of getting the same from her. His information was generally reliable, and once had led to a scoop on an insurance scam for TV4, and she had made certain to reciprocate with a tip on one of their investigative stories.

His front page story today was an in-depth profile of Hillsborough County Commissioner Jack Staley, who had won the office last year on his campaign as a man of the people attuned to the needs of working families and small businesses. Lamar's portrait was of someone who lived in an exclusive gated neighborhood, sent his children to private schools and rubbed shoulders with the rich and powerful at Tampa's most prestigious country club.

"Now there's a news flash, Lamar," she muttered. "Politicians lie."

Still, she enjoyed the acerbic tone of his precision takedown of Staley, whose phoniness was nothing compared to his utter lack of political skills. Only eight months into his four-year term, he had already sold out most of his supporters in county government by cutting deals with the other side, alienating both the clerk of courts and code enforcement office. Lamar suggested he peel off his reptilian skin and run his next campaign from the other party's camp. Ashley didn't disagree with the brutal assessment, and was more than a little jealous that Lamar could get away with saying it and she couldn't. TV4 viewers expected a bit more decorum and restraint.

It wasn't that their news team couldn't be critical of local government. Jarvis loved it when they "got down in the dirt," as long as they got it first and got it right. It was their solemn duty as keepers of the Fourth Estate to hold the powerful accountable, but scattershot hysteria and sarcasm about government didn't play as well on television as they did in a free bi-weekly newspaper.

Her tiny portion of chicken pasta disappeared too quickly as she perused the rest of the paper, and she quickly cleaned up and turned out the kitchen light to avoid the temptation of foraging for more in the cabinets and refrigerator.

For the first time in over a month she found herself drawn to the piano, where she tickled what she remembered of the opening bars of *Rhapsody in Blue*. Her pageant performance twenty-four years ago still stood as her best ever, a three-minute arrangement that had taken her two years to master. The notes and chords were no longer automatic and she occasionally enjoyed the challenge of playing it again. It was true that her visits to Julia's salon had brought it to the forefront of her thoughts, so much that she found herself humming it nearly every day. Julia had said it would be stuck in her head too, but Ashley doubted someone like Julia had much knowledge of Gershwin. She wouldn't either if not for Cassandra.

She banged the last chord abruptly and rose to turn on the backyard lights, revealing her overgrown garden. It was here she spent the hours most people set aside for their friends, but as her mood plummeted over the past few weeks she couldn't whip up the enthusiasm to tend it. Now the area surrounding her tile patio—a cascade of flowering perennials, ferns and palms—was badly in need of attention. It would take all day Saturday to pull out the weeds, a backbreaking day of sun, sweat and grime. Not exactly what the doctor had ordered, but she just couldn't let it go another week. Making new friends would have to wait.

Chapter Four

Ashley muscled the wheelbarrow over the stepping stones that marked the narrow path into her backyard. She could have gotten the landscaper to deliver the two bags of mulch all the way around back, but she prided herself on taking care of this part of her garden herself. It had taken the whole morning to pluck the ambrosia from between her fading angel trumpets, cleomes and gaillardia.

Ambrosia was a much prettier word than ragweed, she mused. Much of her garden she had cultivated from seed, and never once had she sown ragweed. Only her constant vigilance had prevented it from taking over. She had briefly entertained the notion of joining Tampa's garden club in hopes of getting tips on how to rid her yard of these evil weeds once and for all, but then she learned that club members routinely toured one another's gardens. Better to suffer in silence than have strangers traipsing through her yard.

Gardening was therapeutic for a variety of reasons. The physical exertion was good exercise and relieved pent-up stress from the work week, and the methodical tasks gave her brain some time off. Best of all was the sense of control she felt from planning, arranging and tending things to yield just what she wanted, an array of color and texture that she could see from her bed, the living room and the den. She took pride in the fact that she had taught herself, poring over books and online articles, and through simple trial and error. "From the ground up," one blogger had joked. It was a deeply ingrained lesson that perseverance nearly always paid off.

Except in the case of the hybrid tea rose she'd been trying to grow for the last three seasons. Each time she'd been careful to insert her cutting into the stem and bind it up with grafting wax and tape. It grew, all right. It just didn't bud. Stubborn cuss.

Despite the optimism she had felt leaving Dr. Friedman's office, she remained disillusioned over her trip to Missouri. Granted, her feelings about Cassandra should have been put to bed long before the funeral, but seeing her into the ground had only stirred the anguish that had been simmering below the surface for more than twenty years.

When you are truly special, you have a responsibility to excel.

Cassandra had guided her toward excellence, but Ashley's journey had nothing to do with being special and everything to do with her dedication to following Cassandra's path without deviation, the same way she had sculpted this garden. There had been no other way to rise above being raised white trash in Maple Ridge. Putting it that way sounded melodramatic but Ashley had seen one generation after another follow in the aimless footsteps of uneducated parents to wallow in a world of minimum wage jobs, homes and cars in disrepair, and alcohol— lots of alcohol. Only six people in her graduating class of fifty-five had gone on to college, and she doubted half had earned a degree.

She wrestled the first bag from the wheelbarrow, cut it open with her gardening shears and dropped to her knees to spread it beneath her gardenia bush. A perfect blanket would seal the ground from sunshine, starving the weeds of the light they needed to grow. If anyone ever doubted that it worked, she would show them the barren ground beneath the grapefruit tree in her side yard, the branches of which made a canopy of shade as wide as the yard itself.

Expectations had been especially low in her household, where her mother and stepfather had been more concerned about finding ways to buy beer and cigarettes with food stamps than whether she or her brother finished their homework. When Dixon started middle school, he confided to her his dream to one day coach college basketball. By practicing for hours every day, he hoped to earn a scholarship that would take him out of Maple Ridge for good.

Ashley had no such skills, but her dreams of a different life were just as grand. The only thing she had going for her was her looks, and when Cassandra allowed her into the Muldoon Pageant Class at age eleven, she saw her path. It was considered a privilege to take the class, made even more exceptional when Cassandra offered her intensive private tutoring in piano, fashion and cosmetics, all with an eye toward launching Ashley on a pageant career.

It's about sacrifice…about wanting it more than everyone else.

That was another promise Cassandra had kept. Her pageant schedule—annual competitions for titles like Miss Junior Teen, Miss Summertime and Miss Sweetheart—had come at the cost of friends and school activities. More pronounced was the wedge it drove between Ashley and her mother, who abdicated what few parental responsibilities she felt as Ashley carved out her new life with Cassandra. None of it had mattered to Ashley. She was happy for each minute she got to spend with the former beauty queen.

After an hour of spreading mulch she was satisfied the demon ragweed had been choked out, at least until a heavy rainstorm opened new crevasses of light. Then she'd spend another weekend pushing it back into place. A vicious cycle, and yet satisfying.

Around the corner from her patio the Ruby Reds had begun to drop. Sweeter grapefruits would come in the weeks right after Christmas, but these were tangy and plump, good enough to share in the break room at the station. Ashley gathered up a dozen in her woven basket and called it a day.

The most difficult part of her weekend loomed ahead, the internal battle not to order a large pepperoni pizza as a reward for her hard work. Shaking off the thought, she laid a package of frozen shrimp on her counter to thaw and went off to draw a bath.

Why had she chosen a profession where workers were judged like so much horseflesh? Would she be less qualified to do her job if she gained a few pounds? As far as Carl was concerned, she would, and it was no use protesting. Kansas City news anchor Christine Craft had taken that very beef all the way to the Supreme Court and lost, setting the women's movement back thirty years.

After a lifetime of getting by on her looks, it was certainly ironic to be suffering for them now. Someone somewhere was laughing at her misery. Probably Miss Congeniality.

She relaxed in the tub as the warm water reached her bones. The fix was Cancun at Christmas again—two weeks at the Mexican spa, where she'd work out twice a day with trainers, eat measured portions of gourmet dietetic meals, and attend cooking classes and behavior management counseling. She had been there so many times she practically knew the staff by name. It was a grueling regimen but it always worked, and the New Year would see her fresh and invigorated. This was a crisis of her own making and she would handle it with the same determination that had gotten her this far in her career.

With a burst of optimism she yanked the chain on the tub stopper and pulled herself up. The full-length mirror on the back of the door showed her no mercy even as she drew in her stomach and twisted for the slimmest possible angle.

If you fail to discipline yourself, the world will do it for you.

As her shrimp skewer broiled, she tossed fresh spinach, raisins and pine nuts in her favorite balsamic vinaigrette. The moment it all was ready, her cell phone announced a call from Elaine Vandenbosch.

"If it isn't my favorite hippie," Ashley greeted her. She liked Elaine, who personified the sixties with her earth mother wardrobe and disarming sense of spontaneity. There was a genuine sweetness about her, especially when it came to taking care of Robyn, who had a tendency to get wound too tight over work.

"I can't believe a lovely lady like you is home alone on a Saturday night," Elaine said.

"Who says I'm alone?"

"Are you?"

"Yes, but that was just a lucky guess."

Ashley had been hesitant at first to socialize with Robyn and Elaine, knowing it might resurrect the chatter about her sexual orientation. Then the two of them showed up to help at a TV4 beach cleanup, where she saw how committed they were as a couple and decided they were exactly the sort of lesbian friends she wanted. Of course, that was before she'd carelessly agreed to the arrangement with their single friend, Julia.

Elaine asked, "Do you have big plans for Thanksgiving?"

She explained about her brother's tournament in Atlanta. "I'll spend two days sitting in the stands with my sister-in-law pretending to understand basketball."

"It's nice you'll be with family for the holidays. I was actually calling about the week after that. Are you doing anything Tuesday night…seven thirty or so?"

Ashley had learned not to walk into a question like that because of the risk of getting an invitation she didn't want. "You know how it is in the news business…depends on what's breaking."

"It's Robyn's birthday, the big four-oh. We're taking her to dinner at the Columbia in Ybor City. Think you can make it?"

She wanted to say yes, but the "we" part stopped her cold. If it were just the three of them, it would be fun, but she wanted no part of an elaborate surprise party with a dozen people she didn't know. "I'm just not sure, Elaine. I hate to be so slippery."

"I understand, but please try to work it out. It would just be the five of us, counting Julia and Teddie."

"Really? I would have guessed Robyn had dozens of friends eager to push her over the hill."

"She does, but there are people you like and people you *really* like. You're one of the ones she really likes. Quality over quantity, you know? She's been so crazy trying to get this semester wrapped up at school that I think a big party with a lot of people might send her right over the edge."

Ashley's brain was already busy generating possible reasons for why she would likely miss it. She could probably deal with Julia but Teddie made her anxious, going overboard as she had in trying to engage and impress her.

They only want to bask in your spotlight because it inflates their own sense of self-worth.

"Ashley, are you still there?"

"Yes...yes, of course. I'm just trying to think what stories we have planned for next week...and with the holidays and all, people might be taking off. I may have to stay late to write all the copy for eleven o'clock."

"Well, I hope not. We were hanging out at Rhapsody the other night and talking about what to do to celebrate, and Robyn specifically mentioned that she wanted you to be there."

Ashley wondered if that meant she had been a topic of conversation.

"In fact, we should have called you to come down and join us. Julia always does Robyn's hair after hours, and I bring a big pot of something vegetarian that Teddie complains about while she's eating seconds and thirds. She's a piece of work, that one."

"Yes, I met her. She makes quite an impression." Of the outrageous variety.

"Doesn't she, though? Classic baby dyke," Elaine said. "But she's a good kid, sort of our unofficial mascot. One thing you need to know about Teddie is that if you ever really need anything, she'll be the first one there with it. I've never met anybody so loyal."

Julia had also spoken with exceptional fondness for the tattooed biker. Ashley knew she was judging Teddie only on appearance, something that didn't make her particularly proud, but she had no control over her qualms. Dr. Friedman would want her to accept an invitation like this one. All it took was saying yes. It wasn't as if she was pledging a sorority or joining a biker gang. It was a simple birthday dinner for a good friend at a nice restaurant.

"It sounds like it's going to be a great night, Elaine. I'll be there if I can." That was enough wiggle room in case she changed her mind.

Chapter Five

"You suck, dude. That's cheating." Teddie snatched the joystick from Isaac's hand and stomped to a chair closer to the TV, where she could take her turn at annihilating the alien planet.

"It's called skill," he answered smugly. Like Teddie, Isaac was a product of the juvenile justice system, a young African-American who had won the trust of Julia's mother when he helped her start her car. What Bonnie hadn't known at the time was that he had started lots of cars, none of them his. He grew out of his delinquency just in time to avoid what Bonnie called Grownup Jail, and had been a regular at Thanksgiving dinner ever since.

Julia stared at the open refrigerator looking for space. "There's no room for these pies. I'm going to have to take them to my house."

"Just don't let Chuck see you," her mother said, lowering her voice to keep her longtime boyfriend from hearing. "Lord knows, he doesn't need it."

"Thanks for dinner, Mom. Everything was great. Can I sneak back in for leftovers?"

"Help yourself," she said, and with a roll of her eyes, added, "We're going over to Howard's to watch the Packers."

Julia chuckled at the dreary reference to Howard, Chuck's overbearing brother. "I know how much you love that." She balanced two pies on her arm and let the screen door slam behind her.

Across the driveway she entered her place, the garage they had converted to a cottage almost twenty years ago when she got her first job at a hair salon. She had wanted her own place, but didn't make enough money to cover rent and a car payment too. Living in the cottage gave her the illusion of independence until she and Rachel were able to move into a real apartment together. Julia had moved back to save money six years ago when she started looking to buy her own shop.

The cottage was divided into two areas, a living room-kitchen combination, and a bedroom with a bath. It was furnished efficiently, just enough to accommodate a friend or two who might stop by to watch TV, and with a double bed in case Julia had an intimate overnight guest. That had happened exactly once in the last six years, on a weekend that Bonnie and Chuck had gone to St. Augustine. The fact that she had her own front door didn't mean she didn't still live with her mother.

No sooner had she closed the refrigerator than she heard a knock at the door, and she turned to see Teddie rocking impatiently from one foot to the other. "I thought you and Isaac were battling for supremacy of the universe."

"He had to go. Chuck and Bonnie were going to drop him off at the bus stop." She held the door open instead of coming in. "I was hoping you'd take a ride with me over to St. Pete."

To Teddie, a ride probably meant an actual ride on the back of her motorcycle. That wasn't high on Julia's wish list. What she really wanted to do was change into her flannel pants, stretch out on the couch and bury herself in a Patricia Cornwell novel that someone had left at her shop.

"Jordan's not feeling so good, so a bunch of us thought we'd get together at her place and decorate it for Christmas. We were all sort of thinking this might be her last one..."

Julia couldn't say no to that, not when she heard the heavy

emotion in Teddie's voice. "Fine, but can't we just take my car? It has windows, seats and four new tires."

"Aw, come on. Where's your sense of adventure?"

After groaning, sighing and groaning some more, she finally relented. "Where's my brain bucket?"

Their ride across the Gandy Bridge took twenty minutes, after which Julia thought her fingers and nose would fall off. Sixty-eight degrees wasn't all that warm at fifty miles an hour. There were already several cars parked on the grass at Jordan's house, a white stucco bungalow not much bigger than Julia's garage apartment.

They were met by a woman of about thirty wearing ragged jeans and a black V-neck shirt that hugged her torso so tightly she might as well have been naked, especially since she wasn't wearing a bra, which Julia noticed immediately. Her long hair was limp and badly colored in a burgundy shade that couldn't be found in nature, and she sported an unsightly array of studs and hoops on her ears and brow. "Hi, I'm Patsy, Jordan's cousin from Ohio. I just moved down here to help out."

"Good deal," Teddie said, thrusting her hand forward. "She told me about you, something about having another black sheep in the family."

Patsy chuckled. "Yeah, I figure we got the queer gene from our grandma. She would have been happier living on our side of the fence. Come on in."

They stepped inside to find two girls struggling with a seven-foot tree while a third taped a string of lights to the crown molding. Teddie jumped in to push the tree upright while Julia helped Patsy drag a box of dilapidated lawn ornaments back outside.

"You guys are good to do this," Patsy said. "It's going to be a tough holiday."

"She's really sick, isn't she?"

"Worse than most of us thought. And her dad's got emphysema real bad so they can't really help her out much. I figured I'd come down and see her through it, maybe get a fresh start for myself. Life sucks pretty bad back in Toledo."

As Patsy talked about what the doctors had told them to

expect, Julia's respect for her grew, and she felt guilty for judging her so harshly earlier. Though she was far from what Julia found attractive, her maturity and demeanor gave her a special appeal. Under the circumstances it didn't seem right to flirt, but she wouldn't mind getting to know Patsy better. Elaine's crack about her not having a date in the last three years had struck a nerve.

Teddie bounded down the front steps helmet in hand. "Some of the bulbs are burned out. I need to get some more. Anyone want to come?" She was looking at Patsy.

"Sorry, I'm not much for motorcycles."

"It's just a few blocks up to the Walgreens. I'll go slow."

Patsy drew in a deep breath and held it. "Okay, but if I start screaming you have to stop and let me off."

"I don't make girls scream," Teddie said, lowering her sunglasses as she held out the extra helmet. "Unless it's a good scream."

As the horn sounded to signal the half, Ashley came to her feet with twenty thousand others in the Thrillerdome, most of them fans of Georgia Tech, whose basketball team was currently ranked number seven in the country. She was there to cheer for tiny Brunswick College, her brother's team of scrappy Davids to Tech's Goliaths. Going into the locker room, the Brunswick Bears were up by three, which had a lot of people in the arena on edge.

Ashley sat three rows behind the visitors' bench with her sister-in-law, who was assistant provost at the college. Dixon had finally married two years ago after a seven-year courtship. At forty-six, Nancy was too old to have children, but Dixon had always maintained that it was best to let the Giraud line die out so they could put an end to the gene pool that had produced their parents. It was hard to argue with his reasoning, since both he and Ashley wrestled with demons to this day.

While Ashley dealt with her own dubious past, Dixon suffered memories of beatings from their stepfather, who had little use for such trivial things as basketball and even less for another man in the house. Given his traumatic upbringing, it amazed her sometimes to see how calm and respectful he was with his players, though he sometimes showed his fire with the referees in support of his team. With his marriage to Nancy, Dixon had finally healed, and that made her as happy as anything in life ever had.

For years after leaving Maple Ridge they both had found it difficult to keep in touch. It wasn't only that college and careers kept them busy. The biggest barrier was that neither wanted to watch the other still struggling to overcome the hardships of growing up Giraud. It was only after a couple of years with Dr. Friedman that Ashley learned she could reclaim the concept of family by letting Dixon represent all she wanted it to be. When she finally reached out to him, she was overjoyed to find he needed her also, and since then they had made the effort to stay close and share the moments in their lives that mattered.

"Wouldn't it be something if we knocked off Georgia Tech?" Nancy shouted above the pep band that played the Yellow Jackets' fight song.

Nothing would make Ashley happier than to see Dixon's hard work rewarded on national television, especially with such a big tournament audience on Thanksgiving Day. That kind of feat got you noticed by the big-time basketball programs, which was what Dixon had dreamed about since he was a kid.

"I'm so proud of him."

"He's proud of you too. You should hear him go on about how his sister won the Miss Missouri pageant, and now she's on TV in Tampa."

Ashley was willing to bet she was on TV today too, since one of the cameramen had zoomed in several times as she and Nancy watched the game. If these sportscasters had done their homework, they would know who she was from her days at KBC, and she made it a point to guard her expressions and focus her interest on the game. In practice, it wasn't much different from how she behaved everywhere else when she knew she might be recognized.

Tech opened the second half on a 12-2 run to take control of the game, but the Bears hung around thanks to some timely three-point shooting and a generous call by the refs that gave them a chance at a last-gasp heave to win at the buzzer. When it clanged off the front of the rim, it was as if all the air had been sucked out of the gym.

As the crowd erupted, Ashley's eyes followed her brother, who clutched his head in his hands briefly before accepting a conciliatory handshake from Tech's coach. Then he patted each of his players on the back as they filed out of the gym, a gesture that made her swell with love.

"That was a fantastic game! I'm proud of Dixon's boys for putting up such a good fight." She followed Nancy into the tunnel where they waited outside the visitors' locker room while the players showered and dressed. She didn't know her sister-in-law well, but their love of Dixon gave them something in common. "I think we should celebrate as if we'd won."

"Me too. By the way, Ashley, I meant to tell you I was sorry to hear about your friend."

"I beg your pardon?"

"Dixon said you went back to Missouri for a funeral last month, something about the woman who helped you win all the pageants dying in a fire. Did I get that right?"

"Oh, yes. Thank you." The abrupt change of subject surprised her, but not as much as the realization that Nancy, who was now part of her family, knew things about her she had shared with no one. She hadn't even told Dixon much about the pageant class, but he knew it meant as much to her then as basketball had to him.

"He said she had a big impact on your life."

"Yes, she certainly did," she said absently.

The door burst open and one of the assistants waved them in. The players, now showered and dressed in sport coats, were sitting in a circle of chairs with Dixon standing in the center.

"I have some bad news for you, gentlemen," he began. "The Brunswick Bears won't be sneaking up on anyone from this day on. They know now that we mean business and they're going to be ready for us. But the good news is I have a reward for you for playing so well today, because I'm about to introduce you to Miss Missouri."

Ashley laughed and covered her cheeks, stepping forward to the edge of the circle. "I'm sorry, but my brother forgot to tell you that was twenty-some years ago."

The players didn't care. They were all on their feet to shake her hand, probably more out of an effort to please their coach than to make an impression on her. She put on her TV4 news anchor face and thrilled them just the same.

Chapter Six

It was growing more obvious by the minute that Ashley had misjudged her stylist.

Julia stood with her hip jutting out, a look of ire wrinkling her forehead. "It's outrageous if you ask me. They're raising our business license fees, but then giving the big box stores a bundle of tax breaks to open up here and undercut our business. That's like me giving somebody money to open up a salon next door. How much sense does that make?"

It was hard to disagree with the grim conclusion. Ashley had tossed out the topic of the new business fee thinking she would take the opportunity to educate Julia on an important issue that could impact her bottom line. Instead she found Julia not only knew all the details but had been following the city council's deliberations for several weeks.

"And it doesn't even create new jobs. It just takes ours away and gives them to people who will work for less, and then all the profits go to Arkansas or Minnesota…to people who aren't going to spend a dime here in Tampa. Mark my word somebody's getting kickbacks for this."

Ashley chuckled, remembering the blistering front page story in yesterday's *Guardian* that said exactly the same thing. "You sound like Lamar Davidson."

"I love Lamar. He's like a one-man feeding frenzy."

"You read the *Guardian*?"

"I know, I know. It's not a serious paper, but they don't pull any punches in their political stories. The other guys like to say they bring you both sides, but when one of those sides is crazy, all they do is make it seem legitimate."

Ashley was immensely impressed not only with Julia's grasp of local government, but with her news critique as well. "You missed your calling, Julia. You would have made a great news editor."

"I don't know about that, but I can tell when something stinks to high heaven, and that business tax reeks." She rubbed conditioner in her palms and began dabbing it into Ashley's wet hair. Gradually the feather-like touch became a hearty scalp massage.

"I take back what I said about your calling. This is what you were meant to do."

Julia laughed and dug in harder. "Believe it or not, we're all taught to do this in school because our customers find it relaxing. But then we get so caught up in how many people are waiting or if we're going to be able to find a few minutes for lunch. This is usually the first thing that goes when a stylist gets busy, and before long they get out of the habit."

"Then I'm glad we have lots of time. I might talk to Sergio about needing to have my hair done more often." Ashley hadn't yet decided about the invitation to join the group for Robyn's birthday dinner tomorrow night, but her uneasiness about Julia was starting to dissipate. There was no rational reason they couldn't at least be casual friends, especially since she was locked into a contract to come here every month.

Julia was attractive, Ashley admitted. Not in a classic sense, but striking in her own way. Cassandra would have said she worked well with her assets. By wearing her wavy hair short she downplayed the thinness of her face and neck, and the way she styled it away from her face accentuated her brown eyes. Of course Julia knew all those tricks since she practiced them every day on a dozen different people.

"Did you always want to be a stylist?"

"Yeah, I guess. When I was a kid, our neighbor had a salon on her back porch, and she showed me how to do a couple of things. I used to practice on my friends, but then their moms quit letting them play with me."

"I can see how that would have landed you on the No Play list."

"Except now they all come around wanting a discount because they knew me back when."

"You grew up in Tampa?"

"About three miles from here. My mom still lives there and I have the garage apartment."

Julia fired up her handheld hair dryer and began drying one narrow strand at a time with a large round brush. Ashley had learned the same technique from Cassandra.

How can you expect to control your life if you cannot control your hair?

"So you're a genuine Florida native. I thought everyone in Tampa was from somewhere else. And your father, is he…" Ashley didn't want to be too nosy but she found it curious that Julia had never mentioned her dad.

"Dad lives over in the central part of the state. He has one of those little studio apartments with a bed and a toilet…bars on the doors…group showers."

Ashley was stunned not only by the disclosure, but by the look of amusement on Julia's face. "Your father's in prison?"

"He's a career con man. My mom thought she'd married an insurance salesman. He sold insurance, all right—life, home, car, you name it—except the company he represented didn't actually exist. Neither did the cemetery plots or the prepaid funerals, or the gold in those rare gold coins. He's been in and out of jail as long as I can remember. This last time they caught him selling roofing contracts to people who'd been hit by Hurricane Charley."

The revelation startled Ashley so much her own confession slipped out before she could stop herself. "My father died in prison...liver disease. He was driving drunk and killed two men on their way home from work."

Hot air from the dryer blew aimlessly across her lap as Julia stopped her motions. "God, Ashley. That's awful."

"Especially for the families of the two men who were killed," she said bitterly. She had never told anyone but Jarvis about her family tragedy. "I don't remember very much about him, just that my mother moved us to Maple Ridge because everybody in Gallatin hated our guts after that. I was only six."

"I didn't know my dad all that well either. I remember people driving up to our house screaming at us, but I'm sure it was nothing like what you went through."

Ashley couldn't believe she had divulged something so personal, but it wasn't every day she came across someone who could relate to her brand of resentment and shame. "Amazing we have that in common, isn't it? People who haven't experienced it have no idea what it's like to grow up around that."

"My mom divorced him when I was four and spent the next seven years trying to collect child support. As soon as I was old enough to realize what it was, I told her I didn't want his money because he probably stole it from somebody else. I remember us going out for ice cream every time we found out he'd been locked up again."

"Just be glad you had one parent who stepped up and took responsibility. My mother was a textbook codependent, always covering for him and blaming everyone else. She got married again when I was nine to another man just like him...drank all the time, couldn't keep a job." Now she was getting into territory she only discussed with Dr. Friedman. "Look, this isn't something I normally talk about with people...normally as in ever."

Julia chuckled softly. "You'd be surprised what people say when they get in this chair. I'm not a gossip, Ashley. For what it's worth, I think it says a lot about you that you made it so far without much of a springboard."

"Thank you…a lot of it was luck," she answered softly. She had escaped Maple Ridge only because of her looks, which she considered at that time to be her only asset. If there was any credit to be given, it was for her single-minded determination to exploit it.

"If I were betting, I'd say you made your own luck. Anyone who gets dealt a lousy hand and figures out how to play it deserves respect. My friend Teddie, the one who came in last time for her phone…she was raised by an SOB who beat the crap out of her nearly every day. She talks a tough game but the only time she really gets riled up is when you mess with one of her friends. Instead of copying her old man, she copied people like my mom, and like Robyn and Elaine."

Ashley had wondered how someone so young and brash had become part of an older, more subdued clique of friends. Elaine's reference to Teddie as a mascot now made perfect sense. They held her in genuine affection and tacitly accepted a duty to see her along. "That's a good thing you girls do. And I think you left somebody off that list of people she copied."

"Hey, not me. I think she's a brat," Julia said, smirking as she tried to avoid eye contact.

"What's that old saying about protesting too much?"

"Fine, but the chair rule works both ways. No ratting me out." She picked up her scissors and snapped them sharply. "Accidents might happen."

Ashley held up two fingers to signal a truce. She decided she liked Julia, and it wasn't just their shared history. It was her attitude and intellect, the latter of which Ashley had underestimated. Even her reservations about Teddie were fading a bit. The kid had too many people in her corner to be considered a total flake.

Julia applied her finishing touches to the fresh cut and stood back to admire her work. "I'm happy if you're happy. And now I get to use that tired cliché about seeing you next year."

It was on the tip of her tongue to say she'd see her sooner than that—at the birthday dinner for Robyn tomorrow night—but she still couldn't bring herself to commit. Old habits and all.

Chapter Seven

The Columbia Restaurant in Ybor City was a hive of activity no matter the season. As the oldest restaurant in Florida it was a destination for tourists and out-of-town conventioneers, but to locals like Julia and her friends, it was a Tampa icon, renowned not only for its authentic Spanish-Cuban cuisine but also for its nightly flamenco performances.

Julia was glad for the chance to relax after a busy day on her feet, owed to the holiday party season. Knowing that Robyn would probably come straight from work in one of her flashy business suits and Ashley—if she showed up—would be dressed for being on the air, she had taken fresh clothes to her shop. When her last customer walked out, she had hurriedly changed into gray slacks and a fitted teal sweater, and given her hair some life with a hot comb.

"I'm surprised you didn't get a table for the show tonight," she said to Elaine. "Did you tell them we had a birthday?"

"Yeah, but we've seen it so many times and besides, we figured if Ashley joined us, she'd probably have to leave in the middle of it. At least this way we'll be able to talk." She looked at the empty seat at the head of the table. "Although I'm starting to think she isn't going to make it after all."

Robyn smiled weakly, clearly disappointed. "Let's give her a few more minutes. I think she would have called if she weren't coming."

Teddie folded the cuffs on her white tuxedo shirt, exposing the edge of a Harley tattoo on her forearm. She too was neatly dressed in honor of the occasion and had combed her hair to one side, the longer strands tipped in platinum instead of the usual neon. "I hope she comes. I like you guys and all, but I dressed to impress the lovely Miss Giraud."

"Will you knock it off?" Julia smacked her gently with a menu. "She isn't coming to see you. It's Robyn's birthday, remember?"

"And I hate to break it to you, slick," Elaine said, invoking her pet name for Teddie, "but I know for a fact that Ashley isn't all that comfortable with people going on about how beautiful she is. That stalker guy used to send her notes like that all the time."

"So I'm a stalker just because I wanted to look nice? Jeez, Louise!"

"No, you're a stalker because you flirt like a lounge lizard," Julia said. "You should just club women over the head and drag them off to your cave."

Teddie scowled and folded her arms.

"I think you look good, kiddo," Robyn interjected diplomatically. "But don't get your hopes up. I don't really think you're Ashley's type."

"What's that supposed to mean? What kind of type am I?"

"For one thing, you're twenty-three and she's north of forty. And you have to admit there's not anything about Ashley Giraud that says biker chick."

"But you're our favorite punk, slick," Elaine added with a grin.

Though Teddie smiled sheepishly, Julia sensed that their admonitions had hurt her feelings, something they hadn't intended. She wrapped an arm around her younger friend's shoulders and gave her a gentle hug. "Mine too. How was Jordan's chemo?"

"Brutal. Patsy texted me this afternoon…said she'd been throwing up all day."

"Poor kid."

The waiter returned with their drink orders—sangria for Robyn and Elaine, a San Miguel beer for Teddie, and iced tea for Julia, who couldn't stand the taste of alcohol. Since it was already a quarter past seven, Robyn ordered the eggplant Riojana for Elaine and paella for four. "If Ashley doesn't come, we can take the leftovers home."

Julia overheard a woman at a nearby table mention Ashley's name and turned in time to see her stride gracefully through the room behind the hostess. Obviously fresh from her news desk, she wore a long-sleeved navy blue dress with a plunging neckline, a strand of heavy faux pearls and matching earrings. In her hand was a small brightly-wrapped package.

"I'm so sorry I'm late. We had a breaking story and I had to shoot a new promo for eleven o'clock. I hope you ordered already."

"And I hope you like paella," Robyn answered, rising to give Ashley a kiss on the cheek.

"My all-time favorite." Ashley stretched across the table to grasp Elaine's hand and then Julia's. She looked directly at Teddie as she took her seat. "I distinctly remember your hair being green."

Teddie laughed. "Oh, that's just something I spray on when I'm goofing off. Washes right out."

"Who knew?" She looked quizzically at Julia. "Does it come in my color? That's sounds so much easier than what you do."

"Promise me you won't put that junk in your hair. I'd have to commit hari-kari with my scissors."

"You mean if Sergio didn't get there first."

"You know Sergio?" Robyn asked. "That guy is so neurotic, and I swear he has me on speed dial." She launched into a tale of how the assistant producer micromanaged her interns, right down to the quarter hour. "Some days I just want to grind up a

Valium and slip it into his Cuban coffee. Why does a guy like that even need caffeine?"

It was easy to see how Robyn and Ashley had become good friends. They were close in age, hailed from the Midwest, and crossed paths enough at work to know the same people. Both displayed obvious pride in having achieved their ambitions, Robyn as a full professor at the university and Ashley as arguably the most trusted newsperson in the Tampa Bay area.

Ashley propped her phone by her water glass. "Sorry I have to do this. It's set to vibrate, but I have to keep up in case I get called back early."

"We understand. That's part of the bargain," Robyn said. "I'm just glad you're here."

She slid the gift across the table. "Something for the birthday girl."

"You didn't have to do that. Just having all of you here to celebrate is enough."

Teddie chuckled. "I hope so because all I got you is here in this invisible box."

"And you detailed her car for free," Elaine added.

"It looks great, by the way." Robyn reached over and bumped Teddie's fist before tearing into the small package, which turned out to be a fully-loaded paperclip holder with the TV4 emblem on the side. "Oh, my God. I'm never going to live this down as long as I live."

A boy of about twelve in a white shirt and tie appeared at their table. "Excuse me, Miss Giraud?"

Ashley's face lit up in a smile as she appraised him. "Yes, how do you do?"

"May I please have your autograph?" he asked, presenting her with a pen and scrap of paper apparently torn from an address book. He looked sheepishly over his shoulder at his family, who waved in their direction.

"Of course." She scribbled a brief message along with her signature. "What's your name?"

"Jeremy...but it's for my mom. She watches you every night."

"Please tell her that I'm so happy to hear that," she said, returning his pen and paper, "and tell her she has a very handsome, well-mannered son."

He blushed and thanked her before walking away.

"That happens every time we go out," Elaine said. "We're now officially part of Ashley's celebrity entourage."

"I'm so sorry. I hate imposing that on all of you."

"No, I wasn't complaining. I think it's sweet how you always smile and act so glad to see everyone. That kid and his mom will be your loyal fans forever, and probably everybody else who just realized you were here."

Robyn beckoned to the waiter with her empty glass and gestured for another round. "I've published a couple of articles on that. It's called para-social interaction, and it's especially common with those morning news shows. People like to think they have a relationship with the news team they watch regularly. I'm not talking about the stalker thing like Ashley had." She held up her hand for emphasis. "Those people cross the line because they imagine *real* relationships. I'm talking about typical viewers who have these one-sided pseudo-friendships with their local newscasters. They don't have any expectations that Ashley will reach out to them personally, but they're delighted when they actually have a chance to interact in a public place like a restaurant. If Ashley's nice—and she always is—it reinforces what they believe and strengthens the para-social bond."

The labels and nuances were lost on Julia, but she understood what the women at Rhapsody liked about watching Ashley on TV4. "The women I talk to in my shop trust you because they feel like you're one of them."

"I am one of them. This is my home too, and at the risk of sounding like one of our commercials, I think all of us at TV4 care about this community."

"Except for Oscar," Teddie muttered, barely loud enough for everyone to hear.

Julia recognized the knock on Ashley's co-anchor and curbed the impulse to kick Teddie under the table. The last thing she wanted was to see Ashley get offended, even though she totally agreed that Rod Gilchrist was a phony.

Ashley cocked her head to the side and squinted. "Who's Oscar?"

"That Gilchrist guy," Teddie said. "I always call him that because he acts like he's up for an Academy Award or something. Like whenever he does a story that's supposed to be sad—fires or car wrecks...things like that—his face goes all grim and somber, and his voice gets real deep. He's such a poseur."

Several seconds of awkward silence passed before Ashley leaned forward and lowered her voice. "Over the top, isn't it? And that better never leave this table."

Teddie grinned broadly, clearly pleased at getting Ashley's approval. "Never, scout's honor. And I scout for girls all the time so that makes it valid."

"Yes, you do," Julia said, shaking her head as she turned back to Ashley. "I don't care as much about how newspeople say things as what they have to say. Not the words, but the topics. I see all kinds of stories on your channel...good news, bad news, but when you tell us about a problem, you also give us some ideas about what we can do about it. It makes people feel like they matter. In the meantime, those clowns over at Channel 20 try to make you think all that ever happens around here is crime or disaster. I'm surprised people who watch that crap don't just hide under their beds all day."

Robyn was practically jumping out of her chair. "Researchers have been studying that for fifty years. They call it the Scary World Hypothesis."

"Down, girl," Elaine said gently, placing a hand on her partner's forearm. "It's a birthday party, not a seminar."

Teddie ignored all of them. "I want to hear more about your stalker. Elaine told us you had some guy following you."

Ashley made an unpleasant face and sighed. "That was so disturbing."

Julia recognized the expression from when she was talking about her family back in Missouri. "You don't have to tell us about it if it makes you uncomfortable. I'm sure it's not a pleasant subject."

"It's not, but at least it's not a problem anymore. The guy transferred to Texas after the station threatened legal action."

"Wow, I didn't know it was that serious," Elaine said.

"Yeah, it started when we had that telethon for the hurricane victims about eight years ago. His company sent some people over to work the phones, and I told him how nice it was that he volunteered. I always try to speak to everyone individually when we do an event like that, but he obviously read a lot more into it than just me being polite because the next thing I know he's sending me cards every week telling me all about himself and how glad he was that we were able to make a special connection. I just ignored it, but then he started getting weird, telling me that I shouldn't wear blue on the air because it's a sad color and I have too much light in my soul for that." Rolling her eyes, she went on, "Next he sends me a picture of himself. By that time my red flags were up and I turned it over to security. They wrote him a nice but firm note asking him to please refrain from sending personal mail, and for a while I thought it was settled."

"Was he creepy looking?" Teddie asked.

"No, he was just a normal guy. In the photo he was standing there with his arms folded and leaning on this white Lexus convertible, like he wanted to impress me with his car or something. So a few weeks later I go out to dinner with Puze and Melitta, and this bottle of wine suddenly appears in front of me. I don't even drink! And I look over and see him sitting at the bar, and Puze says 'Oh, that's just William, a new guy at my gym.' This man was cultivating my friends to get close to me! I started shaking so much I had to leave."

Julia was concerned about the quaking in Ashley's voice, and would have suggested she drop the subject had she not been riveted by the story.

"Next I get this long rambling apology about how he hadn't meant to intrude on our dinner, and hadn't even realized I was there with his friend Puze—yeah, right. Puze said he hardly knew him. A week after that I'm pulling into my driveway around midnight and see this white Lexus stop across the street from my house. I ran inside and called security at the station, and they sent somebody over just to sit behind him with their lights on bright. The next day they went to where he worked and persuaded him to develop other interests before he ended up in jail."

"You're lucky that was the end of it," Elaine remarked. "Some of these guys...nothing stops them until they get locked up. Creeps."

It now made perfect sense to Julia why Ashley was so cautious about accepting social invitations from people she didn't know well. It was a wonder she allowed herself any new friends at all.

Teddie narrowed her eyes and put on her toughest face. "If anybody like that ever bothers you again, you let me know."

Elaine chuckled. "What would you do about it, slick?"

"I'm not saying, but I guarantee I'll fix it long before the SOB shows up at her house."

"Thank you, Teddie." Ashley looked at her earnestly. "I'm sure you could put the fear of God into anyone."

"I don't know about the God part, but I can do fear. I don't let people screw around with my friends."

Ashley shook her head dismissively. "I appreciate that, but I doubt I'll have any more problems like this. Jarvis had a big meeting with the security company to make sure those situations won't get that far again. In fact, all my mail now goes through one of Robyn's interns, so I don't even see notes like that anymore."

Julia picked up a subtle shift in Ashley's demeanor as she leaned back to put distance between herself and the group, and it was probably no coincidence it came right on the heels of Teddie calling her a friend. It was the same hesitance she had displayed over Julia's invitation to join their group when they got together to hang out. While it seemed she was having a good time, it was clear she still didn't feel totally at ease. Perhaps she didn't even want to and had only come out of respect for Robyn, the one person with whom she had interests in common.

The waiter appeared with a massive dish of paella, and the conversation turned back to Robyn, who vowed to eat one shellfish for every year of her life. By the time they all had their fill it was after nine o'clock, time for Ashley to head back to work.

"Let's hear it for a slow news day, girls. I would have hated to miss this," she said.

"Who's got the next birthday?" Elaine asked. "We have to do this again."

Teddie pushed back and patted her stomach. "Mine's at the end of February, and I probably won't have to eat again until then. But you all have to come to Skate City this Sunday at one o'clock. We're doing a fundraiser for Jordan. Everybody's getting sponsors to pay for however many laps we skate, and we'll probably auction off some stuff." She turned to Julia. "Will you donate a haircut?"

"Sure, but I thought you said she got all her medical bills worked out with the state. What's this for?"

"Everything else. She had to quit her job after she started the chemo. Patsy says she's getting stressed out because they're threatening to cut off her lights."

Elaine addressed Ashley's look of confusion. "Teddie's friend Jordan has melanoma."

"Oh, dear. How is she?"

"Not so good," Teddie said, her nose reddening as her emotions threatened to spill over. "Her doctor says she might have a year, as long as she doesn't get an infection. She's only twenty-four."

"That's awful. Twenty-four is so young."

"It would be really cool if you came to our skate party. It's just for a couple of hours. No telling how much we'd raise if we auctioned off a chance to skate with Ashley Giraud."

Ashley's eyes went wide with alarm. "Oh, no. You'd be more likely to see me in a spacesuit than on a pair of skates. I'm as clumsy as a duck walking backward."

"I wouldn't let you fall."

Julia knew Teddie's persuasive powers all too well and didn't want Ashley to feel pressured into something she didn't want to do. "Teddie, the station probably has someone who coordinates Ashley's appearances. She can't just go wherever she wants and endorse something. They have to approve it."

"She's right. I have to run practically everything through our publicity department. I'll help your friend though," she offered. "I can sponsor you to skate laps. How's that?"

"Cool, but I still think you'd be awesome on skates."

Ashley was relieved to have the evening behind her, not because it had been unpleasant—it hadn't—but because she no longer had to obsess about whether or not to go. In the end her friendship with Robyn had won out. Turning forty was a big deal, something she would remember for years to come, and Ashley didn't want that memory clouded by the fact she had stood them up.

Teddie had been less of a wild card than she expected. Not only had she cleaned up nicely, she had toned down the flirtations and proven herself to be oddly charismatic. As she had talked poignantly about her cancer-stricken friend, it struck Ashley that she wasn't just some weirdo marching to a different drummer. She was a product of her generation, the cohort that pushed its outrageousness into the faces of elders just to proclaim their rebellious youth. It had always been so, and Ashley had to accept that she was now an elder.

She had to admit it was fun listening to Robyn talk about the media theories she had studied in school, but it was even more interesting to hear Julia articulate them from her layman's perspective. The whole news team at TV4 was dedicated to bringing their viewers intelligent, useful news, and Julia got that.

That wasn't all she got. The most welcome moment of the night had come when she keenly picked up on Ashley's panic about Teddie's skating invitation and created the perfect out by suggesting she would have to get the station's approval. It surprised her that Julia had been able to intuit her hesitation given they had known each other such a short time, but their conversations had been among the most revealing Ashley could recall. Now that she had an ally who was sensitive to her social quirks and willing to run interference, she ought to be able to accept a simple invitation every now and then without putting herself through all the mental gymnastics. But not roller skating.

Something else she had noticed about Julia tonight was her appearance. Ashley would never offer anyone unsolicited advice on how to dress, but a woman with fair coloring like Julia looked great in shades of blue such as the sweater she had worn tonight, not the plain white shirts she wore at the salon.

The four friends were an interesting intersection of personality traits. She had thought herself most like Robyn, but their similarities were largely limited to work and their agreement on journalistic values. In fact, it was Teddie who had the most in common with Robyn, like her excitability and strident determination to make things happen. Elaine was at the opposite end of that spectrum, quiet and pensive, more likely to try to understand people than influence them. And Julia was somewhere in the middle, or maybe a mix of all of them. She was introspective at times but spoke with confidence when she had something meaningful to contribute. Ashley had learned to listen to people like that, and to put stock in what they had to say.

She pulled into her marked parking space next to Rod's, which was empty and would likely remain so until the last minute when he appeared just in time to have his nose dusted. *Oscar.* She probably shouldn't have acknowledged her feelings about her co-anchor but Teddie had nailed it as far as she was concerned. Gilchrist was more actor than newsman.

The irony hadn't escaped her, though, that the whole evening had been a performance for her as well, just like all her other social engagements. Despite her bustling arrival, she had, in fact, circled the restaurant several times before finally deciding to park. More important, she had suppressed her doubts about fitting in with the menagerie of women long enough to actually pull it off, even enjoying herself. All it took was keeping her public persona in place, where she treated everyone with grace and charm. The dinner with friends was exactly what Dr.

Friedman wanted from her, a change in behavior that would lift her emotions. She felt better, but how long would it last?

"Hi, Chuck. How are the boys?" She knew all the security guards by name and went out of her way to address them each time she passed through the parking lot. The simple gesture guaranteed her a watchful eye and an escort with an umbrella any time it rained.

The young man who had recently taken over as her office intern met her as she crossed the newsroom. He seemed bright enough but his acne scars and frizzy black hair made him an unlikely candidate for on-air reporting. He had brought himself notice, however, for always wearing a bowtie and sweater vest, prompting some on the news staff to teasingly call him Jimmy Olsen.

"Aaron?"

"Hi, Ashley. A woman came by about an hour ago and dropped off a package for you. She wouldn't tell me her name or what was in it, but she said I had to give it to you...nobody else."

She took the package, a thick manila envelope with her name printed in capital letters. Worst-case scenario, it was something vile from a viewer, either a stalker or someone angry about one of their stories, yet it was hard to imagine anyone delivering something like that in person. Though her instincts told her someone else should open it, her curiosity got the best of her and she tore open the seal.

Most of the contents turned out to be cardboard, inserted to keep a photo from being bent. Pictured was a piece of crumpled blue paper that someone had tried to smooth out, and on it, four alpha-numeric entries followed by dollar amounts ranging from ninety-eight thousand to half a million. A folded note had the name Kathy and a phone number.

"Any idea what that is?" Aaron asked.

"Parcel IDs," she murmured thoughtfully. She checked the clock and confirmed that she had plenty of time for makeup and the sound check. If her teleprompter was set she could squeeze in a short call and shed some light on this mystery. "Is my script up?"

"It's loaded, and I left a copy on your desk."

"Good work." She closed her office door and studied the message. It had no last name but the exchange was the same as her home phone, which meant it was someone who lived near Ballast Point. "Hello, this is Ashley Giraud. I received a message to call Kathy at this number."

"Oh, my gosh! It's her," the woman said, her voice sounding as if she had turned from the phone. "Miss Giraud, I don't know if you remember me. My name's Kathy Finley, and you were behind me in the line at the drugstore a couple of weeks ago when I didn't have enough money."

Ashley recalled her trip to the pharmacy and the mother who was dealing with sick children, but that made no sense in the context of the cryptic numbers she had gotten in the mail. "Yes, what can I do for you, Mrs. Finley?"

"My husband needs to talk to somebody and you're the only one we trust."

"I don't understand. Did you send me this list of numbers?"

A man's voice shouted in the background. "Forget it. Hang up!"

"Kevin, we need to tell her. She'll help us."

Ashley scratched the name Kevin Finley on her day planner in case the woman bolted, and held up a finger toward her producer, who was outside her glass wall waving her to the set. "Kathy, I don't have much time. Why don't you talk to your husband—"

"He's a clerk in the property tax office. Somebody went in and lowered the appraisals on a bunch of properties."

So the dollar amounts were their appraised value. She should have figured that out. "But people are allowed to contest their appraisals, aren't they? Sometimes they get changed."

"I know, but Kevin says they're supposed to submit affidavits so there's a record. They didn't do that. They just changed them, and they used Kevin's terminal to do it. If anybody gets caught, it's going to look like it was him."

Ashley struggled to grasp the scope of what Mrs. Finley was saying, and more important, what she wanted TV4 to do about it. If there was a common thread to these properties that could be tied to malfeasance, it was a potential story. "I tell you what. I'll ask someone to check out these properties—"

"It's not just the ones I sent you. He's been keeping a record and it's"—she turned from the phone to ask her husband—"a hundred and thirty-seven."

One hundred thirty-seven undocumented—and likely unauthorized—changes to the county tax base. This was no longer just a potential story. This was a potential blockbuster.

Chapter Eight

"We're looking for five-oh-seven," Ashley said to Jarvis as he drove slowly through the neighborhood, which consisted mostly of small, single-story homes with chain-link fences around the sandy yards. Kevin Finley had gotten spooked at the last minute about having them come to his Ballast Point house and moved the Sunday morning meeting to his sister's house in Temple Terrace. "There it is."

They parked on the street and were greeted at the gate by Kathy Finley, whom Ashley recognized from their brief encounter at the pharmacy. She was wearing an oversized Tampa Bay Buccaneers jersey which hung to her thighs over faded jeans, and had a toddler perched on her hip. "Thank you for coming all the way out here. Kevin's as nervous as a cat about somebody in his office finding out he's talking to you."

Ashley introduced Jarvis and they followed Kathy inside, where a visibly anxious Kevin Finley paced the living room. Kathy herded the rest of the family down the hall to a den while she and Jarvis gathered around a modest table in the kitchen with Kevin. He was a tall, wiry man, round-shouldered with glasses, and like his wife, wore a Buccaneers jersey. Obviously it was game day.

"Mr. Finley, because we're—"

"Call me Kevin."

"Kevin," she said warmly, taking the familiar gesture as a sign she had his meager trust for now. "Because we're members of the press, we have special privileges that allow us to protect your identity as a source, even from the police or whoever might investigate our story once we make it public. In return for that, we have an obligation to be truthful about the facts and not to twist them in a way that serves anyone's particular agenda. It's very important that we're all on the same page about that."

He nodded. "It's important to me too."

Jarvis began scribbling notes on a yellow legal pad. "Why don't you start at the beginning? Tell us how things work in the property appraiser's office."

Step by step Kevin walked them through the process of how legitimate changes were submitted for entry into the property tax database. The county charter mandated assessments be updated every two years, and those updates were prepared by an appraisal team that evaluated permits, resales and market values on an ongoing basis. Kevin's primary job was to enter those updates, which were used to compute the amount owed each year in property taxes. On occasion, property owners would challenge their assessments, arguing before the tax board that their properties had been appraised at more than they were worth. When these appeals were successful, official paperwork was submitted to authorize the adjustment, and their bill was lowered.

"So I came back from lunch one day…it was the last week in October, and I happened to see this piece of paper in my trash can, the one from that picture Kathy sent you. I only noticed it because it was blue and I didn't have a pad like that." He pulled from his pocket a crumpled blue note which turned out to be the original of what he had sent to the station. "My trash can sits all the way on the other side of my desk, so I knew somebody had been in my office. At first I thought they might have just used my terminal to look up some appraisals. But that night I started thinking about it, and it didn't make any sense for somebody to come in and write all that down, and then throw it away."

Though his knee continued to bounce, Kevin had visibly relaxed, as though relieved to be handing off his problem to someone else.

"So I went in a little early the next day and looked up those four properties on that list. One was in Town 'n Country, one in River Hills, and the other two in Carrolwood, all residential. Turns out they'd been updated the day before sometime between twelve thirty and one when I was down in the cafeteria, and I checked the values against my backup database from the week before and they were all cut by exactly sixty-five percent. The only way we ever get a drop that big is when a building gets bulldozed. Now I'm not saying that doesn't happen, but it doesn't happen four times in one day, and it never happens without an affidavit. So I was going to go ask Bruce—that's Bruce Redmond, my supervisor. I was going to ask him about it when I saw who made the entries. It was my login ID."

Jarvis looked up from his notes. "But isn't that keyed to your computer?"

"I always log out when I leave my desk. Always."

"Who else has access to your login ID, Kevin?" Ashley asked.

"Everybody knows my login. But as far as I know our network administrator down in the basement is the only one who has access to passwords, and I reset mine every week."

"Do you think it could have been a hacker?"

He shrugged. "Maybe, but you can't make those changes just by hacking into the database. There are only two terminals in the building with the software that lets you do that, and the system automatically logs which terminal it came from."

"So whoever did this used your computer," Jarvis said. His notes had become a flow chart with boxes and arrows. "Tell us about the others. How did you find them?"

"Basically, I just looked for them. I went back and sorted all the properties that had been updated in the last six months by the time stamp. Most days there weren't any entries, but sometimes

I'd find ten or twelve all made on the same day during the time I would have been at lunch. But the biggest bunch, fifty-one, was entered last August when I was on vacation. I think that's when it started because I couldn't find anything before then."

Ashley looked at Jarvis and nodded slowly, certain he was already planning resources, graphics and interviews in what would be a colossal effort to tie together the properties in question and identify those responsible for the conspiracy. Kevin Finley had stumbled onto government wrongdoing of the worst kind—unless you happened to be the news team on the inside track. Then it was your biggest story of the year.

"Look at her go!" Julia said, peering over the rail at the rink, where the skate guard had temporarily cleared the floor of slow skaters to allow Teddie and her five friends to rack up as many laps as possible in the closing minutes of their fundraiser. Besides donating a free haircut, Julia had pledged fifty cents a lap thinking the most Teddie would manage in an hour was a hundred or so. In fact, she had doubled that and still had three minutes to go.

Robyn shook her head and sighed. "I hope you brought the checkbook, Elaine. I don't have enough cash to cover this."

"And we still have the auction."

The impromptu event had drawn about twenty of Jordan's friends and coworkers, not a huge crowd but an enthusiastic one by the cheering. Jordan, obviously fatigued from her treatments, watched the goings-on with Patsy from a table in the corner.

Patsy looked tired as well, Julia thought. It had to be exhausting taking care of someone as sick as her cousin, especially without help. She might welcome a break to go out for dinner if somebody—somebody named Teddie—would be willing to sit with Jordan for a few hours. It probably wouldn't amount to anything, but at least Julia could start the clock again on the last time she had a date.

The whistle blew, signaling the end of speed skating and the lap challenge. Teddie slammed to a stop against the rail, sweat pouring down her face and neck. "Two hundred twelve, ladies. That makes…like, three hundred bucks from you guys."

"Three-eighteen," Elaine corrected. "You did good, slick."

"And I got another dollar a lap from Ashley. Are you guys going to do musical chairs? Ten dollars a pop. Winner gets a free haircut at Rhapsody."

Julia held up both hands. "Not me. I'll throw in ten bucks but I can't cut my own hair. That would be like a surgeon taking out her own appendix."

"We're in," Elaine said. "Let's go get skates."

"Elaine's right, you know," Julia said as Teddie skated around the rail to join her. "You did a great job pulling all this together so fast. Jordan's lucky to have a friend like you."

"She could use some luck right about now. And I bet Patsy's going stir-crazy. If the timing didn't suck so bad I'd ask her out to dinner or something. What she's doing for Jordan…well, that's my kind of chick."

It was all Julia could do not to blurt out an expletive. She should have seen it coming after the way Teddie had talked Patsy into taking a ride on the Harley. By voicing her feelings before Julia had a chance to say anything, Teddie had virtually planted a flag in the woman's chest, which meant anything with Patsy was now moot. No way would she compete with Teddie, especially when her interest was only lukewarm. The potential for damage to their friendship just wasn't worth it.

"I need to get this musical chairs game over with so I can get off my aching feet. My legs are shaking so bad I bet I fall on my ass when these wheels come off."

A voice behind them said, "I'm glad I came then, because I would have hated to miss that."

Julia whirled with surprise at the sudden appearance of Ashley. Given where they'd left off on Tuesday, her presence at the skating rink was the last thing she expected, yet there she stood sporting her signature smile. Instinctively Julia extended her arms for a friendly hug.

Teddie just waved. "I'd hug you too but I stink on account

of just having skated for a solid hour. Two hundred twelve laps."

Ashley's jaw dropped and she looked at Julia for confirmation.

"I'm afraid so. I counted them myself."

"And you're just in time for musical chairs," Teddie added excitedly. "You read the fine print, didn't you? It says everyone has to skate. That means you too."

"Not a chance, slick," Ashley said, invoking Elaine's pet name. "I just came down here to watch the rest of you make fools of yourselves."

Teddie scowled but it faded in an instant. "Will you come meet my friend? She's going to be blown away."

"Of course."

Julia watched from a distance as Teddie made the introductions. The sight of Ashley and Patsy standing side by side was jolting because they couldn't have been more different, and there was no question at all as to which Julia considered more appealing.

Next to Ashley, everyone in the skating rink looked ordinary at best. Even her casual outfit—black slacks with a starched red shirt and charcoal blazer—was nicer than any of the clothes in Julia's closet, and though her makeup was not as pronounced as it was on days she appeared on air, it was nonetheless perfectly applied. And, of course, her hair looked fantastic.

Robyn inched unsteadily along the rail until she reached Julia's side. "Where'd Teddie go?"

"See for yourself," she said, gesturing toward the corner.

"Is that who I think it is?"

Elaine grabbed her shoulders from behind, nearly sending both of them to the floor. "Man, that woman can work a room better than anybody I ever saw. She should have been a politician."

"I can't believe she's here."

Teddie called for participants for musical chairs while Patsy collected the entry fees, and one by one the skaters lined up at the edge of the rink to await the start of the game.

"You're not going?" Ashley asked Julia.

"Not me. I'm the prize." She led the way to a small table

on a riser at one end of the floor, where they had a perfect view of the mayhem to come. "I'm really glad you came. You made Teddie's day."

"It's good to see friends take care of each other. It feeds your faith in humanity. We try to do at least one story every day at TV4 that spotlights people doing good deeds because it makes us feel good about our neighbors and ourselves."

"Do you think about work all the time, Ashley?"

Her lips tightened noticeably as what had been a relaxed smile became forced. "I'm sorry. I'm sure it drives people crazy when I do that. It's just a habit that I process things in terms of what stories they tell."

"No, I wasn't complaining. Not at all," Julia pleaded, leaning closer to show that she wasn't put off. "I was just wondering if you ever took the time to relax, or if being in such a visible position means you can't ever turn it off."

The music started and stopped as the game got underway.

"I usually spend the weekends in my garden but I got all of that done yesterday. Then I had an interview this morning for a new story we're working on, and when I suggested to my news director that we go into the station to start laying it out, he told me to get lost. His plan for the rest of the day was football and beer. He said I needed to get a life and there you have it. I now find myself at Skate City, despite being absolutely aghast at the prospect of wearing rented shoes permeated with the collected sweat of a thousand feet."

Julia laughed aloud at how quickly the last words had tumbled out. "Come on, how do you really feel?"

"I don't see you rolling around out there."

"I have a real excuse though. I broke my stupid ankle last year doing something stupid on a stupid skateboard and it took nearly three months to heal. I can't afford to miss that much work again so I have to be more careful not to do stupid stunts."

"I suppose being stupid is a better excuse than just being a big chicken."

"Between you and me, we have to go with whatever works because there's no end to what Teddie would drag us all into otherwise. I've gotten a lot of mileage out of the broken ankle."

Robyn arrived at their table rubbing her elbow. "Did you see what Elaine did to me? That woman is so competitive."

"That's because my haircuts are worth fighting for, and it's almost time for her trim anyway." She turned to Ashley to explain. "She comes in once a year and screams at me if I cut more than an inch off that braid of hers. Her neck muscles must be as strong as goal posts."

The action on the floor intensified as all but two contestants were eliminated. The survivors, Teddie and Elaine, skated with trepidation around the cones that had been placed on the rink, ready to bolt for the last remaining chair the instant the music stopped.

"Smart money's on Elaine," Robyn said with a huff. "She'll cheat."

No sooner had the words left her mouth than the music stopped. Teddie got the jump toward the chair, but Elaine grabbed her T-shirt from behind and slung her to the floor before triumphantly landing in the seat.

"Do I know my girl or what?"

Teddie protested wildly but accepted Elaine's hand as she climbed to her feet, and the two of them skated over to the table. "She cheated. I want a free haircut too."

"When have I ever charged either of you for a haircut?"

"Let's do it Friday night," Teddie said. "I want my head shaved on account of Jordan's is already starting to fall out."

"Are you crazy?" Julia shook her head. "Don't answer that."

"Come on, this is me we're talking about. You think people are going to say I'm weird all of a sudden? Jordan's starting to feel self-conscious about it. This is like telling her it's no big deal."

"Aw, that's sweet." Ashley rose and enveloped Teddie in a hug, prompting Julia and Robyn to trade looks of surprise.

Elaine rubbed her hands together. "All right, Friday night it is. I'll bring dinner."

"Thanks for the warning," Teddie said. "I'll grab a burger on the way over."

Robyn pulled herself up tentatively, gripping the table tightly for balance. "You'll come, won't you Ashley? About seven o'clock."

"Oh, I don't know. It's hard to…I can't really…" She looked from one expectant face to the next. "Oh, what the heck? Sure."

Chapter Nine

With her on-air smile firmly in place, Ashley groaned inwardly at the producer's clock, which showed almost a minute remaining as Puze wrapped up his sports report. Unless she got a cue for something within the next two seconds, she and Rod would have to make nonsense banter until they cut away to the national news. Surely they had stock video of the Christmas shopping crowd or Santa Claus at the hospital.

Rod cleared his throat. "We'd like to leave you with a special clip sent in by one of our viewers. Over the weekend at Skate City, friends of cancer patient Jordan Burgess held a fundraiser to help out with the family's expenses. TV4's own Ashley Giraud was there to lend a hand and she put on this gold medal demonstration."

"Oh, my gosh! I should have known." Ashley grimaced as a video of her skating clumsily with Jordan filled the screen. She had finally given in to Teddie's pleas and agreed to auction herself off for three laps around the rink with the highest bidder. Her four new friends had pooled their money and given the prize to the guest of honor. "Anytime it gets too quiet around here it means you guys are up to something."

"Ashley, you're a regular Peggy Fleming," Puze said.

"Ha!" said Melitta, who along with Puze had joined them at the desk for sign-off. "I have a feeling she'll be channeling Tonya Harding after this."

Ashley groaned and momentarily covered her face before shaking it off and looking directly into the camera. "Join us back here tonight at eleven, where I'll be plotting my revenge."

When the producer called clear, Jarvis jumped to the set to congratulate the team. "Good job, all. I want the 4Team in the conference room, everyone else back here by ten thirty."

She and Jarvis had worked all afternoon on their investigative plan, hand-picking the best personnel for the 4Team, what they called the staff assigned to a big investigative story. They had quickly agreed not to include Rod, since he had little to contribute on the research end, and that was where most of the work was.

Jarvis wanted Mallory for on-the-scene reporting duties. Ashley had chosen the rest of the team—Tim Holland as the segment producer, BJ Henderson behind the camera, and her winter intern Aaron Crum as the assistant producer. She'd work closely with Aaron to guide him through the grunt work of gathering all the data needed to support their story. The challenge, as always, was to pull it together and present it in a way that would draw in viewers and help them understand how this impacted their lives.

After shooting a quick promo for the eleven o'clock newscast, she stopped by her office for her notes and found a text message from Robyn: *Swear 2 god it wasn't 1 of us but we all laughed.*

She had known the instant she saw the video who had taken it—a woman who was there with her kids and had said hello as she was on her way out the door. Her thumbs pounded out a quick reply: *Ha ha all 4 of ur in deep doo-doo c u friday.*

The team was waiting in the conference room, where pizza and sodas were stacked on a credenza off to the side. The men were already at the table digging into the cheesy dough, while Mallory sat pertly to the side munching on crudités she had obviously brought from home. No wonder she looked as though she'd blow away in a strong wind.

"Seriously, Jarvis," Ashley muttered as she took a seat next to him. "You couldn't find something better to eat than pizza at a thousand calories a slice? Whose side are you on?"

"Sorry, I just thought this would be quick and easy."

Quick and easy always got her into trouble on the scales, along with an irresistible craving for whatever tasted fat, salty or sweet whenever she felt depressed. How could Mallory sit there looking perfectly content with her rabbit food while the thick aroma of tomato, basil and sausage permeated the room? Against her better judgment she helped herself to a slice, but then mustered the willpower to set it off to the side without taking a bite.

As Mallory scrolled through her iPhone, her face lit up. "Awesome! I just hit five thousand likes on my Facebook page."

Ashley and Jarvis looked quizzically at each other, neither having any idea what she'd just said.

Jarvis laid out all the assignments and the timeline. A story this complicated could take up to six months to develop, but he wanted it in half that. They all still felt the sting of losing the desalinization plant scoop to the *St. Pete Times*. Another reason for urgency, he said, was that the malfeasance they were investigating was ongoing and there was always the possibility the conspirators would be caught in the act. Still, he wasn't willing to rush out a story that had the strong potential to end up in the hands of the US Attorney. Getting it wrong would be reckless.

For Aaron's benefit, Ashley reminded everyone this was an exclusive, which meant securing their notes and not talking to anyone who wasn't part of the 4Team.

Big stories always generated an adrenaline rush for Ashley and she knew the team in this room shared her enthusiasm and determination. There was an Emmy for investigative reporting in this if they nailed it. She smiled with satisfaction as the team members filed out, leaving only her and Jarvis. "This watchdog stuff is exciting, isn't it?"

"It's why we chose to be journalists."

"Speak for yourself. I wanted to be a professional skater."

He chuckled. "You're not fooling me. You were born for this, Miss Missouri."

"Ugh. I hate it when you call me that." He had used that title the very first time they met when he invited her to interview for a network opening in DC. It was her own fault for including the pageant on her résumé, but she felt she needed to prove her experience in public relations.

"You light up the screen, Ashley. You've been making me look good for fourteen years."

Her mind wandered back to those early years. As a general assignment reporter at the affiliate in Kansas City, she had filed scores of human interest stories on things like street fairs, pet shows and blood drives, typical stories for cub reporters who couldn't be trusted with the serious matters of government. To this day she shuddered to recall her four-part series on beauty tips that had aired during prom season. Her big break had come at the expense of St. Joseph, a town of nearly eighty thousand in northwest Missouri that suffered its worst tornado ever on the day she happened to be there for a story about a ballet class for senior citizens. For three hours she was the only reporter on the ground and her coverage had been uplinked to all the networks. Within a week, her agent had fielded a dozen inquiries but the DC job was the only one she pursued.

That's how the news business worked. You had to be good at your job, but you also had to be in the right place at the right time. And it didn't hurt to have a champion like Jarvis, whose word alone had been good enough to win her the anchor desk at TV4.

She couldn't help but see comparisons in her career and Mallory's. "This is a huge opportunity for Mallory. Once she gets a story like this under her belt, she'll hit the radar of every news director in the southeast."

"I know. I've been thinking about sliding her into the anchor chair at noon. I figure I can keep her busy with that for two or three years. Maybe she'll get married and start having kids, and I won't have to worry about her switching markets. Then when the day finally comes that somebody steals my six o'clock anchor, I'll have a backup."

Ashley chuckled. She was in the prime of her career right now and had no interest in making the jump to a larger market. Besides, the likelihood of a bigger station coming after someone her age was pretty low. "It would take dynamite to knock me out of my chair. You're stuck with me, so don't you dare go lusting after some ingénue to take my place."

A lascivious grin crossed his face but gave way to a frown. "Connie would cut my balls off if she ever caught me lusting after anyone. Remind me again why I married someone with such a violent streak."

"She's perfect for you."

"That reminds me, she has a new friend she wants you to meet, some interior designer. I know you'd rather be sold into slavery than fixed up with somebody, but we can put you both on our next party list if you're interested. No pressure."

It was all pressure as far as Ashley was concerned, since there was virtually no chance a relationship would grow out of her meeting someone at a dinner party, or anywhere else for that matter. The more likely result was that Connie's new friend would have her feelings hurt by Ashley's lack of follow-up. "I don't think I'm up for anything like that right now, but I appreciate that you and Connie look out for me."

Left unsaid was the fact that she never had been up for it and probably never would be, but Jarvis's pensive nod suggested he understood this. "You know it's okay though, right? People know who you are, including Carl. Our viewers bring it up in focus groups all the time and it doesn't bother anybody. If anything, they like you even more."

Ashley shuddered and blew out a frazzled breath. "It gives me nightmares to imagine people discussing my sex life in a focus group. How does something like that even come up?"

"They still remember Valerie…and that interview you gave, I guess. For what it's worth, they respect you for not tap dancing around it like a lot of people tend to do."

She recalled vividly how her stomach had dropped when the reporter asked about her sexual orientation, but she never considered anything but a truthful reply. "Our credibility is pretty much all we've got, isn't it? If we lie to them about one thing, they'll assume we're lying about everything."

The slice of pizza she had set aside, its rim of grease seeping onto the paper plate, was all that remained of the two pies Jarvis had brought into the meeting. No, it wasn't on her diet but if she didn't eat it now, she probably wouldn't get any dinner at all. As she raised it to her lips, the heavy cheese slid off, depositing a dark red glob of tomato sauce onto her chest.

Karma was such a bitch.

"...those stories and more next on TV4 news." It was Ashley's voice on the lead-in but the picture was just the TV4 news logo. After the intro it went straight to breaking news with voiceover, police on the scene of a multi-vehicle accident on I-4.

Julia stretched forward in her worn leather TV chair and matching ottoman to tuck the blanket around her feet. The outside temperature had dropped into the fifties, which to a Tampa native was the equivalent of freezing. The baseboard heater in her small living area had just two settings—off and blazing hot—so she used it only at brief intervals to take the chill off. A blanket was enough as long as she kept it snug.

The TV4 news was a staple of her late nights, at least Monday through Friday when Ashley was in the anchor chair. She had been an occasional viewer of TV news for several years. Like all of her lesbian friends, she watched TV4 out of loyalty to the sisterhood. Now that she knew Ashley personally, she never missed a broadcast, and even recorded them if she wasn't going to be home.

"Good evening, I'm Ashley Giraud. Rod Gilchrist has the night off." Though she was visible only from the waist up, it appeared she was wearing a suit jacket, black with an elaborate silver pin in the shape of an egret. It was different from the turquoise

outfit she had worn for the six o'clock newscast, which made Julia wonder what had prompted a change in clothes.

Yes, she noticed everything about Ashley.

Her latest haircut was a week old today and still looked great. She had mastered the art of separating her bangs into feathered wisps so her cut looked fresh, and the conditioner brought out a shine that glimmered under the set lights.

So why did Rod Gilchrist have the night off? Not that Julia minded. Had it been Ashley who was off, she would have flipped the channel by now. While Robyn might call that a para-social relationship, Julia had another word in mind, one that had plagued her ever since the day at the skating rink when she first recognized the scope of Ashley's appeal…it was turning into a *crush*.

Which was a disaster.

For several reasons.

Not the least of which was that she made it a rule never to date her clients. When things went south—and they always did—she lost both a girlfriend *and* a customer. On top of that, she had learned that the word-of-mouth advertising strategy worked the other way too. The last client she dated—Mickey Varner, three years ago—had talked several of their mutual lesbian friends into switching salons too.

She shuddered and pulled the blanket up around her neck. Thoughts of Mickey always sent chills up her spine, even in August. Somewhere tonight she was torturing another poor soul with her insatiable need to be right about everything in the universe.

A bigger reason to steer clear of Ashley—or at least to keep her feelings to herself—was that she had promised Robyn a safe haven, a place where the celebrity newswoman could let down her public guard and relax without worries that someone would be scheming to get into her personal space just because of who she was. Julia had put her reputation as a professional on the line, and even if she managed to do her admiring from afar, nursing a secret crush on Ashley had creepy stalker undertones.

Groaning in frustration, she changed the channel for all

of five seconds before switching back to Ashley. Why did she always seem to fall for women she couldn't have? Technically she could have had Rachel if she'd been willing to join the Pentecostal megachurch and live without sex forever. With her luck, they would have delivered on their promise of eternal life.

Not that Julia was bitter about everyone in her past. She and Sara Lynn had parted on good terms after almost a year of dating once they agreed their spark had fizzled and they weren't well suited to a long-term deal. These days they kept in touch only by email, even though Sara Lynn lived just a short ride across the causeway in Clearwater.

Ashley returned after the commercial break and introduced a segment from one of the field reporters on the scene at Tampa General Hospital, where several members of the Buccaneers football team were attending a children's Christmas party.

How could someone that beautiful not have hundreds of women lining up to ask her out? Maybe she did but Robyn seemed certain that she wasn't interested in a romance of any kind. Okay, so that was the better question. How could anyone that sexy not be interested in having a sweet, warm somebody there to cuddle on the couch, wash her back or slide around under the sheets?

She groaned again and tossed the blanket aside, her body temperature soaring with prurient thoughts. How bad was it that she was sitting here entertaining images about what sort of lingerie Ashley wore under that black suit? Pretty high on the sleaze scale.

Ashley deserved more respect than that, especially after overcoming her reservations to go out with people she didn't know very well. Having someone get fixated on her the way that stalker had was probably her biggest fear.

Chapter Ten

Ashley turned into the narrow parking lot behind the row of office condos, spotting a space near Rhapsody. She liked that Julia gave her private access through the back door where no one would see her come and go. It was hard to look good in a salon chair with your hair wrapped in a plastic cap or hanging wet in your face, and sneaking in this way spared her the gawkers. Julia said she preferred it that way after hours so she could pull the blinds and hang her Closed sign in the window by the front entrance. Otherwise customers would be walking in at all hours of the night.

She scowled to realize the open space actually contained a motorcycle, probably Teddie's. After parking three spaces down she walked back and stopped to study it. Two simple details summed up all she understood about this contraption: It was a Harley-Davidson and it was blue. No wonder Elaine had been terrified—nothing between her and the crazy drivers of Tampa Bay except the shirt on her back. Jack Nicholson would win the Miss America Pageant before Ashley would ever get on one of these.

Through the back window of the shop she could see Julia talking animatedly to someone out of view. She was dressed with a bit more panache than usual, a gold chain belt hanging low over a flowing white shirt, and long hoops dangling from her ears. The combination lengthened her torso, which made her lanky build look even slimmer. Ashley reminded herself again that Julia was in the fashion business, so to speak, so she shouldn't be surprised by her stylish flair. The real surprise was that it had taken so long for her to notice just how much Julia had going for her.

Just two weeks ago Ashley had been resigned to her isolation, content to have only her job and her garden, plus a handful of weeknight dinners with co-workers to masquerade as a social life. Now she had real friends if she wanted them, this eclectic bunch of women who nurtured one another without demanding anything in return.

"Hi, everyone." A savory aroma enveloped her as she opened the door. "Something smells good, and I bet it's not on my diet."

The shop was modestly decorated for the holidays with a small artificial tree in the corner of the waiting area and strings of tiny white lights that lined the doors and windows. An electric menorah sat on the kitchen counter, one of its bulbs flickering.

Elaine helped her out of her coat and then opened her arms for a hug. "Glad you could make it. We're having old-fashioned black beans and rice. I'm afraid the Cubans never had much use for vegetables and fruits."

"Not true. I picked up some Cuban guava pastries for dessert," Robyn said, jumping to her feet for a hug as well. Though still wearing her skirt from work, she was barefoot and had pulled her shirttail out.

"Do not even wave those things under my nose," Ashley commanded. "It's true what they say about the camera adding pounds."

"Screw the camera. You look fantastic," Julia said, flashing a smile. Her hands held a comb and electric clippers so she gave Ashley a kiss on the cheek instead of a hug. An actual kiss, she noticed, not the kind where they almost touched but didn't.

"Why couldn't I have you for a boss instead of Carl Terzian? The only weight gain he likes on women is when our boobs get bigger."

"Misogynistic asshole," Teddie groused. "Say the word and I'll kick his ass." She was already in the chair awaiting her drastic haircut, and Ashley squeezed her shoulder in greeting.

"I'm so glad I got here in time to see this."

"Step right up"—Julia's clippers gave off a low buzz— "because we're about to make a bowling ball." Row by row, to rousing cheers, she took Teddie's already dramatic style down to a layer of fuzz.

Ashley liked the aura of familiarity from hugging and kissing when they saw each other. It felt genuine, like something "girlfriends" did instead of just an empty social ritual. They were small gestures in the grand scheme of things, but they made her feel accepted as one of the group.

"Looking good, slick," Elaine said. "Now you have a whole new place for a tattoo. Any ideas?"

"How about Spalding?" Julia suggested to guffaws.

"I want a face on the back," Teddie said. "Ashley's face if I can get it. Then people will tell me I'm beautiful and I can whip around and say thank you."

"Careful what you ask for. The upkeep on this face is outrageous."

"Maybe so, but you're doing a great job." Julia took a towel from the steamer and gingerly unraveled it. "Here comes the fun part."

"Ow! That's hot. Are you going to shave it or scald it off?"

Ashley had helped herself to a bowl of beans and rice and sat down in the vacant styling chair, surprised at how comfortable she felt with the foursome, including Teddie. "Teddie, you surprise me. I thought you were tougher than that."

Julia shook her head emphatically. "You should have been here the day she got the Brazilian. We all thought she was being murdered upstairs."

It was unfathomable to Ashley that anyone would subject themselves to such an intimate procedure with a total stranger, and it struck her as particularly funny that it had become such a public spectacle for Teddie.

Teddie folded her arms in a pout. "Needless to say, that was both my first and last trip to the torture chamber. Jasmine enjoyed it just a little too much if you ask me."

"You'll never guess what my girlfriend is giving me for Christmas," Elaine said, perching on the end of the couch to slide an arm around Robyn's shoulder.

"A gift certificate to Bern's Steakhouse," Teddie snapped, earning a light smack on the head from Julia.

"She's going to Sheboygan to stay with Mom while I take Dad out to Tucson to see Uncle Bill. He's wanted to go for a couple of years but couldn't leave Mom by herself."

Ashley recalled vaguely that Elaine's mother was impaired, but she couldn't remember the details. She should have paid more attention. Any decent friend would have asked about her from time to time. "How's your mother doing?"

"Unfortunately, she's totally lost her vision now, but they've got her on a new insulin schedule that seems to be working better. She hasn't had a seizure in over a year."

Right, it was diabetes. That's why Elaine was so strict about her vegetarian diet. As she made a mental note to take more interest in the lives of her new friends, Ashley also chided herself that others did that naturally. Dr. Friedman was right—behavior first, then attitude.

The towel came off and Teddie brushed her fingers against her stubbly hair, catching Julia's eye in the mirror. "Bonnie said you guys were going to Epcot on Christmas Day. Can I come? Unless it's just a family thing…"

"You're as much family as I am. But you'd better wear a hat because this dome is going to burn like a baby's butt." Julia lathered up the gel and began shaving, stopping after every swipe to rinse the blade. "What are you doing for Christmas, Ashley?"

In light of everyone else's plans, she was embarrassed about her visit to the weight loss resort in Cancun and felt compelled to share something a little less self-absorbed. "I'm slated to emcee the children's holiday party at St. Joseph's Hospital next week. And then we're passing out toys at the Boys and Girls Club."

"Will you see your folks?" Elaine asked.

This happened when you kept secrets from your friends. They put you on the spot with invasive questions. Before she could think how to answer, Julia did it for her.

"You saw your brother at Thanksgiving, right? You're welcome to join us at Epcot. It's not very crowded on Christmas Day."

Remembering how badly she'd fumbled Julia's first invitation, she stopped her automatic response of offering another lame excuse. "Actually, that sounds like more fun than what I'll be doing. I'm going down to Cancun for a couple of weeks...not what you think, though. It's my annual self-flagellation pilgrimage to the fat farm." She explained how her weight usually crept upward through the year, but didn't share that her recent bout of depression had caused it to surge. "Like I was saying, it's just a fact of life in television news. If you're on the air you spend all your vacation time getting your eyes pinned back or your lips injected. I'm just lucky this is the only calamity I have to worry about so far."

Julia huffed and assumed what Ashley recognized as her incredulous pose—hip out to the side with an elbow firmly planted in her side. "In the first place, you look amazing. And in the second place, I'm tired of having a size two skeleton shoved at me everywhere I turn. Why can't they let women look normal?"

Robyn went off on a rant about how many of her bright, creative students would end up relegated to researcher or producer jobs because they weren't pretty enough to be in front of the camera, but Ashley missed most of what she said. She was playing Julia's words back in her head, namely the part about how she looked amazing. Not long ago she would have thought such compliments flirtatious and even threatening, but today she was pleased. Even Teddie's brash promise to kick Carl's ass on her behalf struck her as more charming than mortifying.

These women stood up for one another and now they were standing up for her.

Teddie hopped out of the chair to admire her smooth head. "Christ, I look like an Easter egg."

"No one will even notice, slick…except Jordan, and she's going to think you're terrific."

Julia removed a new smock from the cabinet and shook it out. "And now for the main event. Did you wash it already?"

"Sure did," Elaine answered as she took the seat vacated by Teddie, flipping her waist-length braid over the back of the chair. "And you don't need to ask. I'm absolutely sure."

That struck Ashley as a peculiar thing to say and she looked to Robyn, who seemed just as perplexed. With three forceful strokes of the scissors, Julia cut the braid at the nape of Elaine's neck and held it up as if it were a dead rattlesnake.

"Oh, my God!" Robyn screamed. "What did you just do?"

"I just donated two feet of hair to the Leukemia Foundation so they can make wigs." Elaine twisted her head back and forth to examine her new look in the mirror. "And now I'm giving myself whiplash."

Robyn hadn't moved and was standing with her mouth agape, but then a slow smile overtook her face. "For six years, you've been threatening to cut your hair but you always chickened out. I can't believe you finally did it."

"It was the skate party. I kept looking at Jordan and thinking what if that were me. How would I feel if I got sick and all my hair fell out? That's when I knew it was just hair, and it might mean more to somebody else than it does to me."

Julia stepped aside as Robyn wrapped her arms around Elaine's shoulders and nuzzled her shortened locks. "Elaine Vandenbosch, I love you to pieces."

Ashley blinked several times to calm the sting of tears, though not to protect her emotions. "You guys are going to ruin my makeup."

Chapter Eleven

Julia paced her small cottage with the phone pressed to her ear. "How long have you been sick?"

"Ever since I stepped off the plane on Thursday night," Ashley rasped. "So much for being rejuvenated in Mexico. Believe me, this is not how I wanted to lose weight. Even if I felt like eating, there's nothing in my refrigerator because I never even got a chance to stop by the grocery store."

"Sounds like you need some chicken soup and orange juice. I can bring it over, and anything else you want."

"Oh, that's so sweet, but you might catch this and then I'd really feel awful. I can make do."

Julia wasn't going to take no for an answer. "That's what's great about working with the public. I get exposed to everything so I've built up immunity. I haven't been sick in years."

After a long groan, Ashley said, "Everybody's on vacation for the holidays. My house is a mess, my yard is a mess...and I'm a mess. I just hate for anyone to see me like this."

"Here's some breaking news for you, Ashley. Friends don't even notice things like that. What's your address?"

She relayed directions between episodes of coughing and sneezing.

Julia added cold medicine to her list and hurried into her bedroom to change from the tartan flannel pants and T-shirt she'd been lounging in all day. Regardless of what she said to Ashley about friends not caring how she looked, there was no excuse for showing up at someone's house in glorified pajamas.

Though she had forced the invitation, she was convinced that taking food and medicine over was the right thing to do. She would do the same for any of her friends. Admittedly, she wouldn't have been so excited by the prospect. Her crush on Ashley was growing, especially after she had shown up at Rhapsody for their social night and stumbled over Elaine's question about seeing her family at Christmas. She felt like a hero for coming to Ashley's rescue. Because Ashley had talked to her and no one else, she had a sense of loyalty that went beyond their friendship with the rest of the group. For whatever reason, Ashley had a strong need to protect her privacy and feared being judged even by her friends.

Pleased with her well-worn jeans and a light green cable-knit sweater—not too formal, not too sloppy—she exited her cottage to find Teddie polishing her Harley.

"Where are you headed?"

"Just going to run a few errands."

"Want some company?"

She didn't, at least not for this, but secrecy and any hint of wanting to see Ashley by herself could backfire in a major way. Teddie wasn't the sort of person just to let something go, and she'd make a big deal out of it if she put two and two together. "I just got a call from Ashley. She's been sick the last few days, and I offered to pick up some groceries and drop them off at her house."

"Let me go with you." She was already putting away her supplies and as usual wouldn't be deterred.

Given Ashley's reservations about having guests, Julia thought it best to call from the Whole Foods market with a heads-up about Teddie coming along for the ride. As they waited in the car for Ashley to open the electronic gate she spotted an overstuffed mailbox. "Get out and grab that mail," she told Teddie.

"Christ! I just stepped in dog shit. Who the fuck walks their dog in front of somebody's mailbox?" As the gate slid open, Teddie dragged her foot along the gravel at the edge of the driveway to clean her shoe. "Go on. I'll be there in a minute."

Ashley, noticeably slimmer after just three weeks, was waiting at the front door, dressed neatly in dark slacks and a white silk blouse. Apparently she had taken the trouble to make up her face though her puffy eyes and red nose made it clear she was sick.

"Happy New Year," Julia said, pulling her into a gentle hug. "I can't believe you got dressed up for us after I told you friends don't care about those things."

"I couldn't stand myself anymore so I took a quick shower. First one in three days, in fact. If it makes you feel better, I didn't clean up the house or the yard."

"I just discovered the yard part," Teddie grumbled, rechecking the bottom of her shoe as she handed over the stack of mail.

"I'm so sorry about that. For some reason my neighbor insists on bringing his dog to my yard for his business, even after I asked him not to. I was as polite as I could be but it was like talking to a brick wall."

"Which neighbor?"

"Over there in the yellow house. He has one of those giant poodles. It's unbelievable how much one of those…never mind."

"Sounds like somebody needs an intervention. I'll stay out here so I don't track dog shit through your house. You want me to stack those palm fronds next to the street for you?"

"You're such a sweetheart," Ashley said, her voice hoarse. "Oh, and the side yard is full of grapefruit. Help yourself to all you want. There's a basket by the back door."

The first thing to catch Julia's eye as she walked through the entry was the colorful garden patio beyond the French doors of the living room. Two overstuffed white wicker love seats, separated by a matching glass-topped table, sat face to face and were surrounded by lush greenery and flowers. "Wow, your backyard's gorgeous."

"Do you garden?"

"Not a bit. Suzy left me in charge of the plants at the shop once when she was on vacation and everything died."

Their footsteps echoed off the glazed terra-cotta floor as they walked through the expansive living room, which held only a deep green box-shaped couch, a coffee table and a grand piano. Despite the elegance, nothing about the décor struck Julia as personal, as if the room had been designed as a public lobby.

Ashley reached for the grocery bag. "Here, let me take those things."

"I've got them." Julia steered toward the kitchen, where the only signs of life were a few dishes in the sink, mostly glasses and small plates. "If this is what qualifies as a messy house, you're never coming to my place. This is lovely."

"Most of my mess is in the bedroom. I haven't even unpacked from Mexico." The last words were garbled by coughing.

Julia found the glassware cabinet on her first try and poured a small tumbler of orange juice. "Take this and go sit where you're most comfortable while I heat up the soup. I'm also going to look around and see if there's anything else I can do."

Ashley protested, but only mildly as she shuffled down a narrow hallway and disappeared. It probably made her uneasy to have Julia and Teddie there, but the benefits of fresh food and drink no doubt outweighed any apprehension.

When the soup began to bubble, Julia peeked into what looked like the den and found Ashley dozing on a love seat next to a desk piled high with newspapers and magazines. Getting showered and dressed for visitors had probably sapped what little strength she had. Clearly she had too much pride in her appearance to let anyone see her looking like the sick woman she was.

Walking from window to window Julia checked on Teddie's progress outdoors. A basket of grapefruit had been placed on the patio by the French doors, but Teddie was nowhere to be seen.

The master bedroom was every bit the mess Ashley had described. Two suitcases took up most of the floor space, crumpled tissues dotted the room and wrinkled linens were piled in a heap in the middle of the bed. She located the linen closet and put fresh sheets on the queen-sized bed. A cool, clean bed would feel good to Ashley after her shower.

As she worked she noticed that, like the other rooms, the bedroom was devoid of the sort of personal items most people collected over a lifetime…no framed photographs or souvenirs of special places. Even the art on the wall, though tasteful, struck Julia as impersonal. She herself wasn't much for knickknacks either, but still she kept a few tangible reminders of good times or special people. It seemed Ashley's heightened sense of privacy extended even to her own home.

Suddenly cognizant that she had moved past straightening up to snooping, she returned to the kitchen and prepared a tray of soup, fresh crackers and cough medicine. Finding Ashley still asleep, she kept her voice low so as not to startle. "Ready for some lunch?"

Ashley blinked and sat up suddenly. "Sorry."

"No, it's okay. I'm sure you really need your sleep but I bet your stomach needs food too." She set the tray on Ashley's lap and perched on the edge of the love seat, noting that this room seemed to be the centerpiece of Ashley's life at home. "It smells pretty good. Too bad your nose isn't working."

"I'm not sure anything's working. I feel like I've been pummeled," she said, her voice fading in and out.

"Listen to that voice of yours. You might have to stay home another week to get it back."

Ashley shook her head vehemently. "I can't let Mallory Foster get that comfortable in my chair."

"Oh, that's right. I forgot about the paranoia of TV news."

"It's only paranoid if it's imaginary."

"I remember when I broke my foot last year. I worried about all my customers leaving me so I hurried back to the shop as soon as I could move. It set me back at least a month because I spent so much time on my feet and couldn't get the swelling to go down. I hope you won't go back too soon or we'll have to do another one of Teddie's interventions."

"What do you think she meant by that?"

"Probably nothing. You know how she's always talking big, but it's all smoke. That doesn't mean we won't come kidnap you from the station if we see you on the air before you're well."

Ashley sipped from the soup mug and nibbled at one of the crackers. "I can't remember the last time somebody looked in on me when I was sick. Maybe never. Sorry I'm such a grouch. I really appreciate this."

"It's what friends do. It's what you did when you stopped by Skate City that day. You can't believe how much that meant to Teddie. It's times like that when you can tell what people are really like inside."

A faint smile was Ashley's first response, and then she dabbed her eyes and nose with a tissue, clearly overcome with emotion. "I haven't had a lot of practice with this friend business."

"There's nothing to it, Ashley. No tests to pass...no expectations to meet. Just relax and be yourself." It took all the restraint Julia could muster not to blurt out that her door was open for more than friendship if Ashley ever found herself interested. That would surely send her running. "Look, I know you're a really private person, but the reason most people keep secrets is because they're afraid of what other people will think. You don't have to worry about that with us. We've all got our baggage and we help each other haul it."

Ashley nodded but didn't look up. "I have more than the average person."

"Good thing there are four of us."

"Even with four of you, you'll need a lot of patience, because I'm used to being that person you see on TV. She's only about an inch deep and all the other stuff..." She shook her head. "I don't know how far down I can go."

"You'll figure it out. Just relax and try to have fun."

"When does the fun start?" she asked, punctuating her question with another coughing spell before gripping the bottle of medicine and squinting at the label.

"It's the stuff that knocks you out."

"Thank you, Jesus."

Julia laughed and picked up the tray. "Teddie and I are going to scram so you can take some of that and get back to bed. Think you can stay upright long enough to let us out the gate?"

Ashley walked her to the front door and called out her thanks to Teddie, who was waiting by the car. Then she grasped Julia's forearm and squeezed. "Thank you for everything—the groceries, the medicine…and especially the pep talk. It's good to know people care."

"Be good to yourself, Ashley." Julia couldn't resist drawing her into a hug, which she held longer than a simple goodbye when she felt Ashley's arms go around her waist. "I can be here in seven minutes, so call me if you need anything at all. And I'm also telling Robyn and Elaine to drop by tomorrow with a care package too, so don't even try to argue."

As they drove through the gate, Teddie's thumbs pounded out a message on her smartphone. "That was some hug there, Jules."

"It's called comfort, numbskull. The woman's sick."

"I don't remember you hugging me that way last year when I got the flu," she said without looking up, an evil smirk playing at the corner of her mouth.

Julia slammed on the brakes so that the passenger seat belt tightened suddenly across Teddie's chest and threw her back against the seat. "Suppose I just put you out here in the street."

"You have no sense of humor. Let's go. I just told Patsy and Jordan I'd be over for dinner."

"Where did you go, by the way? I was looking for you in the yard earlier."

"I paid a little visit to the man in the yellow house."

"The one with the dog? What did you say to him?"

"I didn't say anything, but I imagine he'll be using some choice words soon."

"You didn't."

"Oh, I think I did."

Chapter Twelve

Ashley laughed to herself in the kitchen as Robyn and Elaine banged out their butchered version of "Chopsticks." Pianos were perfect for entertaining guests, especially those whose idea of a good time was to see who could be the silliest. So far Teddie was winning, thanks to her bizarre talent for playing "Twinkle, Twinkle Little Star" backward.

The last time she had cooked for company was almost five years ago, a gathering that included Jarvis and Connie, along with a handful of people she knew from various community volunteer boards, and their spouses. The dinner had gone beautifully until she discovered near the end of the evening that someone had brazenly gone through her medicine cabinet. It was humiliating to realize that one of her guests had examined her medications and vanity products, and she vowed never again to invite people into her home.

This group of women had managed to break down that wall by insisting on coming over while she battled the flu. Each day there was a new face bringing comfort food or cold remedies. Now that she was better, it seemed only right to have them all over as a gesture of thanks.

It was hard to say who was more pleased at the decision to host this dinner—her friends or Dr. Friedman. Ashley was proud of her progress since the funeral in Missouri, especially since her preoccupation with Cassandra had finally subsided. She saw this evening as a chance to let these women know how much their camaraderie had meant to her over the past few weeks.

Julia in particular had set her at ease, enough that she could see them growing into best friends someday. It didn't appear she had anyone else that close, since Teddie was more of a sidekick and had her own circle of younger friends. It would be fun to have someone she could talk to as easily as Julia, as long as neither of them developed any romantic designs. Not that the idea was distasteful—Julia had a lot of attractive qualities. She was intelligent, mature and independent, and while Ashley hadn't initially found her striking, she carried herself with a confidence that was physically appealing. None of that mattered, though, because Ashley had pulled romance off the table a long time ago. The last thing she wanted was an awkward end to their friendship because Julia made an overture and got rejected.

"Can I help with anything?" Julia's low voice startled her. "I can toss the salad…fetch your earplugs."

Ashley laughed self-consciously, embarrassed even to imagine that Julia might have been reading her thoughts. "It's okay, that piano needs a workout. I hardly touch it."

"And here I was hoping you'd regale us with a little Gershwin."

"Keep dreaming."

"I wish I could play like that."

"I'll let you in on a little secret. I wish I could play like that too. It's one of the many gimmicks behind the scenes at beauty pageants. People think we're classically trained pianists or dancers, but many of us learned only the basics and then three or four routines we practiced like mad. That adaptation I did on Gershwin? All the difficult parts were stripped out. My piano teacher left just enough that it was still recognizable."

Julia dropped her jaw in mock amazement. "Next you'll be telling me those weren't your real teeth."

Ashley decided not to respond on the off-chance that she was being teased. Julia probably knew all about flippers, the mouthpieces worn by beauty pageant contestants to perfect their smiles.

"I think dinner's ready." She removed a broiler pan filled with colorful kabobs. It was a simple recipe—marinated meat, vegetables and pineapple on skewers—and one of her favorites from the cooking seminars at the health spa. Best of all, she could cater to everyone's particular tastes—tofu for Elaine, steak for Teddie and prawns for everyone else. "Go see if anyone's brave enough to try this."

Teddie was the first to arrive at the table. "Wow, a steak popsicle! You married my favorite food with my favorite way to eat. Now how about marrying me?"

Ashley looked her up and down, pretending to contemplate the proposal. Teddie's hair had grown back to almost an inch all over, and had been sprayed neon red on top. Her T-shirt and ripped jeans resulted in virtually the same look she had sported the first time Ashley saw her in the shop, when she had instantly concluded she wanted nothing to do with someone so outrageous. Today, however, she felt no impulse to shy away.

"Sorry, not really feeling it."

"Story of my life." As they started to eat, Teddie peered across the table at Elaine's tofu. "Is that a sponge?"

"It's coagulated soy milk. Aren't you glad you asked?"

"That's disgusting!"

"Good. I'm going to repeat it from now on whenever you make fun of my food."

Julia rolled her eyes and leaned over to Ashley. "Robyn and I have a secret plan to send both of them to a deserted island together."

"It'll be a lot more fun if you can fit them with head-cams so we can watch."

The heartfelt thank you speech she had planned for dinner never materialized, since the ongoing banter between Elaine and Teddie set a much more playful tone. It was a far cry from the stiff atmosphere at most of the dinner parties she attended, and even from the public persona she had put forth at Robyn's birthday dinner only weeks ago. She found it wonderfully liberating not to feel as if she were on constant display.

If she needed another sign these friends were different from others she had entertained, it came when their meal was done, and Julia and Robyn ran her out of the kitchen so they could clean up.

"Wow, look at all this swing music," Elaine exclaimed. "Kay Kyser...Les Brown. I didn't know anyone still listened to this stuff."

"If you wish to imply that I'm old, there are more subtle ways."

"What's swing music?" Teddie asked.

"Only the best dancing music ever made," Elaine said. "My parents used to roll up the rug every Saturday night and put on one of these records. Cab Calloway...Buddy Rich."

Ashley opened the bottom cabinet of her entertainment center. "I think I have those guys too. Here's one of my favorites, Artie Shaw."

She popped in a CD and took Elaine's offered hands for a few simple moves in the narrow space between the coffee table and piano. Then with Teddie's help they moved the furniture against the walls, opening a larger floor for dancing.

Elaine had a decent repertoire of steps but her rhythm left a bit to be desired. Still, after a drought of more than a decade, it was thrilling for Ashley just to have a chance to kick up her heels with someone again.

"Where did you learn to do this, Ashley?"

"We did a swing dance for our big production number at the Miss America pageant. I liked it so much I took two semesters of ballroom dance when I was in college."

"You know who's really good at this?" Elaine hitched her thumb toward the kitchen, where Robyn and Julia had just finished up.

Before she knew it, Julia pulled her into position and led her on a series of triple steps and turns in perfect time with Artie Shaw's "Nonstop Flight."

"You *are* good. Where did you learn to swing?"

"I don't know about swinging. We call this shag. My mom was into beach music, and we used to dance like this at home all the time."

"It looks like all the same steps to me. Show me some more."

Julia executed a back pass, and then flared to perform a flurry of shuffles and twists.

"Wait, wait! Slow down and teach me what you just did."

Robyn and Elaine joined them on the floor and practiced along as Julia slowly demonstrated a few six-step sequences, which they then performed several times to Benny Goodman as Teddie tended to the CD player.

Ashley began to improvise as memories of her pageant routine came back and was delighted when Julia deftly followed her lead. As the steps grew more complex, Robyn and Elaine backed away and cheered them on as they took turns showing off their spins and kicks.

Julia's graceful moves impressed her, but not nearly as much as the self-assurance she exuded on the floor. Best of all, she knew the delicate art of how to lead without pushing her partner around. Keeping up with her was as simple as following the subtle cues from her fingertips.

"I forgot how much fun this is," Ashley said, finally collapsing on the sofa out of breath after nearly an hour of dance. "You're so smooth."

"It helps to have a good partner."

Teddie snorted. "That explains why Robyn was having so much trouble."

Elaine smacked her on the arm. "I didn't see you out there with your dancing shoes, slick."

"Five's a crowd." She held up her smartphone. "I just got a text from Patsy asking if I'd pick up a couple of things at the store. Jordan can't find anything that tastes good to her. Would it be okay if I split?"

"We should go too," Robyn said. "Don't want to wear out our welcome."

Ashley had been having so much fun she hadn't noticed it was nearly eleven. "I didn't even offer anyone dessert. I have snowflake cookies from Kalupa's. At least take them with you so I won't eat them all."

Outside in the circular driveway, Teddie groused about the crisp night air as she zipped her leather jacket and pulled on her gloves. Ashley stuffed two fat cookies into her pocket and kissed her on the cheek before her face disappeared beneath the helmet.

"Thanks for dinner," Robyn said, her arms wide for a hug. "By the way, we have a winter break at school the week after next. Elaine and I always rent a villa in Boca Grande and get everyone to come down for the weekend. You should come too."

Last year she had tap danced around the invitation to Boca Grande, a fishing village two hours south of Tampa. Now she was convinced she'd have a good time. "It sounds great."

She waved goodbye as they drove through the gate and turned to say goodnight to Julia, who seemed in no hurry to go.

"I'm glad you waited, Julia. I wanted to say thank you."

Julia chuckled. "I think you have it backward. For a night like this, I'm supposed to be the one saying thanks."

"Except this night might never have happened if you hadn't insisted on coming over that day I called about being sick. I hadn't let anyone inside my house in years. It didn't matter to you at all. You just bowled me over in my moment of weakness and marched right in."

The look on Julia's face was priceless as she tried to figure out if she was actually being scolded.

"And it's a good thing you did. I needed somebody to shake me out of my selfish little world. I've been taking from people for too long and not giving very much back. So thank you. I had a great time tonight."

"You had me going."

"I know."

"And just for that, I'm tempted to leave before you realize we didn't move the furniture back."

"Some coffee with your cookies?"

Julia chuckled and started toward the house, draping an arm around Ashley's shoulder in a gesture that was clearly affectionate. "Lucky for you I'm a pushover for Kalupa's."

Ashley warmed instantly to the physical contact and responded by wrapping her arm around Julia's waist. They had danced together all night, clasping hands and holding one another close with everyone watching, but this felt more familiar, especially since they were now alone.

After helping to push the furniture back into place, Julia stretched and rubbed the small of her back. "I bet I'll be sore tomorrow. I haven't danced like that in ages. I think the last time was at my uncle's anniversary party about three years ago."

"Only three years? It's been ages for me. I may not be able to get out of bed."

"You're so good at it. I can't believe you haven't kept up."

"Maybe a few times at some of the charity events, but other than that I haven't had anyone to dance with." She set up the coffeepot and took down two mugs.

Julia looked at her pensively and asked, "Do you mind me asking how you got to be such a hermit?"

"It's not a very interesting story." Even though Julia had proven easier to talk to than anyone she'd met in a long time, Ashley was reluctant to reveal how her periodic bouts of depression had driven her into isolation. People just didn't get it. She had tried to talk to Jarvis about it once, and he replied by telling her to cheer up, that it was just the doldrums.

If you must be preoccupied, think about perfection.

She shuddered to hear Cassandra's words erupt in her head, the first time in several weeks.

"I didn't mean to be nosy," Julia said. "I'm just surprised that someone like you doesn't have hundreds of friends."

"I know this will come as a great surprise, but I'm not exactly Miss Congeniality. I don't like to talk about myself, and friends expect you to do that."

"You mean like now?"

"Exactly like now," she said, shaking her spoon in hopes a playful threat would steer the conversation from its potentially serious path. "I'd rather talk about how you take your coffee."

Julia smiled weakly, clearly disappointed at the flippant response.

Ashley didn't mind putting off most people who pressed her on personal matters, but it bothered her to do that to Julia, who had been nothing but a friend and had proven she could keep a confidence.

"Sooner or later people end up asking about subjects I don't want to talk about, like my family or Valerie Reynolds. Or they want to know all about how I could do something as ridiculous as enter a beauty pageant. After all these years, I still haven't figured out how to answer questions like that without saying things I don't want to say."

They delight in telling your most precious secrets.

That had been Cassandra's way of warning all the girls against promiscuity because boys liked to brag about their conquests. Network news stars too, it turned out.

"I just don't want another experience like Valerie. At least I never confided in her about anything really personal, or she might have spilled that in her interview too."

"If you ask me, you've always handled your lesbian identity with a lot of class. She, on the other hand, came off like a major sleaze."

"It wasn't just being a lesbian. Yes, it made me uncomfortable to have it blabbed to the whole world, but I'd have felt the same way if I'd been straight and one of the male anchors had done that. You don't want somebody broadcasting—literally— that they've slept with you." Especially since it had brought Cassandra out of the woodwork. "I think the happiest day of my life was when Jarvis got the news director job at TV4 and asked me to come with him. I was so glad to get out of DC."

"And now you're determined not to let anybody get close like that again."

"Sure makes life easier." It was so much more complicated than that. There were layers upon layers Julia knew nothing about, but if superficial explanations would suffice, why trot out all the ugly details?

"Does that mean you're content...to stay...single?"

The halting cadence triggered uneasiness in Ashley. By her hesitation, Julia seemed aware that her query might be construed as asking about her availability. Now it was up to Ashley to either open or close that door. The coffee sputtered as it finished brewing, which gave her a moment to formulate a noncommittal answer. "I imagine all of us would be happier alone than with the wrong person. It's hard not to envy couples like Robyn and Elaine because they're so perfect for each other, but then I see Jarvis practically begging people to work late with him so he won't have to go home to his wife. Some days I feel pretty lucky that all I have to worry about is me."

"Yeah, the dating game starts to feel like a crapshoot after a while."

"I think Robyn and Elaine work so well because they met when they were young and built their lives together. Once we get older, we have all our own pieces in place and it's almost impossible to make them fit with somebody else's."

Julia tipped her head to the side in a half-nod. "That's a good point, but getting together when you're both young doesn't work if you're still trying to figure out who you are. Rachel and I met when we were both twenty years old and stayed together for nine years...except she was still looking for something else in her life. She finally hooked up with some people from a Pentecostal church and decided God didn't want her to be a lesbian anymore."

Ashley laughed at the absurdity. "You're kidding. She actually believed that?"

"It was bizarre. She had this brilliant idea that we could stay together as long as we didn't have sex, because Jesus wouldn't want us to do something like that. I'm all for religious freedom, but living without sex is not my idea of a healthy relationship."

Ashley stiffened. Here she was again talking with Julia about secrets she had told no one, but she wouldn't be drawn into discussing the subject of sex. "It takes all kinds, I guess," she said nervously.

"Yeah, but I must be a romantic at heart because I still like to dream about the right person coming along. At least all those years with Rachel taught me a few lessons about relationships."

"For instance?"

"That they aren't just magic that happens when two people lock eyes across a crowded room. They're a lot of work, and both people have to be committed every single day. I'm a lot more realistic now about what it takes. I guess I still want it, though. Especially…like you said…when I see couples like Robyn and Elaine."

There was a tinge of sadness in her voice that made Ashley suddenly ashamed that all she ever seemed to think about was herself. Having friends wasn't only about talking, but listening as well.

"You're right, though," Julia went on. "None of that matters if it's the wrong person. But if you're lucky enough to find the right person, you only have to do half the work because she'll do the other half. Or maybe you only have to do all the work half the time or some of the work most of the time…" She grimaced and took a deep breath. "Okay, now I'm starting to sound ludicrous. Obviously I spend too much time alone trying to figure out how the world works."

Ashley laughed heartily, relieved at the injection of levity. "I believe that's called navel gazing."

Julia popped the last of her cookie into her mouth and checked her watch. "It's officially very late."

"I'm glad you stayed, and not just for the heavy lifting."

She helped Julia with her jacket and walked her outside to her car, which she studied for the first time. It was a VW hatchback and it appeared to be well cared for. Low-key and sensible, a lot like its owner.

"I don't know how you do it, Julia, but once again you've managed to get me talking about things I don't talk about with anyone else."

"It's the stylist in me. I'm like the neighborhood bartender." Without a trace of awkwardness, she wrapped her arms around Ashley's shoulders in a bear hug. "Sorry if I got too personal, but it's your own fault for being so interesting."

Ashley stepped back and smiled. "Interesting...that's one of the most ambiguous words in the English language."

"I like you. How's that?"

"I like you too."

There was nothing flirtatious in their manner, just two friends putting it out there. As Julia drove through the gate, Ashley grasped that for those few moments, her mind and body had physically relaxed to allow her words to come out unguarded. That, she realized, was how normal people behaved.

Chapter Thirteen

Julia licked her fingertips one by one and slumped back from the table, unable to eat another bite. "That was the most delicious grouper I've ever tasted."

"Nothing but the best for my friends," Ashley said, waving a hand with false modestly. She had been wearing the same wide grin for the past four hours, ever since she landed the twenty-eight-inch fish that would become their feast.

"Dinner's always better when you catch it yourself," Robyn said. "Watching you pull that sucker in was a sight to behold. Even Elaine was excited and she usually cheers for the fish."

Teddie snared the last of the hush puppies, and with her mouth full, proclaimed, "If this grouper had been a vegetarian, he wouldn't have swallowed that pinfish in the first place."

"Can't argue with you there, slick. I liked how Ashley kept saying, 'No, no...I just want to watch.'"

It was Julia's fourth year in Boca Grande with Robyn and Elaine, and her third time out on a fishing charter. The thrill of catching her first big grouper two years ago was something she'd never forget, but even that didn't compare to the excitement of watching Ashley reel in her catch this afternoon. After spending most of the day tucked under the boat's awning out of the sun, she finally gave in to Teddie's relentless nagging, all the while complaining about the irreversible damage she was doing to her skin, and how she'd lose her job if she started looking old. Then her line jolted and before their eyes she became as manic as a five-year-old at Christmas.

"I only said yes so Teddie would finally get off my back. I figured I'd hold that pole for a few minutes and hand it back to her."

"Then that fish hit your line and you were like, 'Out of my way. This baby's mine!'"

For Julia, the more astonishing transformation was the one that took place once they returned to the villa. For the first time since they'd met, Ashley appeared from her shower without makeup, not even a foundation to cover spots and blemishes. It was all Julia could do not to stare at her imperfections with admiration. She was proud of Ashley for finally letting down her guard about her appearance, but didn't dare say anything for fear of making her self-conscious.

Her efforts to bring her crush on Ashley under control had failed miserably. If anything, the attraction had only gotten stronger, especially since the night she stayed late after dinner. Ashley had seemed genuinely happy to have her stick around, a fact that fueled Julia's hope there might be at least a hint of mutual interest. If she had been anyone else, there was no question Julia would have asked her out by now.

But this was Ashley Giraud, a woman everyone in Tampa recognized. She was also Robyn's friend, and she'd been promised a safe haven from exploitation of her celebrity. If all of that weren't enough, she was also a salon client whose satisfaction impacted Julia's business and reputation. The only way—the *only* way—there could ever be anything between them was if Ashley initiated it. That meant Julia had to get a handle on what she was feeling before she inadvertently crossed a line and ruined everything.

Teddie's phone roared in her pocket, and she stepped out

onto the balcony and closed the sliding glass door.

Elaine started clearing the table. "Is it my imagination, or does her phone ring every time it's her turn to do dishes?"

"She probably has it programmed," Julia said. "Her birthday's next weekend, by the way. She mentioned something about wanting to go bowling."

Ashley huffed. "First she makes me put on skates. Now she expects me to wear bowling shoes. What's with her and the rented shoe fetish?"

"But you're coming, right?" Robyn asked.

"I guess…and I'll be sure to dress up for the video somebody will send to TV4."

As Ashley disappeared into the bathroom, Robyn turned to Julia and whispered, "Can you believe the change in Ashley? She's like a whole different person from just a few weeks ago. She got so excited about coming down here with us that she called me practically every day last week, and now she's ready to go bowling of all things. Remember when we had to practically beg her to come to my birthday dinner?"

Elaine sidled closer and kept her voice low as well. "I told Robyn she was acting like someone who was bipolar. Nobody changes that much overnight. And if she is, we'd better look out because she could crash"—she snapped her fingers—"just like that."

Julia didn't like the direction of the conversation, or that they were having it at all. "I don't think she changed overnight. She didn't know us before and now she does. What's so weird about that?"

"It's more than that. It's like she's—"

"We shouldn't be talking about her like this," she said sharply. "If you guys want to speculate, fine, but leave me out of it."

Teddie returned just as Ashley did. "That was Patsy. Jordan's in the hospital. Apparently she's running a high fever."

The situation with Jordan was growing steadily worse, and Julia knew it was taking a toll on her young friend, who was running errands for Patsy at all hours of the day and night. "Do you need to get back to Tampa?"

"Nah, she'll probably go home tomorrow. I told her I'd come by Monday when I got off work." She looked around the kitchen. "You guys finished already. It was my turn to clean up."

Robyn chortled. "Funny, we were just noticing that you always disappear."

Teddie glowered at each of them. "Do you guys talk about me every time I leave the room? Because that would be really shitty."

It was all Julia could do not to snort.

Ashley's phone vibrated against the coffee table for the third time in the past half hour, and she looked up from their dice game to peek at the incoming message. No matter what else she was doing or how enjoyable it was, her journalist side never took a day off.

"Must be a big breaking story," Robyn said.

"No, just a couple of updates from Aaron. I asked him to look into something for me this weekend and to keep me posted."

"My intern Aaron? You must be investigating something. Is it juicy?"

"It's getting more interesting. We're studying some public documents and trying to tie people together through all these social networks. It's unbelievable how much personal information some people put on these websites where everybody can see them." Aaron had put together profiles of dozens of the property owners they were investigating.

"What kind of documents are you looking at?"

She didn't want to share too much information, especially in the preliminary stages, but she needed a polite way to deflect the question instead of just refusing to answer.

Julia saved her from having to come up with anything. "They were probably deposit slips for the city council's monthly bribe, which explains why they keep sending all of our tax dollars out of state. That reminds me, I'd better give somebody bail money because Larry and I are going to that council meeting next week."

Ashley smiled, not only at the mental image of seeing Julia marched off in handcuffs after a lively council protest, but also at recalling her erroneous first impression. It was out-and-out stereotyping on her part to assume that Julia—because she was a hair stylist and not a white-collar professional—wouldn't keep up with the important news of the day. Not only did she follow it, she understood many of its implications far better than some of the people from Ashley's newsroom, which instantly earned her Ashley's respect.

She had underestimated Julia in other ways as well. The idea of these laid-back get-togethers with their small circle of friends had seemed preposterous when she was first invited, but now they were unquestionably the centerpiece in the rebirth of her social life. All the fears about how networking with people she didn't know would expose her to exploitation had proven unfounded. These four women were as trustworthy as any she'd ever met, and Julia had been absolutely right to think she'd enjoy their casual brand of friendship.

The person she had misjudged most, however, was not actually Julia but herself. Up until now her desire for privacy had been strong enough to shut down interest in someone before it could manifest as romantic or sexual desire. Now she found herself scrutinizing everything Julia said or did for a sign that her offer of friendship held more. While that didn't mean anything would come of it—there was a good reason she had extinguished that part of her life—she was encouraged for once not to hear Cassandra's snide voice in her head.

"Hotness!" Teddie exclaimed, lunging for the TV remote to turn up the sound as a voluptuous pop singer was being interviewed on an entertainment program. "Drool, baby, drool. She always reminds me of my first."

"Your first what, slick? Restraining order?" Elaine's quip earned her a swift pinch and a round of laughter. "I don't remember you having any girlfriend who looked like that."

"I didn't say girlfriend. It was back when I was in the seventh grade. Her name was Kristie Fulenwider, and she looked just like—"

"Wait a minute," Robyn said, her face contorted with apparent disbelief. "You lost your virginity when you were twelve years old?"

"No, I got held back a year. I think I was thirteen."

"But still…"

"What? It was just dyke sex. Everybody that age has dyke sex."

"I beg your pardon."

"That's what I always called it," Teddie said. "Remember how all the girls in school would talk about letting some boy reach into their pants and touch their business? But they didn't actually screw so they still called themselves virgins. Except dykes don't screw, so what straight girls don't even call sex is the whole enchilada for us."

Elaine nodded thoughtfully. "As much as I hate to say it, you're right. I had dyke sex too."

Robyn stiffened with a look of horror. "I thought you said I was your first?"

"You were my first woman, but both of us were with guys before that. By Teddie's definition, I lost my virginity in the ninth grade when I was fourteen."

"What about you, Julia? How old were you when you had dyke sex?" Robyn asked.

It won't make you a woman…just a girl with nothing to give.

Ashley's stomach lurched as she realized the discussion was working its way around the room, and it was all she could do not to bolt. There was nothing fun or interesting about explicating such a deeply personal and serious issue with silly overtones.

"I don't even think about a first time," Julia said, shaking her head. "Teenagers fooling around is all about hormones. Why should I even care when the first time was? It's no more significant than the first time I parallel parked."

Teddie sniggered. "That explains a lot."

"So if it isn't the loss of your physical virginity that you mark, what is it?" Robyn asked. "The first time you made love? The first time you had an orgasm?"

"To be honest, I don't really think about any of them, at least not in a way that I memorialize as the first time. I'd rather pick the moments I think are worth remembering because of how I felt than because it was the first time it happened."

"I like Julia's thinking on this," Elaine said. "A lot of the historical emphasis on virginity has been about women as property…"

As Elaine expounded on her feminist perspective, Ashley looked down to find her hands shaking, and she realized with embarrassment that Julia had seen it too. She was about to excuse herself when Robyn finally turned to her.

"What's your thinking on this, Ashley? Do you remember losing your virginity, or was your first time as forgettable as Julia's?"

She couldn't speak, afraid her voice would crack. "I…I don't…"

Suddenly Julia's soda and a half-dozen ice cubes splattered across the coffee table as her glass tipped from her hands. "Oh, shit!"

Teddie was nearest the kitchen and grabbed a towel to mop up the mess. "Way to go, Your Grace. I'm usually the one who does something like this."

"You're rubbing off on me," Julia said as she picked up the wet game pieces. "I must be ready for bed if I can't even hold a glass in my hands. Being out in the sun all day drains me."

Ashley seized the opening and started for the bedroom, hoping that a night's sleep for everyone would push this unpleasant topic off the radar. When she turned to say goodnight, she caught a wink from Julia and realized the spill had been no accident.

Ashley slowly turned the knob on her bedroom door so as not to wake Teddie and Julia, who were sharing the foldout sofa in the living room. Just a quick trip to the bathroom and she would go back to her room and wait for the others to come to life. It wasn't like her at all to awaken so early, but she had gone to bed before midnight, which wasn't her usual style either.

The distinct odor of coffee drew her from the bathroom to the kitchen. Teddie was stretched diagonally across the sofa bed and Julia's bare feet were visible on the balcony. Ashley poured a cup of coffee and tiptoed to the door, where she paused to study Julia in her blue flannel pajamas staring out over the water. She had such a peaceful, contemplative look that Ashley considered leaving her be, but then Julia spotted her and waved her out.

"You're up early," she said as Ashley quietly closed the sliding glass door behind her.

"Strange bed."

"Tell me about it. I'm not used to sleeping with a turbine. For a little thing, she sure takes up a lot of space."

"It was sweet of you both to double up and let me have the bedroom."

Julia tipped her head in the direction of the living room. "We didn't want to scare you off the first year by making you sleep with Teddie. Or with me, for that matter."

"I don't know. You look pretty easy to push around." She tapped Julia's toe with hers. "And by the way, I appreciate that little move last night, though I'm sure you're going to say you have no idea what I'm talking about."

Julia gave her the same wink as the night before. "We've all known each other for a long time, so there isn't a whole lot on our private list. I'm sorry if things got uncomfortable for you."

"Don't be sorry. It's just more of my eccentric baggage. It's been a long time since I was asked to talk about something like that."

"It isn't eccentric. You shouldn't feel like you have to divulge things you want to keep private. We learn each other's limits and respect them."

That approach seemed to Ashley like the perfect way to balance having friends with maintaining privacy. There was just one problem—it didn't work. "So you're saying it won't hurt anybody's feelings if I don't share all my secrets when they do, or that they won't whisper about what I'm hiding."

She had meant it only to show how difficult it was in practice, but it came out sounding like an indictment of Julia and her friends, and she groaned dramatically, hoping the exaggerated display would lighten the tone of their discussion. "It's no wonder I don't have any friends. I'm probably the most paranoid person you'll ever meet."

"What was it you said…it's only paranoid if it's imaginary?" Julia flashed a gentle smile that kept the mood light. "Just relax and be yourself. If certain topics are off-limits, say so and we won't talk about them. Simple as that."

She followed Julia's eyes out to the water where a man navigated a sailboard back and forth along the shore. It seemed almost effortless, as though he was gliding on a current, and it only added to the serenity of the morning. With a deep breath she allowed the calm to engulf her. Having friends was every bit as hard as she thought it would be but it was proving worth the effort. Julia's support and understanding made her want to try harder to face the issues that kept her in knots.

"I've been burying my problems for so long I'm not even sure who I'd be if I ever relaxed and became myself. That's the beauty of being a public person. I get to project whatever I want."

"We all project the parts we want other people to see. I don't usually talk about my personal life with my clients…unless, of course, they happen to ask me point-blank about my father," she added with a chuckle.

"See, that's a perfect example of the difference between me and everyone else in the world. You didn't get all anxious about it and clam up like it was some deep dark secret."

"You didn't either, Ashley. Something told you it was okay to confide in me that day and you did. You can do that any time you want, but you don't need to feel pressure to do it if it doesn't feel right."

It was true their conversation about their fathers had happened without all the usual angst and dithering on her part, and it had marked a change in how she perceived Julia—from acquaintance to potential friend. Not once since that day had she felt threatened by what she had revealed.

"It was nice to talk to somebody who knew where I was coming from," Ashley admitted. If she was ever to make any progress toward honesty in her relationships, it would have to start with someone like Julia. "A lot of my life is like that... unpleasant things I don't like to revisit. Unfortunately, I've learned the hard way that not dealing with them tends to make them fester. I can barely stand to think about the first time I..." She couldn't even say it. "You guys talk about it with all the nonchalance of what you had for breakfast."

"That was my point, though—that we should choose the pieces we want to hold onto and throw the rest away."

If only she could. Her whole life since leaving Missouri might have been different if she could have purged the memory of her first sexual experience. "Unfortunately, no one gets to choose their memories."

The door slid suddenly and Teddie appeared with her phone in her hand, her eyes streaming with tears.

"She died."

Chapter Fourteen

The speckled bowling ball teetered into the gutter despite Robyn's grimaces, twists and kicks, and she slogged dejectedly back to her seat. "Whose bright idea was this?"

Julia nodded in the direction of Teddie, whose somber mood on her birthday reminded all of them it had been only a week since Jordan's death. They all had stood by her through the funeral, and took it as a good sign that she still wanted to have a bowling party, though no longer with forty of her closest friends. Today was just for their usual gang, which now firmly included Ashley, along with Patsy, and Julia's mom, Bonnie.

"Did you really go out and buy those?" Elaine asked, gesturing toward Ashley's brand-new burgundy suede bowling shoes.

"Do you even have to ask? Not only did I buy them, I also paid for overnight shipping so they'd get here in time. Laugh at me tomorrow when the skin starts peeling off your toes." She got up and took her turn, drawing the eyes of several bowlers on nearby lanes. A few flashes from camera phones suggested a new picture would soon be shared with the news team at TV4.

"You might have to get your own shoes too, Robyn," Julia said. "Ashley's kicking your ass."

"Beginner's luck."

They had taken two lanes side by side with an automatic scorekeeper that broadcast their collective ineptitude to everyone in the building. Only Bonnie seemed to have a clue about what she was doing, but their general lack of bowling prowess wasn't getting in the way of their fun. The whole day was about camaraderie and support for Teddie.

As Elaine took her place on the lane, Ashley slid into the seat next to Julia and whispered, "Is it my imagination, or is there something cooking between Teddie and Patsy?"

The pair had been practically inseparable, with Teddie gallantly responding to Patsy's every need, from hanging up her jacket to fetching drinks. They looked comfortable together, and Julia nearly laughed aloud to think she had once entertained the thought of asking Patsy out.

"Teddie's been interested in her for a while but didn't want to start anything while Patsy was still taking care of Jordan. She got the big lecture from Mom this morning about not jumping into anything, and she promised they were going to take it slow."

"This is a whole different side of Teddie, like she's grown up all of a sudden."

"I hope so. What I like best about Patsy is that she hates motorcycles. We'll know it's serious when Teddie gets rid of that Harley."

"You're up, Jules."

Julia hopped to her feet and found herself standing beside her mother in the next lane. In perfect synchrony they marched four steps and rolled their respective balls down the alley, both striking off-center to leave several pins standing.

As they waited for their balls to return, her mother turned her back to the group and lowered her voice. "I like her."

"You mean Patsy?"

"No, I mean Ashley. Teddie said she thought you two had a thing going on."

Julia groaned, knowing that any protest would probably only

fuel further speculation. One of the hardest bits about coming out years ago was listening to all the people who said they knew it all along, which taught her that hiding her real feelings only made it harder to admit them later. "We don't, but it would be fine with me if we did."

She had worried all week about Ashley. By the time they left Boca Grande, it was obvious Ashley trusted her more than she did the others, and was making a serious effort to open up. The discomfort she harbored about her first sexual experience—so pronounced she couldn't even say the words to describe losing her virginity—stoked Julia's fears about how horrible it must have been.

"From the way she keeps watching you, I'd say it would be fine with her too."

Feeling her face grow hot, she looked to find that it was true. "She's only watching me because it's my turn to bowl."

"If you say so." Her mother picked up her spare and dusted her hands with satisfaction. "No pressure."

Julia's ball found the gutter almost as soon as she released it. With the idea of Ashley watching her now firmly planted in her head, she self-consciously returned to her seat, trying not to make eye contact. Of course she wanted their friendship to lead to something more, but it wasn't going anywhere until Ashley decided she was ready. So far she'd given no such sign.

When Patsy got up to bowl the last frame of the afternoon, Teddie came to sit beside Julia. "Patsy and I were thinking about taking a ride out to Pass-a-Grille but there's just one problem."

"Neither one of you has a car."

"And Patsy doesn't want to go on the bike. Think you could get a ride home with Bonnie?"

"I can take you home," Ashley offered. "Maybe we could grab some dinner."

That was the sign Julia had been looking for, and even if it meant grist for Teddie's rumor mill, she was glad to get it. "Sounds good," she said, deliberately avoiding Teddie's eye as she handed over her keys.

Ashley's plans for a private evening with Julia were scuttled when Robyn and Elaine suggested dinner at The Reef, a laid-back seafood restaurant that had just opened on the Hillsborough River. At least the short ride downtown gave them a few minutes alone in the car—not enough time to start another deep discussion like the one they'd begun on the balcony last weekend, but enough to reaffirm her trust in Julia.

She was glad to find most of the restaurant's patrons casually dressed, since they had driven over straight from the bowling alley. It was remarkable how little thought she'd given the idea, since only a few months ago she would never even have considered going anywhere unless she was meticulously coiffed and made-up. Though she was sure to be recognized, it seemed silly to be self-conscious about how she looked now after making a total fool of herself all afternoon at the bowling alley.

The minute they were seated, a gray-haired man in a sport jacket approached their table. Ashley recognized him at once as Jack Staley, the at-large county commissioner whom Lamar Davidson had lambasted with his *Guardian* profile.

"Miss Giraud?"

"Commissioner Staley," she said, taking his extended hand.

"Please, call me Jack. How have you been?"

She was pretty sure he couldn't have cared less, but making nice with influential media personalities was a big part of the political game, especially in a public venue like The Reef. She introduced each of her friends and listened politely as he made small talk.

"I'll let you get back to your dinner. I just wanted to stop by and say hello."

Ashley followed him with her eyes back to his table, where he joined an elegant woman she presumed to be his wife and a younger couple. There was something familiar about the young man, a face she had seen recently. Suddenly it struck her that his was one of the social profiles Aaron had shown her.

"Excuse me just a minute." She fished her iPhone from her purse and rushed over to the commissioner's table. "Jack, I hope you'll indulge me one little treat. Any chance I could get a picture with all of you?"

"Of course." He introduced his wife, along with the younger couple—his daughter and son-in-law.

She thanked them and hurried back to join her friends. "Sorry about that," she said as she typed a short message to Aaron. "One of the stories we're working on just got very interesting."

When they walked into her cottage, Julia flipped on the light over her stove and propped open the door to let in some fresh air. "Have a seat on the couch. I'll bring over a couple of sodas."

The downside of living in an apartment behind her mother's house was that privacy was impossible, but her Mom was over at Chuck's tonight, and Teddie was out with Patsy in Julia's car.

Ashley poked her head into the bedroom on her way to the couch. "This is very cozy, and no, I'm not using that word to mean small. It feels comfortable."

"It's enough for now. I've been back here about six years. After I split up with Rachel, I decided I wanted to buy my own shop so I had to save some money. Teddie was kind of peeved about it because she wanted to move out of the house, but I think she got over it when she bought that Harley and had to start making payments." She took the opposite end of the couch and leisurely tucked her bare feet underneath her.

"I bet you've had a hard week with Teddie," Ashley said.

"It's been tough watching my little buddy fall apart. She knew Jordan's chances for pulling through were pretty slim, but I don't think she was ready for it to happen so fast. Now she feels guilty for not going back on Saturday night."

"Guilt is such a useless emotion. Nothing good ever comes from it."

"I know, but how do you get rid of it?"

"If I knew the answer to that, my psychiatrist would be collecting unemployment."

With her reference to years of psychotherapy from last weekend, it was the second time Ashley had mentioned being in therapy, and it almost made Julia wonder if she was inviting comment.

"It's not any of my business, but I'm glad you're working your issues out with somebody. I know you say you have a lot of baggage, and it takes a lot of guts to face that. I admire you for it."

"I'm not sure I'd call it guts." Ashley chuckled softly. "Not sure I'd call it working my issues out either. But I have friends now, and it wasn't long ago that I couldn't say that."

"You sure do." Julia held up her soda in a toast. "What about your week?"

"Up and down...down, mostly. We covered three different news stories about somebody Jordan's age getting killed. It made me appreciate how much of what I do involves real people."

They sipped their drinks somberly for a long moment and Julia decided to get something off her chest. "Ashley, I really appreciate that you've started to open up more. It means a lot to know you trust me."

"It means a lot to know I can," she said, punctuating her words with a direct gaze. "I need to stop treating every single detail of my life like it's a national secret. I spend a ridiculous amount of energy trying to hide things that don't even matter all that much."

"That's what I was trying to tell you last weekend. But everybody is entitled to their privacy, even with their friends."

"Which works just fine as long as I have you around to run interference for me. But how long will it be before Elaine notices that you always manage to change the subject or throw your drink across the room right when they're waiting for me to put in my two cents on something?" There was distinct antipathy in her tone, but it wasn't clear exactly which part she resented.

"If you want me to butt out, I will."

Ashley sighed with obvious frustration.

"Sorry," Julia said. "I didn't mean for that to come out whiny. I'm just saying I'll step back. It's hard to do that though when I see that look of panic on your face."

"You can actually see it?"

"I saw it that day at the shop when I asked if you wanted to hang out with us sometime, and again when Teddie tried to get you to come to her skate party. Your face freezes, but your eyes dart away like they're checking to see what your brain comes up with."

"That's exactly what they're doing...watching the wheels turn and waiting for the best excuse to fall out. Great to know I've had so much success at hiding it," she said sarcastically.

"Give me a little credit. I study people all day so I'll know what they *really* think of their haircut." She peeled the foil off a small chocolate from a bowl on the coffee table and held it to Ashley's lips.

"Mmm...have you forgotten that I told you they'll fire me if I get fat?"

"You're not fat. You look great." Julia took a candy for herself before feeding Ashley another.

"That's good but you have to stop. I'm serious."

In the process of feeding the sweet, Julia had slid closer on the couch, enough that her knee rested against Ashley's thigh. "So what kinds of national secrets have you decided to stop hiding?"

She leaned back against the pillow and folded her arms as if settling in. "Think you're up for hearing *The Chronicles of Ashley Giraud*?"

"Do they have a happy ending?"

"The jury's still out on that one, but it wasn't a very happy start."

She began with the story of Cassandra Muldoon, who Julia learned was the woman whose funeral Ashley had attended last fall.

"She was the most gorgeous woman I had ever seen, and I'll never forget how fascinated I was the day she came to our sixth-grade class to tell all us little girls what it meant to be ladies."

Julia had never heard of a pageant class and had no idea such things existed.

"It was just a glorified charm school, but all the good mothers wanted their girls to attend after school. It probably wouldn't have gone anywhere if Cassandra hadn't singled me out and asked me to come to her class—probably because I was a talkative, eleven-year-old lesbian-in-waiting and couldn't resist telling her how beautiful she was. But of course, my mother wasn't going to pay for something as silly as that, so Cassandra worked it out that I could come early and help her set up, and do a few little chores for her on the weekends, like ironing and polishing the silver. Then I could take her class for free."

"She must have seen something special in you."

"I'd never had anybody pay attention to me like that before…no one encouraging me to do better, and certainly nobody complimenting me on how pretty I looked and how much potential I had. I woke up every day thinking about what I could do to make Cassandra like me even more." By the faraway look in her eyes, she was remembering the emotions as if they were alive today. "I was so intent on pleasing her that I drank up everything she said. And let me tell you, that woman had more rules than Congress."

She had always wondered how Ashley could have gotten caught up in something as demeaning as a beauty pageant. Now it made sense—it was the only place in her life where she had been made to feel she could excel. "No matter how hard I try, I just can't picture you in one of those pageants. You're the last person in the world who would call attention to herself."

"How dare you imply I'm not vain," Ashley said, making an elaborate display of fluffing her hair and blotting her lips. "It's a fair question, especially when you see how these mothers doll up their five-year-olds with lipstick and off-the-shoulder tops. My experience wasn't like that at all. I was in it at first because I was infatuated with Cassandra, but as I got older I realized it was my best shot at getting out of Maple Ridge. I can honestly say I've used every single trick I ever learned about appearance and poise."

"But not the piano."

"Or prancing around in a swimsuit and high heels," she added drolly. "Anyway, one of the first things I figured out when I started the pageant class was that you didn't have to be the prettiest or the most talented to be recognized, and you definitely didn't have to be the most congenial. All you had to do was follow Cassandra's rules better than anyone else, and she'd put you out there in front for all the big events. We were like thoroughbreds out of her stable."

"I see now where you get your discipline."

Ashley rolled her eyes and leaned forward to snatch another chocolate. "Discipline was Cassandra's middle name. She said winning was all about never letting someone else take control. Every little move was choreographed, and every line scripted. We learned not to ad-lib anything because that opened the door for somebody to trip you up."

"I had no idea it was all so strict."

"It was, where Cassandra was concerned. She knew my background would be a liability at the pageant level because of my father, so she taught me how to talk about Maple Ridge without ever mentioning my family. 'It's just the prettiest place, especially in the fall.' Sound familiar? I got so used to it that I even found a career where every word I say gets written down ahead of time."

"I think I get it. You don't like to talk about something unless you've thought it all out ahead of time."

"Exactly. Remember that interview I did a few years ago with the *St. Pete Times*? The one where I said I was gay?" Her words were momentarily garbled by the chocolate, and she paused to take a drink. "It was set up by our public relations department because I'd just been appointed to the board of United Way. He asked me all about what our goals were for the year and what sorts of interests I planned to focus on. The interview was practically over but then he tossed off a question about what I liked to do in my free time. I told him a little about my garden—I even made some silly joke about growing the finest ragweed in Tampa Bay—and then, bam! He launches right into the whole

Valerie business and says, 'That means you're a lesbian, right?' The first question was just a setup, and once I told him about my stupid garden, he figured the door was open for whatever else he wanted to ask. I should have seen it coming, given that I learned all the same tricks in journalism school."

"For what it's worth, I have a lot of respect for how you handled that. It's discouraging when you know somebody's gay and they won't admit it. They wouldn't act that way if they were married with kids."

"I know, our news director—my friend Jarvis—said the same thing. Juicy little tidbits like that tend to spike the ratings," she said cynically. "My being a lesbian isn't a secret, but it's not really something I want to talk about either. I'm sorry if that sounds discouraging...but the only way to keep personal subjects off the table is not to talk about any of them, no matter how innocuous. My bio on the TV4 website is pretty much all I want people to know about me. It's the only way to keep control of what gets out there. I've been handling everyone in my life that way for as long as I can remember—shutting down their questions by not talking to them at all."

Her intonation had become more pointed with each word, and from the way her feet were fidgeting, she was growing agitated.

"But if it isn't about being a lesbian, then what is it? You're a success story, Ashley. You pulled yourself up out of nothing. You should be proud of that."

Shaking her head vehemently, she bolted from the couch and began pacing the small space in front of the kitchen counter. "You don't just pull yourself up out of a life like mine. There's a price for everything and once you pay it, you have to live with it."

Julia's gut tightened at the implication, remembering the revulsion with which Ashley had spoken of her first sexual experience. It sickened her to think that incident might have been coerced or even nonconsensual. On her feet now, she clutched Ashley's shoulders firmly and dipped her head to find her eyes. "Look at me, Ashley."

Her face was a mask of torment, shame and anger.

"Whatever happened then, happened then. You don't have to talk about it if it upsets you like this, but I promise I'm on your side, no matter what." She drew Ashley into her chest and hugged her tightly.

Several seconds passed before Ashley's rigid body relaxed, and she laid her head on Julia's shoulder and slid her arms around her waist. "Every time I think I'm ready to put this behind me once and for all, it comes back like it was yesterday."

"It's okay." Overcome by the urge to comfort, Julia stroked her hair and pressed her lips firmly against her temple, savoring a long, heady moment of physical closeness. Her feelings for Ashley were soaring more than ever, and it was all she could do to hold her in this silent embrace.

Until Ashley turned inward and released a warm breath against her neck.

Julia's pulse quickened as she waited for another sign, any hint at all that Ashley felt the same need. When Ashley's hands began gliding gently across her back, she boldly answered with a tender trail of kisses along the contours of her brow to her cheek. There she lingered, scarcely breathing as Ashley tipped her head, allowing the corners of their mouths to meet. That was the affirmation she needed, and she brushed her lips in a soft kiss.

As the seconds ticked off, her desire grew to the brink of losing control. Her hands wanted to wander and her hips to grind, but there was no mistaking Ashley's uncertainty. She had dropped the embrace and placed her hands on Julia's shoulders as if to push her away at any instant, all the while keeping tentative contact with her lips. Whatever conflict was playing out in her head, it was too much a part of her to simply slough aside, and Julia knew instinctively to take it slowly, no matter how torturous the wait.

Suddenly Ashley's lips parted and her arms went around Julia's neck with an urgency that seemed almost desperate.

Unable to hold back any longer Julia gave in to her wants,

swirling her tongue with Ashley's as she pulled her closer, her daydreams of the past few weeks not doing justice to the exquisite discovery of their mutual desire. Her mind darted from one sensation to the next—the rhythmic sound her hands made as they stroked Ashley's back, the taste of chocolate between them and the fragrance of delicate perfume—until her focus came to rest on the feel of Ashley in her arms. She imagined herself a fierce protector against whatever had dealt this anguish, poised to slay it once and for all, and give Ashley back her life. The surge of feelings caused her to deepen their kiss to the edge of passion.

It was too much for Ashley, who abruptly leaned back, shaking her head. "No, I can't do this, not again…and not to you."

Unwilling to let her withdraw, Julia drew her back into an embrace and cradled her head, determined to ease her doubts. "Ashley, I know there's something under there that's hurting you, but it isn't me. And no matter what it is, I'm not afraid of it. I can wait as long as it takes for you to work it out, or I can help you unravel it. What I can't do is let you pull away."

"But I'm afraid of it, Julia. I don't expect you to understand. Just trust me…all the roads go to the same place. The only decision that's mine is whether it hurts a little now or a lot later."

"It doesn't have to hurt forever. We can do this."

Ashley stepped back, breaking all contact between them. Even in the dim light, it was impossible to miss the tears that smudged the mascara on her lower lashes. "It's me. I'm the one who can't do it. Please don't ask me to."

Julia had no answer for the plea. She didn't want to cause more suffering, and that meant accepting Ashley's retreat for now. But there was no chance she could erase the memory of their kiss. "I won't…but don't expect me just to stop caring about you. I can see what a big deal this is for you, and I won't stop worrying about you until you've put it behind you."

"I don't want to be worried about." Ashley sighed with palpable frustration, slung her purse over her shoulder and ambled to the door, her jaw set grimly. "At least now you can see why I try so hard not to let conversations like this one even start."

Only moments earlier, Julia had been filled with joy and anticipation. The closing door left only misery.

Chapter Fifteen

"…and, as you can see, whatever she put on my hair was just disgusting. I'm never setting foot in that beauty shop again."

It's called a salon, you moron. Julia bit her tongue to keep the words inside her head. No way had this color job been done by a professional stylist. She winced as she studied the texture of the young woman's shoulder-length, albino-white hair, which was broken and split beyond all repair. "I think we should take it all the way down to the new growth and leave it natural so your hair can build back some strength in the shaft."

"But I like being blond," she whined. In addition to having the worst hair Julia had ever seen, she also had a dreadful sense of how to dress. Pajamas were not daywear, but who could expect fashion sense from someone stupid enough to use laundry bleach on her hair?

"Blonde we can do, but this Annie Lennox look…it's only going to work if you keep it under two inches. And even then, you're getting breakage all the way down to the scalp, which isn't all that big a deal if you're okay with the bald patches."

Suzy cleared her throat and sought out Julia's eyes in the

mirror. Her raised eyebrows and forced smile were the cautionary cues they sometimes shared when one of them struggled overtly with a client. More often than not it was Suzy who was having a bad day, since people seldom got under Julia's skin.

Ashley was under her skin now, and had been for the past five days. A four-word text message on Monday—*Sorry for the meltdown*—had been Ashley's only communication. Julia had answered it with a voicemail, clumsily apologizing for misreading things, and asking her to call. The fact that she hadn't spoke volumes.

As screwups went, it was difficult to imagine topping this one. The total loss of Ashley's trust was bad enough, but she had also broken her pledge to Robyn to provide a safe setting where Ashley wouldn't be bothered by people trying to get into her personal space.

Or kiss her.

When the TV4 news logo appeared, she turned up the volume with the remote.

"Oh, it's time for the news," the young woman proclaimed. "Can you switch it to Channel 20?"

We don't watch crap like that here.

Ashley looked ready for a trim and was due back in the shop on Monday…unless Sergio called and canceled the contract between now and then.

"We don't get that station…something interferes with the reception on our satellite dish."

It's our garbage filter.

"That's too bad. They have news that people actually care about—like murders and stuff."

There was probably a bottle of bleach in the laundry room.

Ashley followed the red light to Camera Two. "Police are on the scene of an accident with injuries slowing westbound lanes of the Courtney Campbell Causeway. For more, we go live to…" The producer had cued the reporter's name through her earpiece only seconds ago, but she had lost her focus. The result was dead air until it came through again. "Chris Lumke, on the scene."

Jarvis eyed her pointedly and she looked away. He couldn't possibly scold her more than she did herself.

Rod sent it over to Puze for sports, after which they traded lines by rote through their usual sign-off. Ashley wasted no time shedding her mic and exiting the set, leaving her co-anchor to shoot the eleven o'clock promos whether he liked it or not.

Moments later Jarvis darkened her doorway, still scowling from her on-air gaffe. "Having a nice vacation?"

"I'm not in the mood for jokes."

"Fine. What if I just tell you to take your head out of your ass? Is that better? I don't like it when my anchor gets caught in the headlights like that. It makes us all look bad."

Though she seethed at his crudeness, she couldn't deny the truth of his words. Nothing was worse in her book than being unprofessional, and blaming it on a faulty earpiece would only eat up someone else's time checking it out. "I'm sorry. It was a lapse in concentration, and I won't let it happen again."

He nodded slowly, squinting as if studying her. "I know. I bet it bothered you more than it did me."

Her whole week had been dotted with moments like that one, but at least the others hadn't occurred while she was live on the air. She was distracted and irritable, and back to wrestling with insomnia and listless grazing at her refrigerator. A part of her wanted to call Julia and put the whole ugly incident to rest. The other part—the part that was currently winning—didn't want to confront the reasons behind why she had gone off the rails.

"Let's go get some dinner," he said. "We need to talk about the tax office story…and yes, I'm avoiding going home. Connie's sister just got here from New York, and that old saying about fish and houseguests stinking up the place after three days is off by two and a half."

She didn't want to have dinner with Jarvis—or anyone else for that matter—but five days of relentless introspection had gotten her nowhere in terms of sorting out her emotions over the incident with Julia. Maybe after a couple of hours of distraction, she could even call it a kiss instead of an incident. What she needed was to own the fact that she had liked it.

It wasn't exactly true that she'd made no progress at all since Sunday night, she realized as they rode silently along Kennedy Boulevard. At least she had admitted to herself that she didn't want to run from Julia. The problem was with what came after kissing—at least for normal people—and even thinking about it now was enough to stir a sense of panic that sent her hand to her chest. None of that was Julia's fault, and she'd tried to say as much in a short text message in which she had taken responsibility for the way things had unfolded on Sunday. Julia had responded by voicemail with a generic apology of her own— small wonder since no one not currently living in Ashley's head could guess precisely what was wrong with kissing someone you cared about. Her regular hair appointment was three days from now, and she needed to get up the nerve to call before then. More than once she had picked up the phone only to put it down when her heart began to race.

"This okay with you?" Jarvis asked as he pulled his black Mercedes S-80 into the valet circle at Capital Grille. It seldom occurred to him to ask anyone else where they wanted to go for dinner, since he never ate anything that didn't bleed all over his plate. He was on a first-name basis with the door staff at practically every upscale steak place in town.

Ashley made her usual entrance, nodding and smiling at those who recognized her as she made her way to their table. Jarvis usually relished the attention his star anchor commanded, so it surprised her when he asked for a booth not in a high traffic area.

"Johnnie Walker Black, neat and…"

"Iced tea," Ashley said, noting with displeasure his lecherous admiration for the derriere of their departing waitress.

"I had an interesting talk with Carl this afternoon," he said as the young woman drifted from sight.

"Let me guess. He wants me to get implants."

"Probably, but that didn't come up today. He wanted to know if we were working on something related to his good friend, Jack Staley."

"And I trust you told him to keep his nose out of the newsroom."

"He's the boss, Ashley. I don't have that luxury." When the waitress delivered their drinks, he held up a finger for another before pounding the first one back.

"But you got him to agree to the Chinese firewall between what we cover and the business side of the station. Surely he realizes that also includes his personal interests."

"Yeah, he gets it. That's what made our little talk so interesting. It was actually like he was warning me that Staley was on to us. I wanted to get your take on how that might impact our story. Does it even matter?"

It was nearly impossible to investigate people without tipping them off, but it didn't change their set of facts. "We've got all the changes to the database documented so it's not like he can go back and move the numbers around and make it all okay. All the ones we identified paid a lower tax bill. That's a permanent record."

"What if he just has the tax office send out a revised bill, like it was a clerical error? No harm, no foul."

"It won't fly. We've connected a lot of these so-called errors to people he knows," she said, lowering her voice. "If we go all-out, we can probably trim a week off the timeline...but that means I should probably send regrets to doing the emcee gig for Connie at the stage guild next Friday. I don't want to be out of pocket when we're this close to breaking the story."

"Are you trying to hasten my next divorce? Because we both know that's what'll happen if you no-show. She'll serve papers on me faster than you can say 'lump sum alimony,' and yours truly will be leasing a Chevrolet for the next four years." He accepted his second drink and this time sipped it judiciously as they ordered dinner. "We still have plenty of time to pull this together. BJ and Mallory already shot half a dozen spots in front of some of the properties, and that kid of yours—"

"Aaron Crum."

"Yeah, he's been working with Tim on the graphics. Sharp fellow...too bad about all those acne scars."

Ashley was annoyed by his dismissive critique of her intern, but that battle had been fought and lost years ago. What bothered her more was hearing that Jarvis's young and beautiful star reporter Mallory was slated for so much of the screen time on her exclusive, but that was a useless battle too. The 4Team was supposed to be just that—a team—and she was nothing if not a professional.

"Jarvis, I'd feel better if we knew exactly who was making the changes to the database, and how they were cracking Kevin's ID. Aaron has a theory, but he won't give me any details just yet...which makes me think he's up to something sneaky."

"I hope you read him the riot act."

"He knows not to break the rules, but he's a smart guy and a pretty creative problem solver. I promised to work with him this weekend. Maybe something will pan out."

"Keep me posted." He opened his mouth to say something else then apparently thought better of it.

"What?"

"Something else came up with Carl today. It seems his youngest son pals around with Lamar Davidson, and he asked if you might be willing to grant him—"

"No."

"At least let me—"

"No. I like Lamar as much as anyone, but I'm not sitting down for another interview with a newspaper reporter." She hated to think this was an effort to generate some titillating publicity for the station before heading into February sweeps. "You'd provide more fodder for gossip than I would, don't you think?"

He shrugged. "Skirt-chasers are a dime a dozen, and we're all scoundrels. Everyone likes lesbians. So what's up with you lately? You seeing anybody?"

"No," she said icily.

"You know, Connie has a friend who—"

"No."

He chuckled and held up his glass in a toast. "I've got to hand it to you, Ash. No one's ever going to call you fickle."

She felt bad for hedging with Jarvis, of all people, who had never been anything but supportive of her ups and downs. "The truth is that I've been spending more of my free time with friends...one in particular." She held up her hands as his face brightened. "Don't read too much into that. It's way too early to know where it's going...or if it's going anywhere at all. I'm not very good at this, in case you haven't noticed."

"It's because you haven't had any practice. It takes the average person at least four or five marriages to get it right." No surprise that he considered himself average. "You know, Connie and I would love it if the two of you would join us for—"

"No."

"At least tell me what she—"

"No." She laughed at his dejected look. "Give me some time, okay? A couple of years ought to do it."

"Connie's loss. I'll probably be married to someone else by then."

Feeling good for the first time all week, Ashley enjoyed her Alaskan salmon and vowed anew to get her life back on track without rushing to Dr. Friedman for crisis management. Her feelings for Julia weren't going away just because she'd decided not to face them. There was no mystery in what she had to do, and when she excused herself to the ladies' room and found it empty, she pulled out her cell phone and placed the call she'd been unable to make until now.

"Any chance you're still talking to me?"

The sound of Ashley's voice was music to Julia's ears. "I never stopped. In fact, I talk to you twice a night during the TV4 news."

"A pleasant conversation, I hope."

"Always." She caught herself smiling at Ashley's calm

demeanor, a 180-degree turnaround from Sunday night. "I'm really glad you called."

"I'm sorry I didn't do it sooner. It always takes a while for me to sort my problems out, but I always knew it was me and not you. I apologize for all the drama."

"No apology necessary." Julia didn't want to say anything that might spook her into running away again, even if it meant pretending they hadn't kissed. "It's all in the past, and we don't ever have to talk about any of it again. I just…I want you in my life, however that has to work. Friends…whatever."

Several agonizing seconds passed before Ashley replied. "Are you brave enough to let me try talking again?" There was uncertainty in her voice, but Julia had no way of knowing if it was because Ashley was still afraid to share her secrets or simply doubted her ability to do it.

"Absolutely. How about I come over when you get off work?"

"You mean tonight?"

"Why not? We don't have to talk it all out until you're ready, but I've been sick about this all week. I just want to see you so I can feel like we're okay again. Maybe I'll finally get a good night's sleep."

"I could use that too." A sudden burst of laughter in the background told her Ashley was in a public place. "I have to go."

"Midnight."

Chapter Sixteen

Ashley had raced home to change from her business suit and was putting the finishing touches on a pot of coffee when the buzzer sounded for the gate. The hours past midnight had always been her favorite time of the day because of their utter solitude, but tonight was different. Like Julia, she needed a dose of reassurance that all was good between them again. After her quick call from the restaurant, she had returned to work with a calm resolve to take it forward, to share the truth about what a mess she really was and let Julia decide what she wanted. At the very least, she was confident of coming out of this with a friend she could trust.

And at the most…

Julia appeared at her door dressed in jeans and a denim shirt, and presented her with a colorful Christmas tin. "Kalupa's was closed, but I managed to throw together some oatmeal raisin cookies. Sorry about the box. It was a fruitcake from one of my aunts and it deserved to die."

"There you go again, trying to get me fired." She set the package on the table by the door and opened her arms. "I am so sorry," she murmured into Julia's shoulder.

"You don't have to be."

She enjoyed a long moment of serenity in Julia's strong embrace. With her eyes tightly closed, she envisioned them standing together, the whole of their bodies in contact. It felt more intimate than even their kiss because she was fully aware and in control of her feelings. It was a deliberate step this time, not one that got away from her and rendered her powerless to physical desires. A major part of her control came in knowing this new intimacy didn't have to mean romance if she found she couldn't handle it. Julia had offered friendship.

"I smell coffee."

"I was hoping you'd stay a while but I know you have to work tomorrow."

"Not until eleven. I'm a night owl too, remember?"

As Ashley filled their mugs, she began to feel the magnitude of what she was about to do. Other than Dr. Friedman, to whom she paid two hundred dollars an hour to listen, she had never shared with anyone what she was about to tell Julia. Reconciled to the fact that it might end the romantic aspects of their relationship, she took comfort in knowing at least that Julia would finally understand the mysteries about why she held the world at arm's length. That didn't mean she wasn't still afraid of her judgment.

"How do you feel about sitting in the dark?" Ashley asked.

"I do it all the time, actually. It takes out some of the clutter when I'm trying to focus."

She led Julia to the couch before flipping the light switches one by one, leaving only the up-lights of her garden shining faintly through the French doors. "I like to sit here at night sometimes because I can see better through the full-length glass. I get home with these awful stories still in my head and need to let go of them before I can even think about going to sleep. My favorite nights are when there's a little breeze because the fan palms and hibiscus sway back and forth, and it lulls me into a quiet place."

"Too bad there's no breeze tonight."

Ashley turned sideways on the couch. "You can't see anything from that end. Why don't you come down here?" Her request had little to do with Julia being able to see the garden. Rather, she wanted her facing away from the embarrassment and shame that would follow once she started talking.

Julia settled her head against Ashley's chest and draped her feet over the end of the couch. "This is peaceful."

After letting that peace settle over both of them for several minutes, Ashley began her tale with a deep sigh. "That stuff about me not wanting to answer personal questions and pulling away when people invite me somewhere...it all comes from the same place. I never want people to get close enough to see who I really am. It's not just because I came from white trash, which I did. And it's not because I stepped on people to get out of Maple Ridge, though I did that too. The real reason is that you can't truly get to know me without realizing that most days I'm just holding it all together by a thread. You got to see that up close and personal last Sunday."

"I didn't see that at all. What I saw was you needing a friend and me stepping over the line."

Ashley let out a small groan of disbelief. "We both know that wasn't just a friendly kiss, and it wasn't just you stepping over lines. What you didn't know—what no one knows—is that a kiss like that scares me more than anything else in the world. That's why I haven't kissed anyone since Valerie—and before I met you, I never even let myself get close enough to anyone to want to."

Julia had found her hand and was lightly stroking the back of her palm, not remotely suspecting the bombshell Ashley was about to drop.

"The fact is I could have kissed you all night. What I couldn't do was what usually comes after that, at least for most people. I don't..." She drew a deep breath and turned her hand over to clasp Julia's. "I have really serious issues with sex. I don't enjoy it like normal people. Even thinking about it makes me panic, like someone's standing on my chest."

After several seconds the only response to her confession was a tightening of Julia's grip.

"I've learned to control my reactions by not even starting down that road in the first place. I'll spare you all the unpleasant details of how I got to be this way, but the bottom line is I don't want to lead you on because I honestly don't think I can go there." It was only when the words left her lips that she realized she had already staged the outcome in her mind without ever offering Julia the chance to change it.

Never give anyone else control over you.

"I've tried, Julia...a couple of times, even, but when it was over I just wanted to get out of there as fast as I could." She hadn't thought in years of the encounter with her classmate from Mizzou...Patrice something or other. It was emotionally so insignificant that she hadn't even bothered to remember the woman's last name. The whole episode had been easy to dismiss since Patrice was only experimenting with lesbian sex and laughingly came down on the other side the next day. What she hadn't known was that Ashley had spent the whole night in the bathroom throwing up. "I never even talked to Valerie about what was wrong with me. I just ran. It's no wonder she treated me like a cheap whore."

Julia tried to sit up but Ashley held her firmly in place. "Ashley, I—"

"I can't look at you right now, not when I'm talking about this. I've done some things in my life that I'm not proud of. I even convince myself sometimes that I'm actually the victim, but the truth always finds its way back." Her victim rationale fell apart each time she remembered her own seductive role in what had transpired back in Maple Ridge.

"Remember what I said, Ashley. I'm taking your side, no matter what it is." Julia lifted her hand to her lips and kissed it softly. "I've been worried about you ever since Boca Grande when you said you couldn't bear to think about your first time. If something happened that shouldn't have, then you really are a victim."

"It wasn't like that," she said quickly, shocked to realize Julia might have thought she had been raped. "I just had a bad experience is all."

"Which is why you don't talk about sex."

"Right."

"And why you don't want to socialize, especially with other lesbians."

"Exactly."

"And why you never let another woman get close enough to kiss you."

"Never."

"Not even me."

Recognizing that she'd been set up, Ashley groaned again. "Aren't you clever?"

"I wasn't trying to be...okay, maybe I was." She kissed Ashley's hand again but made no more effort to turn around. "I was just trying to show you that something must be different about this time. You didn't kiss just anybody. You kissed me, and I think you did it because you wanted to. That's the same reason we're sitting here in the dark talking about secrets you never share with anyone else—because you don't think of me as just anyone. Isn't it worth asking yourself why that is before you decide you don't want to lead me on?"

Ashley wasn't accustomed to arguing her points, and the idea that she secretly craved the intimacy she denounced—while true—did nothing for her sense of control.

"And isn't it also worth asking, 'Say, Julia. How do you feel about any of this?' Because I keep listening for something that says you aren't worth the trouble and I'm not hearing it. I think you are." She wriggled her shoulders and finally pushed herself up. "You're scared. I get that. New relationships are scary as hell even under normal circumstances because it takes time to build trust. If you hadn't told me any of this, I might have done something that caused you to run away again. Now that I know you're afraid, I'll be careful to follow your lead. We don't ever have to go out of your comfort zone."

Julia was being entirely too reasonable. "Did you not hear what I said? I might not ever be ready for sex, no matter what you do. This is all about me."

"I heard that. I also heard you say that you could have kissed me all night. That doesn't sound like someone who really wants to run away."

There was no denying she was trying to have it both ways. If she truly had wanted to be done with Julia, she would never have called her again, and certainly wouldn't have laid her problems out there like a challenge. "You have no idea what you're getting into."

"So tell me." Julia returned to her position, pulling both of Ashley's arms around her as she nestled into her chest. "Or if you aren't ready to do that, we can sit here some more and look out at all the pretty flowers. Either way I'm not going anywhere."

Julia hoped she sounded more confident than she felt. The one wrinkle she hadn't expected tonight was for Ashley to try to end their relationship before it even started. The desire to know everything about her was now tempered by the recognition that too many questions might send her back into her shell. But she didn't doubt for a moment that Ashley wanted something deeper than friendship. The warnings that they could never have a sexual relationship seemed like a defense mechanism, an automatic reaction to someone getting too close.

"What is it you need from me, Ashley?"

"For you not to have any expectations," she answered without hesitation.

"About anything…or just about sex?"

This time she didn't hurry, waiting several seconds before her response. "Just sex, I guess."

Julia tried to stay focused on Ashley but was bombarded instead by thoughts of Rachel. What awful irony it was to be facing once again the possibility of a relationship without intimacy. While she never doubted the sincerity of Rachel's religious beliefs, she also knew Rachel still wanted her sexually even as she deprived herself. It was maddening that something outside their relationship was able to dictate how they behaved, and she would never forget her feelings of frustration in being powerless to change it. This could very well be the same path, which meant that now Ashley wasn't the only one with a reason to be scared.

"I know you feel safe where you are, Ashley, and it's tempting to want to stay there. I promise not to pull you anywhere. I won't plead with you or try to make you feel guilty about what you can or can't do. What's most important is that you feel safe, especially with me. I can color inside the lines but you're going to have to draw them for me." Regardless of whether or not it was true, she sensed it was what Ashley needed to hear. Now she had to deliver.

"No expectations?"

"Nope…but can we still kiss all night?"

Ashley chuckled softly. "I don't think either one of us would be able to do that. Things just have a way of taking off whether you want them to or not."

"So you still feel it…the excitement?"

"Yeah, I feel it. I just respond to it differently. As soon as I start to feel like I'm losing control, I panic."

"So what if we make a deal, like a safe word?" The only way she could earn Ashley's trust was by demonstrating respect for her limits. "I don't ever want you to feel threatened by me. But I don't want to give up just because you think it might not work. I like you too much to just throw that chance away."

Ashley lifted her hand and kissed it. "I don't want to either, but I think you're underestimating me. I'm a total basket case, Julia."

"Basket case is a terrible safe word. What if we just went with safe?" She hated to end the evening, but something told her Ashley had been through enough for one night. "I should go, and I'd really like it a lot if you walked me to the door and kissed me goodnight. If for any reason you don't want to do that, you know the word."

Their simple parting proved more awkward in practicality, since each of them seemed to be waiting for the other to initiate.

"See, I've already scared you off," Ashley said.

Julia hissed as she drew in a breath. "Let's not make this so hard. Give me those lips."

They both laughed as they came together in a kiss. It wasn't passionate but it was warm, and certainly more than friendly.

Julia was careful not to linger too long, breaking it off well before she was ready. "I have appointments until seven tomorrow but I'm free after that…and all day Sunday."

"I've scheduled some work with Robyn's intern. I'll probably be at the station all weekend." Ashley must have read her skepticism because she followed quickly with a genuine smile. "Honest. I'm not just blowing you off."

"Monday then." She brushed Ashley's bangs aside and planted one last kiss on her forehead. "Because somebody needs a haircut."

Chapter Seventeen

Julia stifled a yawn as she ducked into the pantry to check their towel supply for the day. Despite her prediction about finally getting a good night's sleep, she had awakened early with excitement over what she felt was a new direction with Ashley. Just twenty-four hours ago she had been coming to grips with the fact that their kiss might have been only a flash in the pan. Now their relationship had new life, as precarious as it was. Ashley definitely was traumatized by her past, and any missteps in their plans to take things slowly could send her reeling. But Julia was glad at least for the new start they had gotten last night, and that Ashley trusted her enough to take a chance.

As she came out of the pantry, she saw Robyn walking down the stairs, her hands held daintily as if she were afraid to touch anything.

"I didn't know you were here. What's with the nails?"

"Elaine dropped me off. I have a wedding this afternoon, one of our associate professors. I hardly know him but that's department politics for you." She gently shook her arm until her purse fell from her shoulder to the couch. "Suzy said you weren't coming in until eleven."

"There's always something to do." The tightness in her stomach was unusual, and she knew right away the cause. It was only a matter of time before the others learned she was seeing Ashley, and besides the issue of breaking her promise to Robyn, there was the whole matter of keeping secrets from her friends. That wasn't their style, and while she was anxious to get it all out into the open, she only wanted to share it if it was good news. "So where's Elaine this morning?"

Robyn groaned and rolled her eyes as she perched on the arm of the couch. "One of her online friends talked her into going to a meeting at the Greyhound Rescue Society."

"Sounds like a dangerous hobby."

"You're telling me. Apparently she believes we don't have enough complication in our lives already. You'd better watch out. You know as well as I do if she throws herself into this, she'll be hitting on you and Bonnie and Ashley to take in dogs too."

"Just what I need—another creature to share my four-hundred square feet."

The back door opened and Teddie shuffled in, dressed snugly against the chilly February air in tight leather pants and a studded jacket. She nearly ran over Suzy, who was sweeping up after her customer.

"Hiya, Suze. How's my little buddy?"

Not missing a beat, the stylist replied, "He's all yours if you want him. Two is such a wonderful age."

"You'd better say no," Julia said. "Elaine's off getting you a dog as we speak."

"Dogs are cool. I hope he fits in my pocket so he can ride."

Robyn shook her head. "Nope, she's looking at greyhounds. Maybe you can get one that'll just run along beside you."

Teddie nudged Julia with her elbow as she walked by her to the couch. "You were out late last night. You have a date?"

Julia felt her face growing red. "God, it's like living in a fishbowl. Don't you have better things to do than watch me out the window?"

"That wasn't exactly an answer, now was it?" She slumped next to Robyn, smirking with way too much satisfaction. "Come to think of it, I seem to remember you had a late visitor last weekend when I got home…somebody in a red Avalon."

Robyn's face lit up as she put two and two together. "Julia?"

She held up a finger and shook it toward both of them. Keeping her voice low, she commanded, "Don't go there—neither of you. When I have something to tell you, I will. Until then I'd appreciate it if you didn't try to stir something up just so you'd have something to gossip about."

"Hmm, methinks thou protects too much," Teddie chided. "Or however that saying goes. Normal people don't really talk like that, do they?"

From the corner of her eye, Julia could see their conversation had gotten Suzy's attention. "Upstairs, both of you."

She led them into Jasmine's vacant waxing studio and closed the door. Teddie wore a mischievous grin while Robyn seemed clearly irked.

"Seriously, I need some space on this."

"You promised me you wouldn't do this, Julia."

She looked pointedly at Robyn. "I promised a safe place for Ashley and I'm trying to give her that, but it won't be possible if you two start wagging your tongues."

"So it's true. You're dating."

"It isn't that simple." Julia folded her arms defiantly and leaned her back against the door. "If you know anything at all about Ashley, it's that she values her privacy above everything else. This kind of jabbering—what you're both doing right now—is her worst nightmare. I'm asking you one more time not to go there."

"No way," Teddie said. "It's too much fun watching you squirm."

"She's right, Teddie. This would bother Ashley way too much."

Julia clasped her hands skyward. "Thank you!"

"You guys are no fun. Now unless I'm a hostage, I need to go." Teddie pulled an envelope from inside her jacket. "I just stopped by to drop this off. Bonnie said it came to the house by mistake."

The tax bill for Rhapsody. This day just kept getting better and better.

Robyn didn't budge after Teddie left. "You realize if this goes south, it's probably going to ruin my friendship with Ashley too, to say nothing of our work relationship."

"Come on, Robyn. Would you say something like that to Ashley?"

"Fair enough." It was a stretch to say she was satisfied, but she seemed to accept it. "But I hope you'll both come clean about what's going on. It's hard to be comfortable around people when you feel like they're keeping secrets."

"Just give us a little time, please. We have a lot at risk here too."

Robyn left and Julia checked the clock—five minutes until her first appointment. What had started as a great day had now lost its shine, as she was sure to spend the rest of the day worrying about whether she should let Ashley know they were now the subject of speculation among her friends, or start off this new stage of their relationship by keeping secrets.

Ashley squirmed to fit her "bucket" into the bucket seat of Aaron's economy car. He had persuaded her he should drive since his student parking sticker would allow them a space on campus, and he kept checking his mirrors as if to make certain they weren't being followed. She hoped for all their sakes that this clandestine meeting would bear fruit, since it would establish once and for all that Kevin Finley wasn't part of the conspiracy.

"What can you tell me about the person we're going to see?"

"Not much," he said. "Just that she's willing to be a confidential informant."

"Right, and I'm going to need a confidential legal opinion about whether or not we can use her, and I can't get that if I don't know who she is."

"I don't even know her real name, just her handle. She goes by Tobias and she's a computer genius."

"How did you find her?"

A sheepish look crossed his face and he stared straight ahead so as not to meet her eye. "I'd rather not say."

"That isn't going to fly, Aaron. We need her credentials even if she's confidential."

"What if our source isn't exactly...clean?"

Ashley had already surmised he was taking her to meet a hacker who, unless the woman was working for the government or doing private network security, routinely trespassed into the data domains of others. "It depends on how dirty she is. We're ethically and legally bound to color inside the lines."

She smiled to hear herself use Julia's expression from the night before. Recollections of their evening had peppered her thoughts all day, but having their issues resolved meant they were no longer a distraction. With luck, she might even wrap up her work in time for a spontaneous dinner.

"I asked around. There was a rumor she might have helped one of my fraternity brothers on his LSAT...sort of after the fact."

A cheating scandal. "I suppose we should be grateful your fraternity brother chose law school over the medical profession. That said, I don't think you need to retell that story to anyone, especially since it's just a rumor."

Aaron found a parking space in the sparse lot behind historic Plant Hall, the architectural and academic centerpiece of the university. "There's hardly anybody in this computer lab on Sunday."

They entered through a door at the end of the building and descended a narrow marble staircase to the lower level, where a row of small rooms were lit only by dim computer displays. About half of the rooms were occupied, all by solitary students who never even looked up as they walked by.

Aaron stopped in front of a door marked L6 and craned his neck to see through the tiny window. "Tobias?"

A young woman ushered them in and closed the door. She was not at all the Goth or grunge that Ashley had envisioned when she conjured up her image of a hacker. In fact, this girl looked like any other coed with her long blond hair and preppy style of dress. What stood out for Ashley, though, was the quality of her threads—definitely discount, exactly like the ones she had worn during her years at Mizzou—well out of the norm for this expensive private school. Tobias, or whatever her name was, clearly wasn't here because her parents were rich, and Ashley felt an instant kinship with her.

"I recognize you," the girl said with a hint of awe.

She was used to that from strangers. "That's good, I guess. You know I'm who I say I am. Aaron says you've been helping him. Can you tell me why?"

"Because I can."

"Have you been compensated or promised anything?"

"Just that I wouldn't be identified."

"She's doing it because she's nice," Aaron chimed in, his coy smile suggesting he was smitten.

Ashley nodded. "I think we can work with that. What have you got?"

The three of them pulled chairs around the screen as Tobias's fingers clicked rapidly over her keyboard. Familiar images of the Hillsborough County official seal appeared several times, only to be replaced by what looked to Ashley like gibberish, a series of letters, numbers, slashes and symbols.

"It's pretty simple, actually. If we were in Hacking College this is what they would teach you in Hacking 101." She pointed to a small line of code at the bottom of the page. "Right here is where everything is happening, and it only took me about three minutes to find it the first time. Unless you're a top secret defense contractor or guarding the Colonel's eleven herbs and spices, you build a back door into your system. That lets you access the network when the boss calls you on Saturday night to say there's something goofy going on with his email. Otherwise you have to drag your butt back to your desk to fix it."

"So you're saying someone is hacking into the county database and making unauthorized changes."

"Not exactly. Now we're in Hacking 102. The admin for this network set up a pretty neat system of checks to keep people from doing that. If I wanted to make a permanent change to the database right now, I'd have to convince the system that this terminal was one of only two in the whole system that allowed that particular input. That's pretty tricky, even for me."

Ashley admired how Tobias showed confidence without coming off as cocky.

"And even if I were able to do it, there would be a log with a big red flag saying that my entry had violated the parameters they set up for this system. You can't alter anything in this database without leaving a trail. Normal trails don't get flagged, but that one would and then they'd close the door."

"That means the changes had to be made from our guy's computer," Aaron said glumly.

"Right, but it doesn't mean they were made by him. Anyone with physical access could have done it," Tobias clarified.

"Except they need his password," Ashley reminded.

The young woman clicked through a few more windows of various sizes so fast that Ashley couldn't keep up. "You mean like 'walter34payton?'"

She peered over the girl's shoulder at the list of nonsense words and remembered Kevin's point about the administrator keeping a log of passwords. "In other words, anyone who can get through that back door like you just did has access to all the user passwords."

"Which means I can log in as anyone as long as I can sit at their desk."

It wasn't ironclad proof that Kevin wasn't somehow involved, but it bolstered his story that someone had in fact made the changes from his desk while he was out of his office. "And how can I prove any of this when I have a..."—hacker seemed so pejorative—"computer expert who doesn't want to go on the record?"

Tobias had obviously anticipated her question and drew a folder from a backpack on the floor. "I made you some screen shots of everything I just did. There are at least a couple of dozen people in Tampa alone who can get through that back door without leaving a footprint. The problem with most of them is that they want credit for it, so they like to tag their work, usually by imbedding their trademark somewhere in the code where it won't get flagged. This guy goes by the handle Obviosity. Probably a kid. It's a song by a local techno-band called Gigadrone."

"You've been very helpful," Ashley said, furiously scribbling the last of her notes.

Aaron stammered, "Yeah, it's…you've…maybe I can buy you a burger or something."

Ashley shook her head. "Except that would be like paying a source, and we don't do that."

"We could go Dutch," Tobias offered.

Their nascent mutual interest was charming. "If that's the case, then it's not really any of TV4's business, is it?"

Chapter Eighteen

There was a lot of variance among the small group of diners at the all-you-can-eat Chinese buffet. Ashley could never manage more than one trip, and was amazed to see Teddie and Patsy going back for the third time. Not that she blamed them. It was probably the only meal out all week for the budget-conscious pair, and they seemed determined to make the most of it.

She would have preferred a quiet dinner at home with Julia, but by the time she called from work their plans were set. At least they were together, if muted somewhat by the company of others.

Robyn gnawed on a chicken wing barbecued the same color as her copper hair. "You'll never guess who we booked for the Women in the Media conference next month—Katie Couric!"

Ashley had so far dodged Robyn's request to commit to a panel, especially when she'd said the planning committee had mentioned Valerie as a possible keynote speaker. "That's a coup. You'll draw a nice crowd and probably get some local coverage too."

"The only local coverage I care about is getting TV4's anchor to sit on my panel too. What do you say?"

"Why would you care about me when you have Katie Couric?"

"Because she'll make me a nervous wreck and you won't. Come on, Ashley…please?"

The conference was at the Don CeSar Hotel on St. Petersburg Beach, a fabulous resort built in the Roaring Twenties to pamper the rich and famous. She'd have no trouble getting the day off for something their PR department was sure to find interesting. "Can you promise me Valerie Reynolds won't be coming?"

"I'm positive she won't be there!" Robyn was already beaming with excitement. "This is so cool. My panel's going to be the best one—Katie Couric and Ashley Giraud."

Ashley rolled her eyes with genuine modesty. "Katie Couric and anybody would make it the best panel there."

"Hardly. You've won what, three regional Emmys and a share of a Peabody Award? Nobody else in town has credentials like that."

Elaine swiped a snow pea off Teddie's plate when she slid back into their long booth, setting off a mock sword fight with chopsticks. "That's a Friday. I think we should book a couple of rooms and hang out on the beach. We could even see about a fishing charter on Saturday if anybody's interested."

Ashley hedged on making a weekend of it, since Julia and Teddie would probably have to work, and she didn't want to be a third wheel with Robyn and Elaine. "I have to check first and make sure I can get the whole night off. There's this hotshot reporter nipping at my heels."

Robyn scoffed. "I wouldn't worry about Mallory if I were you. She's good—I should know because I trained her myself— but she doesn't have your para-social rapport."

"Here we go again," Elaine said. "Honey, if you promise not to talk about your research tonight, I'll promise not to get a greyhound…tonight."

Julia's thigh pressed against Ashley's as she made room for Patsy at the end of the bench. A week ago it might have gone unnoticed but no more. For the first time in years, Ashley was experiencing hyper-vigilance about someone, even finding herself excited tonight when she spotted the familiar black VW in the parking lot. From that moment on, she had soaked in every imaginable detail about Julia, the most riveting of which was her adroit mastery of chopsticks. While trying not to let her thoughts wander, she concluded that Julia was quite good with her hands.

"I'm already resigned to getting a greyhound, honey. I just don't want four of them." Turning back to Ashley, Robyn said, "I've noticed Mallory getting a lot more airtime. How's that going down with the old guard?"

Ashley's first reaction was that *she* was the old guard, and it wasn't sitting all that well with her. It wasn't that she felt genuinely threatened, since Mallory was way too green to sit in the anchor chair, but there was creeping insecurity among everyone in the television business when younger talent began commanding more attention. "You know how it is. It doesn't matter if you've been there twenty years or twenty days. Everybody scraps for the best assignments. I wish we'd brought Chris Lumke in on our 4Team story. We could have used his experience and connections."

"When are you going to tell us what you're investigating?"

The restaurant wasn't crowded but she lowered her voice anyway. "Not a word to anyone, okay? We're looking into a tax scandal at the county courthouse."

"When is it going to break?"

"Looks like the Monday after your conference. That's another reason I don't want to stay out of pocket too long. We'll be finalizing the details that week. But I might be able to stay over on Friday if everyone else does."

"I can probably do that too," Julia said. "I've been keeping my schedule open that week for a hair show in Ft. Lauderdale, but this sounds like a lot more fun."

"Will you get a double room?" Teddie pleaded.

"Fine, but I'm not sleeping with you again. I'm still black and blue from the last time."

It was settled then, as far as Ashley was concerned. Another gathering like the one in Boca Grande was just what they all needed to snap back from Jordan's death. Ironically, now that she had begun to enjoy feeling like part of a group, she found herself craving the tranquility of having Julia all to herself. The thought made her reach for Julia's hand beneath the table and when their fingers entwined it felt like the greatest secret ever.

"...I wasn't your typical tomboy because most of the time I was trying to cut everybody's hair."

"I bet you were so funny chasing all the other kids around with scissors."

"It wasn't just kids. It was their dolls, their pets...I did a show-and-tell in the fifth grade on how to trim your own bangs. Even the teacher liked it, but then I got in trouble the next day because everyone went home and tried it. The whole class looked like a bunch of freaks."

They were back on Ashley's couch with the lights off but tonight their positions were reversed, with Ashley's feet dangling off the end while her head rested in Julia's lap. The invitation had come in secret after dinner when Ashley passed her a remote transponder for the electronic gate. All Julia was missing was a house key, but if tonight was any indication, that would come soon enough.

"Were you a happy kid?" Ashley asked.

"Pretty much, I guess. We didn't have a lot since my asshole father supremely sucked at the whole concept of child support. I remember when mom finished her criminology degree and got promoted from being a guard at the juvenile detention center to a probation officer. It was a huge raise and she went right out and bought a brand-new car—our first one ever—and we drove it all the way to Daytona and back with the radio cranked up all the way."

"Sounds like a fairy tale."

The long ensuing silence was a reminder of Ashley's discomfort with the subject of family. In fact, it was surprising to Julia that she had brought it up in the first place, though she suspected it was Ashley's way of easing into the topic.

"We didn't have much either. I didn't know what it was like to have nice things until Cassandra bought them for me. Dresses, makeup…jewelry. She encouraged me to wear them whenever I was with her, but then I'd change back into my old clothes before I went home. I was like Cinderella walking in two different worlds."

"You were lucky to have someone who cared about you like that. It makes me sad to think about what home must have been like for you."

This time there was no response at all for a couple of minutes, which she took as a sign that Ashley was struggling with her memories. It was hard to imagine a child having virtually no relationship with her mother. Without a doubt Ashley had lingering problems over it, yet she had come remarkably far for someone who felt profoundly unloved as a child.

Ashley rolled onto her side to face away, but kept her head in Julia's lap. "I thought my life was perfect when Cassandra took me in. I didn't care that the other girls whispered about me…and the boys too, for that matter. They all knew I was a lesbian because I couldn't hide the fact that I was in love with her. I talked about her all the time, how beautiful she was, and I raced to her house every day after school because I couldn't wait to see her. As far as I was concerned, she was the most wonderful creature to ever walk this earth."

Julia sensed her melancholy and began a fingertip scalp massage, something she knew Ashley enjoyed. Holding her would have been even better, except that her body language wasn't particularly inviting, and besides, she didn't want to do anything to break the spell that had started her talking again.

"I would think about her all the time…like late at night when my hormones were acting out. I'm pretty sure I discovered that part of me long before any of the other girls my age, but they weren't crazy in love like I was. My obsession got so distracting at one point that my grades started slipping. My mother didn't even notice but Cassandra did. She told me to imagine her there in school with me, like she was always watching from the corner of the room. It worked. Straight A's from that day on. Even now—thirty years later—I sometimes feel her watching me."

There was a subtle change in Ashley's tone, and what had begun as a tale of inspiration took on an aura of foreboding.

"I was fifteen. She was forty-one, the same age I am now. I pretty much threw myself at her thinking it would be the most glorious and romantic moment of my life." Her voice trailed off. "It wasn't, of course. Once the reality set in, it became frightening and then repulsive, everything about it...the way she touched me...the things she had me do to her. Mostly it was what she said...nothing about love or feelings...just comments about our bodies that made it feel dirty. I changed my mind and tried to get her to stop but she kept saying it was what I wanted."

Julia's heart broke at the pain in Ashley's voice. The idea that the one woman she had trusted had used her that way was sickening, and she instinctively leaned forward to cradle Ashley in her arms. All that kept her from an outburst was relief Cassandra was now dead. "God, Ashley. No wonder this has all been so hard for you. It makes me furious just to hear about it."

"What it makes me is ashamed."

"It wasn't your fault. That woman took advantage of you. You should have told someone and had her arrested."

"Told them what? That I seduced her? I remember it vividly and that's pretty much what happened. It wasn't enough for me to be her favorite student, or to have her lavish me with attention and pretty gifts. I needed to have her choose me as her lover too."

"You were a child." Julia shook her head adamantly, astonished to realize Ashley didn't consider herself the victim. There was no other term for this than statutory rape but those words were loaded with equal horror. "No matter what your body was telling you then, you weren't ready to make a decision like that at fifteen. Nobody is. The decision was hers, and she was bound by the law to say no. What she did wasn't just immoral—it was illegal, and the whole reason those laws exist is so people like her won't be able to justify exploiting children."

"I know all of that in my head," Ashley said dismally. "But it isn't something you just write off to being immature, not when it comes back to slap you in the face every time you try to have a normal life. If I had been younger, I would have dealt with it like I did all the other wretched pieces of my life…just by moving on. But I was old enough to share responsibility. At least now you know why I said I had so much baggage."

"This isn't baggage between us, Ashley. You don't have to feel shame about something you did when you were fifteen years old."

Ashley had carried this around with her for so long she wasn't likely to be placated by assurances now, but Julia was determined to convince her it wasn't something she needed to be ashamed of. She understood now why Ashley trusted no one, why her secrets mattered more than anything, and especially why sexual situations sent her into a panic. No wonder her relationships had failed. After what she'd been through, it was a miracle she had even tried to have relationships at all.

"You can't tell anyone, Julia."

"I promise I won't." She could keep secrets for Ashley, but not from her. "But there's something I think you need to know, especially since we're all supposed to meet at Rhapsody on Wednesday night. The others are onto us. Teddie saw your car on the street a couple of weeks ago, and then she caught me dragging in late the other night. She happened to bring that up at the shop yesterday morning when I was talking to Robyn."

"What did you tell them?"

"As little as possible. I didn't want them speculating though, and I asked them just to leave it alone. Robyn wasn't too happy with me because when we set up the arrangement for your hair, she made it a point to tell me how important it was for you to feel safe from people getting into your personal space. I promised her I'd see to it, and I think she sort of feels like she left the fox guarding the henhouse."

Ashley sighed but didn't seem perturbed by the news. "I guess that's what happens when people entertain your paranoia. They treat you like you're fragile. Do you want me to say something to her?"

"Nah, let's see how long they can keep quiet. I appreciate that Robyn's looking out for you, but she ought to know after twelve years that she can trust me."

The trust that mattered most was Ashley's, and Julia felt privileged to know she had it. Otherwise Ashley would never have revealed these secrets from her early life, not only what had happened to her as a teenager but also her admissions about the role she had played. The fact that she had never told anyone before gave Julia hope it would be a turning point, a victory over the problems from her past. Whatever was happening between them was important enough to make her willing to take a chance.

She was glad to have her conversation with the others at Rhapsody out in the open too. With Ashley putting so much on the line tonight, it seemed frivolous to be hiding details of little consequence. If she was relieved over confessing such a triviality, she could only imagine what Ashley felt after shedding such a monumental burden. By her body language, it had left her exhausted. Her eyes were closed, her breathing was slow and steady, and her body was limp. Only the occasional movement of a foot or hand confirmed she was still awake.

"I bet your hands are getting tired," she finally murmured, suddenly sitting up and running her fingers through her hair to straighten it. Then she slid under Julia's arm and pressed a light kiss to her lips. "I'm taking it as a good sign that you haven't run out of here yet."

"You haven't told me anything that makes me want to run." If anything, she felt more determined to stay—perhaps even for the long haul if Ashley wanted her.

"The story isn't quite over." She laid her head on Julia's shoulder and drew a deep breath.

"Cassandra put me up for Junior Miss a few weeks after we... you know. That was a whole year ahead of schedule because I was her new pet, though she told everyone it was because she didn't have any promising sixteen-year-olds in her class. I won first runner-up in the statewide pageant, or as she liked to say, I lost. I got nervous and dropped two whole bars out of Beethoven's 'Für Elise' in the talent competition. She didn't believe in second chances for the big pageants—she said it made you look desperate—so that was the only shot I got at Junior Miss. There were a handful of minor pageants up in Illinois and over in Kansas, and I managed to keep busy for the next couple of years. I practiced that Gershwin piece so many times I could play it in my sleep. Over that period she had sex with me four more times. I remember every single one like it was yesterday."

The thought of Cassandra touching Ashley filled Julia with rage, but even more pronounced was her sorrow at what Ashley had endured. Hearing her speak with such shame was heartbreaking.

"I couldn't bring myself to tell her no. I was afraid she wouldn't put me up for any more pageants when I was so close to reaching my goal. I told myself it didn't matter after the first time, that you couldn't save something after you'd already given it away. I had to make it to the Miss Missouri pageant. That was the big ticket because the winner went on to Miss America, and all I needed to do was place at the state level to get enough prize money for college. God, I can't even stand to think what I would have done if I hadn't won."

Julia hugged her and pressed her lips to Ashley's temple. "But you did."

"Cassandra always said the optimal age for Miss America was nineteen, because that's how old she was when she went. I knew I wouldn't be able to stand it for two more years so I betrayed her. She put up Lori Spearman that year, but I paid my own entry fee—all of my savings plus what I got from selling some of my trophies. I'll never forget the look on Cassandra's face when she saw me backstage that night at the Miss Adams County pageant. She was absolutely shaking with rage and asked me how I could betray her after all she'd done." She chuckled cynically. "All she'd done indeed."

"And you won."

"Yes, and then I won the Miss Missouri pageant, the youngest ever. I came in fourth at Miss America, and that got me all the scholarship money I needed. I never lived another day in Maple

Ridge. I only heard from Cassandra once after that, when she tracked me down at the network to rub my nose in what Valerie had done."

With every detail Ashley's story had grown more remarkable. "Have you ever stopped to think how much strength it took to pull yourself out of all that? You keep calling it blame but I call it credit. You put your whole life on the line that night. Most people would never have the guts to do something like that."

"It taught me not to trust other people with decisions that matter. Only one person looks out for Ashley Giraud, and that's me."

"That's not true anymore." Julia followed her words with a warm kiss, all the while fighting a protective urge that made her want to squeeze Ashley and never let go. The tenor of their conversation, amazingly, had quieted her sexual desires, yet intensified everything else she was feeling. Ashley had suffered enough for one lifetime, and Julia was determined she wouldn't be hurt again.

The real surprise of the moment was that Ashley didn't seem to share her sense of self-control and had deepened their kiss to the point of showing arousal, allowing her hand to wander along Julia's hip.

"Do you have any idea how much you're torturing me right now?" she asked as she placed Ashley's hand back in her lap.

"This is precisely why we can't kiss all night."

"Though it makes me want to try."

Ashley leaned away to signal an end to their brewing intimacy. "It crossed my mind to ask you to stay tonight, but I would probably attach so many restrictions that we both would be too nervous to sleep."

"Restrictions like what?"

"Oh, I don't know…like you have to wear a strait-jacket and sleep on top of the covers with a row of pillows between us. Any accidental touching would result in an electric shock."

Julia chuckled. "You're really that scared of me?"

"I'm scared of myself."

The idea of sleeping together under any circumstances

fueled Julia's excitement, but it was too soon to allow their desire to escalate. Ashley was emotionally vulnerable tonight and if she couldn't protect herself, Julia would have to do it for her. "I'm okay with all your rules, Ashley. Just think about what you need me to do—or not do—and keep talking to me like we did tonight. In the meantime"—she delivered one last kiss—"I'm going to scram before we start kissing again and I forget all about what I just said."

Chapter Nineteen

"Robyn, make sure that front door is locked," Julia said. "I'd be screwed if the health inspector walked in right now."

Elaine was sitting on the couch, softly scratching the ears of her timid two-year-old fawn greyhound, Henry. "Didn't I tell you he was a sweetheart?"

Julia had never thought of herself as a dog person but had to admit this one was special. It was beyond cruel that someone would breed such a peaceful animal for sport, and then callously abandon him when he didn't respond to training. "He looks like a mama's boy to me."

"I'm trying to hold the line on just one dog," said Robyn, who was laying out the fixings for meatless tacos. "Elaine wants half a dozen."

"How could I not? Look at him. They kept him in a crate with another dog that attacked him all the time."

Teddie, who was in the stylist chair awaiting the finishing touches on her latest outrageous haircut, had already offered her services as a dog sitter. "I'd like to get my hands on the asshole that bred him. Wonder how he'd like living in a cage and being terrorized his whole life?"

"You need to be still," Julia cautioned as she taped the pattern into place on one side of Teddie's head. "Otherwise you'll end up with New Jersey instead of New York."

"What's with the Yankees logo anyway, slick? I never knew you were a baseball fan."

"They're in town for spring training. I'll pick up an extra hundred bucks in tips next week just because people think I care."

"Yeah, until they ask you a question and find out you don't know jack about baseball."

"It's all about perception. You wouldn't believe how many people come in there with Yankees crap on their car. If this works I'm going to try it during football season too."

"Where did you even learn to cut designs like that, Julia?" Robyn asked.

"One of my recertification classes a couple of years ago." Which reminded her…she had only four months to complete her license renewal requirements of sixteen credit hours. Since she was trading her Ft. Lauderdale workshop for a couple of nights at the Don CeSar, she'd have to scour the offerings on the state's website. "I need to find something fun like that again. I hate sitting in the same old lectures about blunt cuts."

Teddie snickered. "Let's hear you say that five times real fast."

The back door opened for Ashley, who looked even more dazzling than usual in a deep red dress. She went straight to Julia for a luscious kiss on the lips, much to Julia's delight and everyone else's obvious astonishment. "Did all of you see that, or do I need to do it again?"

Julia laughed at their surprise and couldn't resist goading them. "I missed it. Can I see it again?"

Ashley obliged and proceeded with her greeting ritual, squeezing Teddie's shoulder before giving a hug to Robyn. She turned to address Elaine and noticed Henry for the first time. "Oh, my goodness. Who is this gorgeous baby doll?"

Elaine proudly introduced the new addition and they all watched with interest as Ashley got acquainted, talking in a sweet, melodic voice that finally drew a soft thump from Henry's tail. Clearly impressed, Elaine said, "I didn't know you were a dog person, Ashley."

"We did a story a couple of years ago on puppy mills and I'm sorry to say I got a chance to see some of these creatures up close in awful circumstances. They were so pitiful, it just broke my heart. At least we were able to shut two of them down."

"That's what good reporting can do," Robyn said.

"Any more problems with your neighbor's dog?" Teddie asked.

Ashley turned and looked at her quizzically. "Now that you mention it, no."

Remembering Teddie's secret scheme, Julia began to chuckle. "You should tell her."

"Tell me what?"

"Remember that day at your house when I stepped in the dog shit?"

"When I was sick?"

"Yeah, you said you had already asked your jackass neighbor to clean up after his dog. I gave him a little extra incentive. I scooped up a pile of it and smeared it on the underside of the door handle on his car. Most people would've taken that hint, but not Mr. Jackass. I stopped by a couple of days later and he'd done it again, so this time I put it right in the driver's seat. And I left him a note that said shit happened to people who didn't clean up after their dogs."

"You're leaving out the best part," Julia prodded with a grin.

"He actually brought his car into Sterling Wheels where I work the next day to have it cleaned. I nearly laughed my ass off. He's a cheap bastard too—gave me two bucks on a thirty-dollar detail with dog shit."

"My hero!" Ashley took Teddie's face in both hands and planted a kiss on her forehead.

"I keep telling you guys, all you have to do is say the word and I'll kick some ass."

"I believe you now. I'm going to start a list of all the people who've wronged me in this life."

Julia shook her clippers playfully at Ashley. "Don't encourage her. If she ends up getting arrested, my mom will come after you."

Henry whimpered at the threatening gesture, sending Ashley back to his side to cajole him.

"Wave the clippers again, Julia," Teddie said. "Let's see if Henry jumps over here and takes a bite out of your leg."

"Let's see if I clip a hunk out of your ear."

Ashley fixed a taco from the spread and walked around the shop as she ate. "Julia, did you see our big story tonight on the city council? They're rescinding the tax hike. In fact, I have to get back to the station as soon as I eat this because we're doing a recap for eleven o'clock. We'll probably lead with the fact that you and your militant friends prompted the reversal by storming city hall, so you can pat yourself on the back for being a citizen soldier."

True to form, Robyn launched into a commentary on civic activism and the role of the press, though Julia barely heard a word as she found herself locked in a gaze with Ashley, who was sending intriguing signals with her eyes as she ate.

Elaine whispered loudly, "No one is listening, sweetheart. Save it for your book."

As Ashley switched her focus to Robyn, Julia realized an unfortunate fact—she didn't want to share Ashley, not even with her friends. She wanted her undivided attention, and as many opportunities to kiss as possible. That would pass eventually, but probably not anytime soon.

She concentrated on finishing Teddie's NY design and then brushed her down. "Who's next? Ashley?"

"Oh, right. I'm such a sports fan. And on that note, I've got to go. Want to walk me out?"

Julia waited self-consciously at the door while Ashley said her goodbyes. She knew her friends well enough to predict their tongues would start wagging about their kiss the moment they stepped out.

By the time they reached her car, the flirtatious bravado Ashley had exhibited with her eyes had wavered. "You told me once you were a night owl…and I was thinking midnight's been working pretty well for us."

The surprise invitation told her Ashley was as eager as she was to spend time together. Being careful didn't have to mean moving at a snail's pace, especially when the biggest issue was trust. Obviously Ashley trusted her.

Also, Ashley wasn't afraid to ask for what she wanted. That was critical for setting her comfort zone.

"I'll be there when you get home…now that I have my trusty gate doohickey."

"Right, the gate doohickey." She fished a TV4 key ring from her purse. "You should take this too in case I'm running late."

Another nice surprise. "You want me to bring anything?"

"Just yourself. We don't have to talk about anything heavy tonight. I just want to be with you. I've spent the last two nights sitting around wondering what you were doing and trying to decide if that's healthy or not."

"I hope it's healthy because I've been doing it too," Julia said. New relationships were exciting enough but never more than when the other person confessed they had it as bad as you did.

"I was going to suggest you bring your toothbrush but I chickened out."

That, she hadn't expected at all. It had been only three days since they decided such a step was too much too soon. But Ashley had just gone from semiconfident to nervous wreck in a matter of a few words, suddenly twirling her keys and staring down at her hands. Julia rescued her with a quick hug and a kiss on the cheek. "I think you should pick up an extra one sometime and keep it on hand for emergencies."

As Ashley's taillights disappeared around the corner of the building, Julia focused on her recertification, civic responsibility and the horrors of puppy mills—whatever it took to wipe the smile off her face before she walked back into the salon.

"Distracted much, Ashley?" she muttered to herself as she pulled out of TV4's parking lot for the second time. Of all nights to walk off without her phone, she had picked the one when Julia was waiting at her house. It was tempting just to leave it there but Murphy's Law dictated that the biggest story of her life would break overnight and she'd miss it if she didn't have her phone.

She had come out of the weekend with a brand-new outlook about the potential to build something special with Julia, and had ruminated nonstop to come up with a plan for how to go forward without screwing this up. In the back of her mind were the nagging doubts that she wouldn't be able to follow it all the way through, but Julia made her feel like sex might be possible again. There was certainly no shortage of desire, and if she hadn't been so afraid of Cassandra invading her thoughts again, she would have let her body have its way by now.

Julia was already relaxing in the den, looking freshly showered in cargo pants and a blue silk shirt with three-quarter-length sleeves.

"Have you been here long?"

"I came over a little early so I could watch the news—hope that was okay. I'm having a para-social relationship with that news anchor on TV4."

"It's fine," she said, bending over the love seat for a kiss. It was more than fine. She was delighted by this new burst of familiarity, not only at seeing Julia making herself at home in her den, but also at how comfortable she was at having someone else in her space. "It was nice coming home and seeing your car in my driveway, but I have to admit it's kind of weird. I've never come home to anyone before, not even once."

"So we treat it like any other day. What do you usually do when you come home at night?"

"You mean like my twelve-step skin rituals and the thirty minutes I spend in my closet trying to figure out what I'm going to wear tomorrow?"

"From where I'm sitting, every minute you spend is worth it. You look amazing all the time." Julia followed her through the house to the smaller of her guest bedrooms, which she had converted into a walk-in closet. "Wow, the last time I saw this many clothes in one place I was in a department store."

Ashley normally came to this room to undress and hang up her clothes, but realized she wasn't comfortable enough to do that with Julia watching. "They're pretty generous with my clothing allowance. I try not to wear the same outfit more than once a month, and I have an elaborate system for keeping track."

"I think you should wear red every day."

"Red is once every two weeks, max. Same with pink and yellow. They aren't very good news colors unless you're sure the news is going to be good. I have to keep a gray suit in wardrobe in case I need to tone it down."

"Fascinating." Julia strolled through the closet, stopping to run her fingers over the suede lapel of a brown suit.

"Those are my fat clothes on that side. I haven't worn any of them since before I went to Cancun." She rapped her knuckles on the doorjamb. "Knock on wood."

Julia's eyes lit up as they came to rest on her sequined, aquamarine evening gown. "When do I get to see you in this?"

"Is Friday soon enough? There's a fundraiser for the stage guild at the Tampa Theatre. Jarvis's wife, Connie, is the program chair and she asked me to emcee."

"Where can I get a ticket?"

"Sold out. But Rod's covering the news desk on Friday night so maybe you'll be here when I get home."

She still hadn't taken her eyes from the dress. "What time are you going?"

"They're sending a car at a quarter to seven."

"Then I'll be here at five thirty to do your hair."

Ashley was surprised to find she liked her assertiveness. Valerie's brashness had been difficult at times, but then she had been brash about everything. Julia had every right to be confident about her hair skills and her cockiness didn't bleed over into other parts of her personality.

She excused herself to change into loose-fitting knit pants and a top and came out to find Julia back in the den flipping channels with the remote. Foregoing her usual reading chair, she took the open space on the love seat and snuggled next to Julia's shoulder. "This might be the oddest date I've ever had, meeting someone in my den after midnight."

"It's okay, though?"

"It's perfect. Do you mind that I'm not entertaining you?"

"Who says you're not?" She muted the TV. "Tell me something that made you laugh today."

"That's easy—Teddie's story about my jackass neighbor. You?"

"Elaine bought her dog a free-range chicken at Whole Foods and wouldn't let Robyn have any of it."

"Those two are such a pair. I just love them together. I've always found it interesting that they keep to one small circle of friends since they're both so outgoing. You and Teddie too. I'm surprised you don't all have parties to go to and friends hanging out all the time."

"Teddie's like that, but she usually drops everything if the rest of us are doing something together. Elaine's deal is that she doesn't suffer fools. The older she gets, the less patience she has. And Robyn's like you...she has a high-profile job where she has to be careful about who she hangs out with."

She tickled Julia's forearm and smiled to see goose bumps. "And what's your story?"

"That kind of socializing lasts all day long for me. My real friends aren't just the people I want to do things with—they're the people I want to do things for, and I know I can count on them to feel the same way about me."

It was one of the best distinctions Ashley had heard, and she had no trouble identifying who was inside her circle. "Outside of you guys, I think Jarvis is the only one who fits that description for me. Without him I think I would have washed out after the Valerie episode."

"I'd like to meet him one of these days."

"He's been the perfect mentor...for me, at least. The sexual power plays are just as rampant in TV news as they are in Hollywood, but I can always count on him to be in my corner.

Carl Terzian—he's our GM—is a chauvinist pig who doesn't care one whit about news values as long as he can put a pretty set of boobs in front of the camera. Jarvis cares about the news, and he also cares about me. If it ever comes down to scratching and clawing for my job, I know he'll have my back."

"I hate to break it to you, Ashley, but you aren't exactly unattractive."

"And I hate to break it to you, but that para-social crush you have going on has made you just a little bit biased." She leaned into a kiss that quickly generated more heat than she expected, and she soon found herself practically in Julia's lap. Her first effort to pull away only bared her neck to Julia's lips, and she closed her eyes to drink in the searing sensations. "Oh, this isn't going to work," she groaned.

"And here I thought it was working perfectly."

"I can't go this fast," she said as she scrambled to her feet.

"Safe. That's the safe word, remember?" Julia said without even a hint of exasperation or reproach. "Just tell me where the line is, and I won't go past it."

"You aren't the problem, Julia. Lines won't make any difference if I'm the one crossing them." How could she have thought they could spend a whole night together and just lie there without touching?

Julia grasped her hand and pulled her back down to the love seat. "There are two of us here. I know you aren't ready for sex, but I'm perfectly happy just making out on the couch. If that feels like too much we can sit here and talk, or we can watch something on TV. There's no reason for you to get flustered about anything."

To Ashley, all of it was intimate and therefore plenty of reason to get flustered. They could ride their passions all the way to the bedroom but no amount of physical pleasure tonight would be worth it if it made her push Julia away tomorrow. "I just don't want to screw up."

"Then I should go."

Ashley grimaced. "This is insane. I feel like a little kid trying to wade into the ocean but then running away when the wave rolls in."

"Big deal. That's how little kids build up their courage. When you start to feel anxious about whatever we're doing, just step back. It's okay."

Julia's maddening reasonableness ended Ashley's brave foray into possibly, perhaps, maybe at least sleeping in the same bed, and she dismally waved goodbye from her doorway. There might never come a point when she didn't panic about sex, and trying to build up resistance while Julia nibbled on her neck seemed to defeat the whole purpose. What was the point of foreplay if not to become aroused?

Chapter Twenty

Julia wrapped a towel around her torso and slapped her wet feet across the freezing tile floor to peer through the blinds. The only person who would come knocking on her door at nine o'clock on a Monday morning would be Teddie, who was standing underneath the small awning of her porch with her hands in her pockets. "Come on in," she said as she pulled the front door ajar. "How's that haircut working out?"

"Eighty extra bucks in five days. Do I know my customers or what?" Teddie reached out and poked the sunburn on the back of her neck.

"Ouch!"

"Where'd you get that?"

"Ashley put me to work in her garden yesterday. I pulled ragweed all day, and then we planted two gardenias and I helped her graft a rose bush. That was kind of interesting…but she says it never works."

"Didn't you tell her that everything you touch dies? Bonnie calls it your black thumb." Teddie helped herself to a soda before sinking onto the couch.

"Very funny. Maybe that's why Ashley kept pointing me back toward the weeds." Julia retreated to her bedroom to get dressed but didn't bother closing the door since Teddie was facing the other direction.

"How come you're cleaning up? You doing Ashley today?"

The only way to stifle Teddie's childish references was to ignore them. "Mom asked me to come down to juvenile hall and do a few haircuts."

"Good ol' juvie hall. If you see that wrinkled old ball-buster with the purple eye shadow, be sure to give her my finest regards."

"How'd your weekend with Patsy go?"

"It didn't. She finally got that job at the print shop—nights and weekends. Perfect, huh? It's like they looked at my work schedule and made hers just the opposite."

"When are you going to see each other?"

"Pfft. I'm not sure it even matters. It's all weird now."

It was hard to sympathize with her loss of a playmate since Patsy had been in dire need of a job. Julia zipped her jeans and walked back out to the living room, rolling up the sleeves on her yellow Oxford shirt. "What's weird?"

Teddie scowled and shook her head. "I don't want to talk about it."

"Okay, fine." She didn't have much time to talk anyway.

"I don't think this deal with Patsy is going to work out."

"How come? I thought you guys were getting along pretty well."

"We were, but…" She twisted the tab on her soda can, concentrating as if it were brain surgery. "So after a month of sitting around on our hands, we finally spent the night together last Friday and it was the biggest bust of my entire sexual life."

She was used to Teddie's overblown boasting of her conquests and charms, but it wasn't like her to talk about her actual sex life, especially the shortcomings. The unusually serious tone suggested this was more than just a gripe session. "What happened?"

"Nothing. It was about as exciting as one of those insect documentaries on the Nature Channel."

"I wouldn't have guessed that. You guys were practically hanging on each other that day at the bowling alley."

"It was just flat. We were trying to be so mature about everything after Jordan died and not rush into anything. Then we finally did and it turns out I have more chemistry with Elaine."

Julia scrunched her nose as she tried to imagine those two together. "I could have done without that image, thank you. What do you think happened?"

"I guess we just waited too long. Two weeks ago we were making out and getting all hot and bothered, but we kept pushing it down trying to behave ourselves. Then all of a sudden we decided to go for it and it's like we couldn't get the burner lit. Like I said…weird."

Not as weird as thinking they could have been talking about her relationship with Ashley. It had never occurred to her that fighting their desires might ultimately snuff them out. "Surely you must have realized it was cooling off."

"Not until we were both naked. I kept expecting to heat up and I never did. Might as well have been reading a newspaper."

That couldn't possibly happen with her and Ashley. They were both ready to combust. "What are you two going to do now?"

"I don't know. If I had it to do over again, I never would have gone there. We could have been best friends," she said miserably.

"I'm your best friend," Julia said, giving her a gentle nudge.

"So I can hang out with you and Ashley instead?"

"No."

Ashley's eyes adjusted quickly to the ambient light in Dr. Friedman's office. She had never before thought to appreciate the contrast between this and the white-hot studio lights that had come to symbolize her life on display. That she revealed more of herself in the dark was certainly an ironic twist.

"What is it that scares you most, Ashley?"

"Losing her…or given the way I am, running away from her."

"Because you're afraid of having sex?"

"It's more complicated than that." Up until now, all of her sessions had focused on hypothetical circumstances and deep-seated emotional issues that caused her to withdraw from the people around her and suffer depression. Now it was about Julia, and Ashley's choices would have real consequences. "Things are going pretty well between us. I feel comfortable talking about my past without fear that she'll judge me, and I like being with her. She's a wonderful person…and this feels special. What I worry about is that taking our relationship to the next level could ruin what we have."

The doctor, primly dressed in a tweed suit and scarf, sat perfectly poised in her stiff leather armchair, occasionally scribbling a note on a pad she kept on the table beside her. "We meet lots of people whom we like but don't want to know sexually. Could it be that Julia is just one of them?"

"No, Julia definitely isn't one of them. I want to be with her, but I get freaked out every time I start thinking about it that way. That's the whole reason I'm here." Ashley sighed with frustration at the onerous process. They could cover twice as much in half the time if she would just talk. "I'm in love with her, but I'm sure she isn't looking for a platonic best friend."

"Are you?"

Ashley shook her head.

"Listen to yourself. I hope you recognize what tremendous progress you've made just in the past few weeks. You're here tonight looking for a way forward with someone you love and you never thought that possible."

It was hard not to be cynical. "It won't matter much if I crash and burn again, now will it?" In fact, it would probably be the final nail in the coffin on her love life.

"Do you feel pressured to have sex?"

"By her, no." She related Julia's idea about having a safe word. "The pressure I feel is from inside myself. It's natural for people to want to express their feelings sexually. So no matter how patient she is now, Julia has every right to expect we'll have sex eventually if we have a romantic relationship. The problem is I start to panic every time I think about it."

"Tell me how that panic feels."

"Like the worst sense of dread I can imagine. Sexual thoughts have always dredged up those times with Cassandra, how she'd leer at my body before she touched me. And all the nasty things she'd whisper…about my breasts or my skin…telling me to relax so I could feel her inside me." She shuddered with disgust at the thought of Cassandra's hands all over her. She could never share those ugly memories with Julia.

"Are you afraid Julia will do that…leer at you or whisper nasty words?"

"Not really. She knows how anxious I am about all this so she'd never do anything without making sure it was okay."

"It's good that you've begun to communicate your feelings with Julia. Having these issues out in the open enables both of you to work together on this as partners, and it sounds as if she's being patient and understanding. She's allowing you time to trust her."

"I trusted Cassandra too."

The doctor shook her head. "Cassandra obviously wasn't worthy of your trust. What you had with her was never a partnership because she had all the power. Believe me, every teenage girl who idolizes someone the way you idolized her thinks what she feels is love. You know now that it wasn't."

Ashley nodded. That had been her consistent message throughout their years of therapy.

"What about the intimacy exercises? Have you continued those?"

"Yes…and yes to your next question as well," Ashley answered swiftly, heading off an explicit inquiry about whether or not she had been able to have an orgasm while masturbating. She touched herself only rarely, focusing solely on physical gratification, never as part of a fantasy. The moment she imagined it as a real episode, the intensity of her sensations evaporated.

"Do you fantasize about Julia?"

"Not sexually. I try to imagine how we would go together… sharing a home, cooking, gardening, being out with our friends." Though not sexual, her dreams often had a sensual component. "I think about sleeping in her arms or just lying in bed together on a rainy Sunday morning. It feels foreign to think about someone like that but it's exciting."

Dr. Friedman went quiet for almost a minute as she wrote in her notebook. It usually signaled the end of what Ashley had come to recognize as the information-gathering phase of their session, and marked the start of her action plan. "Whether you call that a fantasy or not, it seems clear to me that you're thinking about Julia in an intimate way. Would you agree?"

Ashley nodded.

"And you understand that if you make love with her, she'll probably touch you the way Cassandra did, and maybe use some of the same words, both of which may trigger your memories. So the challenge is to disentangle those memories of Cassandra from your feelings about intimacy with Julia. One way to do that is to recognize that real intimacy is only shared by consent."

"I don't see what difference that will make. I consented to Cassandra. And every single time I've consented to intimacy with someone else, she's rushed into my head to make sure it's an awful experience."

"Ashley, you did not consent to being subjugated. Put yourself in Cassandra's shoes now. If a child of fifteen flattered you sexually, how would you handle it?"

The question was too absurd to warrant a reply.

"Cassandra was the aberration, not you. And what transpired between you was not intimacy, but exploitation. You have a chance to redefine with Julia what you want all of these concepts to mean—intimacy, sexuality and even love—but first you have to acknowledge that your old definitions are wrong."

I'm powerless to deny you…my pretty Lolita.

She closed her eyes and drew a deep breath to chase the voice away.

Lolita.

It had been three years later in a literature class at Mizzou when Ashley discovered with humiliation that Cassandra had compared her to a pubescent temptress. It still roiled her with anger that Cassandra could never have seen through her own narcissism to recognize herself as the lecherous Humbert.

"What scares me even more than sex is that my feelings for Julia could change if we make love and it causes me to panic. That's what happened before. I loved Cassandra and I had feelings for Valerie too, but after it became sexual I couldn't bear to be with either of them. I'd almost rather forget all about having sex with Julia than risk losing what I feel for her."

"Almost, you say, but you really don't want to forget about it." Dr. Friedman patted her knee warmly. "Those are your coping mechanisms, Ashley. When we're faced with threats, we're programmed for fight or flight. You weren't able to do either with Cassandra so you adapted by disassociating yourself from the situation. By negating your feelings, you're able to distance yourself from the act. Same with Valerie."

"But how can I keep from doing that? I don't want to distance myself from Julia."

"It's a learned response, like your reaction to the sexual act itself. If you choose to fight one, you may have to fight the other as well."

Ashley resisted the urge to shake her head, knowing she'd be admonished for not believing in herself. The problem was that Dr. Friedman laid these challenges out as though fighting them was as simple as clicking her heels.

"How is your depression, Ashley? Any more trouble sleeping? Difficulty with overeating?"

"No, that's all over with. Getting out with friends broke that cycle just like you said it would. Emotions following behaviors… all that."

A strange smile crossed the doctor's face as she leaned forward and clapped her hands softly. "I honestly think you've begun the process of closing the book on Cassandra. She plagues you through these sexual memories because it's the last thread she has, but you're the one in control of those thoughts now.

You've always been a master of self-discipline. What if you just decided to reach for what you wanted and not think about her anymore?"

Ashley had faithfully followed the doctor's advice throughout her treatment, and nearly always with positive results. Strengthening her relationship with Dixon had helped her redefine the concept of family, and giving her home life more structure had fostered a sense of control. The greater challenges all had to do with Cassandra, and while it was undeniably true the woman's death had signaled the beginning of the end of her clout, there were pieces that wanted to live inside her forever. Gone were the daily torments and the horrid threat that she would re-emerge with her taunts, but Cassandra's greatest power had always been as a wedge between Ashley and fulfillment with someone else.

"Ashley, it's time to overwrite those old definitions. Anticipate the difficulty but commit yourself to the larger goal. If you're persistent, you can replace your memories of having sex with Cassandra with ones you want to hold and keep."

There was indeed something satisfying about admiring one's own handiwork, Julia thought. The fan palms of Ashley's garden swayed unfettered where only a day earlier they had been bound by the demon ragweed.

She smiled at hearing the garage door go up. Ashley's late invitation to meet her at the house had come as a mild surprise since they had spent most of the day together on Sunday. At the risk of seeming too available, Julia hadn't hesitated for a second. Sleep was highly overrated when you had this many endorphins.

The lights came on suddenly in the kitchen. "Julia?"

"I'm sitting here in the dark," she said, leaning over the back of the couch to watch Ashley enter, all business in a dark blue suit and beaded necklace. "Did you have a good day?"

"Productive," she said, dropping a small plastic shopping bag from the neighborhood pharmacy in Julia's lap.

"What's this?"

"What you asked for."

Julia's stomach fluttered as she removed a toothbrush.

"It's time to find out if I can make it through a whole night with someone in my bed." Ashley pounded her forehead with the heel of her hand and sighed. "I'm sorry. I bet you would have preferred something a little more quixotic."

"As long as it's coming from you, I'll take it however I get it." No, it wasn't the romantic invitation she had dreamed about, but Ashley's worried tone told her this was another big step. "Just tell me what you want me to do."

"I want us to sleep together without me having a panic attack. Just share my bed."

"Okay, but the safe word still applies. You can change your mind anytime, and I'll get up and go home."

Ashley led her into the bedroom and showed her two drawers that held an array of pajamas, gowns and T-shirts. Then she disappeared inside the master bath for nearly thirty minutes, leaving Julia to wonder if indeed she was already panicking. Just as she was ready to knock on the door, Ashley emerged wearing long, light blue silk pajamas and a matching robe.

"You could have gotten into bed."

"I wasn't sure which side." That wasn't quite true since the alarm clock was on the side nearest the bathroom. She had donned a pair of Ashley's knee-length pajama bottoms with a drawstring waist and an oversized United Way T-shirt, and then waited at the foot of the bed so she could save them both from an embarrassing scene in case Ashley changed her mind. Noting her ongoing nervousness, she casually pulled back the spread and gestured toward the TV. "Want to find a movie?"

"I love you."

It was said so softly that Julia was afraid she had misheard.

"I wanted to sleep with you without all the warnings and caveats but I can't. I haven't done this in a long time, and I don't know how I'll handle it."

Julia didn't care how many caveats and warnings there were. "You love me?"

Ashley was frowning as though she'd just made a troubled confession. "I don't want to lose you."

"I'm not going anywhere." She closed the distance between them and took Ashley in her arms, wishing they could fall into bed tonight and make love without any constraints, but it was plain to see Ashley was more afraid right now than ever. "I just want to be as close as you'll let me."

Ashley returned her embrace and released a tense breath. "I don't know where the lines are anymore. I'm not even brave enough to draw them, but I promise you I'm going to try."

"I believe you." Julia walked on her knees to her side of the bed and fell against the pillow, shrugging off the sexual desires that had been soaring since their kiss. It could take weeks to break down these walls, and tonight she needed to show her willingness to let Ashley set the pace. "Let's just lie here and talk. No lines to worry about, no pressure."

She tried not to stare as Ashley removed her robe and tentatively slid into bed. Her full figure was plainly outlined beneath the silk, and the sight of her generous breasts falling outward as she lay on her back served notice that a goodnight kiss could easily send them both rocketing out of control. There was no way she would lose her desire for Ashley while she waited for her to come around.

Ashley hugged her knees and rocked herself gently in the bedside chair. At a quarter to three, it was obvious sleep wouldn't be possible tonight, not as long as Julia was in her bed.

Julia's efforts to calm her with casual conversation had lent a layer of absurdity on top of the already surreal. Two women who claimed to love one another, in bed together fully clothed and somehow not touching. This was progress?

No, this was painful reminiscence. In her time with Cassandra, they had spent only one night together—at a hotel in St. Louis on the night of Missouri's Junior Miss Pageant. Cassandra had booked a room with two beds. Months had passed since their first sexual encounter, leaving Ashley to hope it was a mistake they would both forget. Then she had awakened to find Cassandra's hand beneath her gown, and her pleas to be left alone drowned by kisses she didn't want.

The memory of that awful night—so vivid she could practically smell Cassandra's putrid lavender perfume—had jolted her from the edge of sleep. It didn't matter how much she trusted Julia, not when she feared Cassandra's assault each time she closed her eyes.

She had to fight through this, one step at a time. It was the only way to write over the old definitions.

Tonight, however, was a lost cause. As quietly as she could, she tiptoed into the guest room and crawled between the crisp cotton sheets.

Chapter Twenty-One

A familiar chime announced a text message and Ashley checked her display: *meet 4 dinner @ the reef?*

The past three days had been a struggle, but not because of anything Julia had done. Ashley found herself dancing at the water's edge again, poised to run but wanting desperately to feel the joy others found in the swirling sea. If she couldn't manage a simple sleepover, how could she even think of doing more?

Julia had said all the right words the day after, but her actions told a different story. She had come into the guest room already dressed at seven thirty to say she was leaving, and wouldn't even stay for coffee…something about giving Ashley her space. It was only a setback, Julia had promised—no big deal—except then she dropped off the radar until just now. No calls, no texts, and instead of another intimate rendezvous at midnight, Julia was asking to meet for dinner.

Not that Ashley had taken the initiative—she hadn't. It was pathetic to go chasing someone after leaving her alone in bed, and she couldn't blame Julia at all if she was having second thoughts. The sad part was that she'd actually seen two signs of progress in this recent debacle. First, though she hadn't been able to talk herself into getting back into bed with Julia that night, she had successfully forced Cassandra from her thoughts long enough to fall asleep, and had suffered virtually no Cassandra "hangover" the next day. It was the first time she could remember willing the rancid emotions away, and it gave her an extraordinary sense of power to know that she could.

The second was her awareness that, while a part of her wanted to escape from the stress, none of her wanted to escape from Julia. For the first time in her life, she had someone who made her want to confront and conquer her past, and if they could hold on through—

Thunk! Aaron dropped a stack of mail on the corner of her desk. "It's basically junk except for your registration packet for the women's conference at the Don CeSar. Wish I could go to that."

"Only in drag," she told him.

After a quick confirmation that her mail contained nothing important, Ashley shook off her earlier thoughts of Julia and returned her focus to work, squinting at her computer screen, then the diagram on her desk, and back to her screen as she tried to replicate even a small piece of Aaron's work. He must have logged dozens of hours tying these fifty-four people together in a network linked to Jack Staley. A second chart showed another network—eighteen of the property owners linked either by family or workplace—but there was no crossover with the group tied to the commissioner. A third circle of six was also charted. That confirmed there were at least three conspirators among the groups represented here, and probably more. Staley was unquestionably involved but it was unlikely he was the one going into Kevin Finley's office to change files. That would have to be someone who walked freely on the eighth floor of the courthouse without arousing suspicion.

Following Aaron's trail, she clicked through one of the digital photo albums posted for public view on a social networking site. There was Staley at a picnic, his arm around a young woman who had tagged him as Uncle Jack. That woman lived in a house in

Citrus Park, purchased two years ago for $305,000 and assessed last summer for $106,750—which reduced her annual property tax bill by $3,000. That was a sweet gesture from Uncle Jack, and there were dozens more like it to people who belonged to his country club, whose children attended the same private school as his, and who had reported donations to his campaign fund. All told, his circle alone amounted to a taxpayer giveaway of nearly half a million dollars a year.

Aaron Crum had been a godsend with his avenue to the hacker Tobias, and also his diligence in building the diagrams. Ashley was aware that some of her co-workers used these networking sites to keep up with family and friends, but she was continually shocked at how much personal information people were willing to share with total strangers. Using the strategy Aaron had shown her for connecting people to the commissioner's network, she scrolled through the young woman's family photos to see how the circle was connected. One showed her sitting on the couch with a teenage boy who seemed bored and unaware of the camera, as if trapped in a family gathering he hadn't wanted to attend. As she clicked to advance to the next photo, something caught her eye and she abruptly returned to enlarge the previous image. The boy's black T-shirt was covered in what looked like binary code that spelled out a word she was sure she'd heard before: Gigadrone.

It took several seconds to lay her hands on her notebook but she found the word again in her scribbles from the meeting with Tobias. "Aaron, get back in here!"

An hour later they identified the teen as Jason Robinson, a nephew of Staley's, and had linked him to a series of video and forum postings about the rock band Gigadrone, whose lyrics were packed with words Aaron recognized as computer programming jargon. "This guy could be Obviosity."

"Find out all you can. I want to know if any of his friends are on our list." She located Jarvis in what had become his favorite hangout of late—Mallory's cubicle. His increased attention to the young reporter was irritating because she knew what a flirt he could be. Even if he weren't married, he had no business behaving that way around a woman half his age, especially one who worked for him. "I need to see you."

She resisted the urge to scold him, instead turning her focus and his toward their newest discovery, the possible avenue by which Staley had accessed Kevin Finley's password. "I can't wait to see the look on Staley's face when I ask him if investigators will find any evidence of messages or phone calls between him and a hacker known as Obviosity on the days these changes were made to the database," she said.

"I like that," Jarvis said, committing her words to a yellow legal pad. "You have a gift for cutting through the crap and going right to the questions that tell the whole story. I wish they could teach that in J-school but it's all instinct, and you were born with it."

Getting praise like that from Jarvis meant as much to her as all the awards and recognition she had garnered over the years. He was the gold standard of newsmen, the professional she aspired to be.

They all were excited to be sitting on the brink of a story this big. It was certain to dominate news coverage for months to come—the indictments, the trial, the sentencing for public corruption. All the media outlets in the Tampa Bay market would be playing catch-up for weeks. Ashley had no qualms about taking credit for the exclusive, despite the fact that it had practically dropped into her lap. Sources were cultivated through trust, and this was no exception. Kathy Finley was a living example of one of Robyn's para-social viewers who learned to trust Ashley because of her news coverage.

She smiled as she walked back to her office, thinking this was the best day she'd had in weeks. A celebration was in order and there was only one person she wanted to be with. Her thumbs hammered out her reply: *c u @ 6:45*

Julia watched the door anxiously as she waited for Ashley to appear. Her plan to arrive early—along with five bucks to the hostess—had paid off, yielding a booth near the back of the restaurant. Ashley would have to walk past dozens of people to reach the table, but would be tucked out of sight once she got there. She had no idea what to expect tonight, since Ashley had warned her that her *modus operandi* was to pull away in the face of conflict, and she'd certainly done that. Their night together had been an abject failure. She hadn't been invited back—not even to talk—and had only pressed the issue of dinner tonight to get a feel for where they stood.

Finding Ashley asleep in the guest room had been discouraging, but she'd tried to downplay it. Something had unnerved her in the middle of the night, and Julia had no way of knowing if it was only a hiccup or a sign she was shutting down again. What worried her most was that Ashley would react by impulse and push her away, so she'd dashed off without giving her a chance to back out again on the spot. She hoped a few days apart would help fortify Ashley to try again.

Julia had tried not to think that Teddie's experience with Patsy was repeating itself here—that after sharing a bed, Ashley had decided she didn't want that kind of relationship after all. There had been no mention of love the next morning, just a feeble apology for failed expectations. Possible translation: No one ought to sleep with someone just to keep from hurting their feelings. Julia half expected to be told as much tonight.

Another explanation was that she had underestimated Ashley's struggle with her past, and Ashley had as well. If that were the case, the answer was greater understanding, more patience and stronger commitment...which still wouldn't be enough without the same resolve from Ashley. That she had wavered on something as innocuous as sharing a bed didn't bode well, but at least there was a glimmer of hope in the fact she had agreed to meet for dinner.

At six forty-five on the nose, a murmur spread across the restaurant as Ashley walked through the door. No doubt the whole roomful of people would watch TV4 news tonight just to claim this connection to Ashley Giraud, who smiled radiantly as she crossed the room to their booth, nodding along the way to those who acknowledged her. She was fresh from the set in a sparkly black and silver top with black slacks and slightly more makeup than usual.

"You look amazing," Julia said, keeping her voice low. "I've never seen that top before. I would have remembered."

"A Christmas present to myself. I wore it to the Gasparilla brunch last week." When the waitress stopped by for their drink orders, Ashley placed her dinner order as well, and Julia followed suit. "I hope you don't mind the rush. I have to get back to the station right after dinner. I'm working Robyn's intern overtime on our 4Team story, and I feel a little guilty for running out on him."

"It's okay. I'm just glad you could get away." The way Julia saw it, she had two choices. She could tap dance through an abbreviated dinner trying to gauge Ashley's feelings, or she could put her cards on the table. "Look, I've missed you these last few days. Is everything okay?"

Ashley closed her eyes for a moment and smiled. "If you mean my little panic episode the other night, I'm feeling pretty silly about it. I hope you haven't given up on me already."

"Are you serious?" Julia felt a surge of irritation that Ashley was being so flippant. Did she actually expect her to blow it off and act like nothing had happened? "I've been wringing my hands for three days thinking you were going to tell me to get lost and all that time you thought I was the one giving up? Why didn't you call?"

"Why didn't you?"

She checked the neighboring tables and pasted a pleasant look on her face. "Because I wasn't the one who disappeared in the middle of the night. Any reasonably intelligent person would take that to mean you wanted to be left alone."

Ashley didn't bother with the charade of a pleasant face, squaring her jaw as she too lowered her voice. "Disappeared in the middle of the night...such a compassionate choice of words."

"I just meant that you got up and went to the other room." Julia clenched her teeth as she drew in a breath, weighing her next words more carefully. "I told you it was no big deal. What do I have to do to get you to trust me? It's your job to draw the lines and mine to color inside. That's all I was trying to do."

"And I told you I loved you. Do you think I'd say something like that on a whim and forget all about it the next day? I was afraid. I'm sorry. If I could handle my fears better, we wouldn't be having these problems in the first place."

One thing was becoming crystal clear to Julia—that she wasn't going to win even a shred of this argument. She had promised to be there and when Ashley really needed her to step up, she had stepped back instead. It was also true that she had trivialized Ashley's declaration of love. "You're right."

"I'm not trying to be right. I'm trying to be understood."

They paused long enough to smile sweetly at the waitress, who deposited their drinks and salads. Julia then discovered her smile was quite real.

"What's so funny?"

"I'm not laughing. I'm just happy. You're totally right and I'm totally wrong. And believe it or not, I actually do understand you now better than I did, because I let my fears keep me from doing what I really wanted to do, which was show up at your door the next night with my own pajamas."

Ashley squinted suspiciously. "Are you jerking me around now?"

"No, I'm trying to apologize. And I'm also telling you that I love you too, though I didn't really want my first time saying that to happen at a fish restaurant."

There it was finally, Ashley's first genuine smile of the evening, a sly one with a trace of mischief. "In that case, I accept. I especially like that whole bit about me being totally right and you being totally wrong. Who could ask for a better apology than that?"

"I'm not afraid to admit when I'm wrong. And you heard the second part of that too, right? That I love you."

"Oh yes, I really liked that, but the 'me being totally right' part"—she touched the tip of her thumb to her middle finger and kissed it—"*perfecto*."

Julia buried her head in her hands. "I may as well wave the white flag. My life is over."

"Victory is mine."

"Does this mean I can come over tonight? I don't really have to bring my pajamas...or maybe I'll leave them in the car just in case."

Ashley shook her head. "I may not get home until late...that 4Team story. Tomorrow night, though."

"So you weren't just blowing me off about having to rush back to work?"

"Trust me, when I want to blow you off, there won't be any doubt in your mind."

"When?"

"I meant if."

"You said when."

"I meant if!"

Chapter Twenty-Two

"...intelligent, conscientious, dedicated, and did I say intelligent? Doesn't matter, I'll say it again. Intelligent, as in the brightest intern you've ever sent me."

Robyn beamed with obvious pride at the superlative evaluation. "Even better than Mallory?"

Ashley checked the door to make sure no one was within earshot. Tuesdays were quiet since Jarvis and Carl played golf and there was no one else at the station to impress. "Mallory's very gifted. And she's also very beautiful, which frankly helps her get some assignments she might not otherwise get. I don't say that against her at all—Lord knows, I rode that gravy train too—but Aaron succeeds despite his...ordinary features." That was the kindest description she could think of.

Using a scratchy mechanical pencil, Robyn made notes in her black leather binder. "So you're saying he might struggle in a career as on-air talent?"

"I'm saying he has the potential to be one of the best segment producers in the business, and I'd recommend TV4 hire him in a heartbeat." It was the strongest endorsement she had ever given an intern.

"For what it's worth he says the same about you. He put on his career prospectus that he wanted to be a magazine writer someday, but now he's been bitten by the TV bug. And he adores you." She closed her folder and dropped the pencil into her purse. "That takes care of Aaron. Can we talk about a couple of personal matters?"

Ashley chased a tiny piece of black lint from her pink suit. She'd been expecting Robyn's queries ever since the demonstrative kiss she'd given Julia at the shop. "Sure, I'd love to know how Henry and Elaine are doing."

"Fine and fine…but I was more interested in how you and Julia are doing."

Sorely tempted to parrot the same trite reply, Ashley looked at her clock to see if a meeting somewhere might save her from this conversation. She was still getting used to the idea of having a girlfriend, but Robyn and Elaine were on the short list of confidantes who already knew that, so there weren't really any secrets to protect. "We moved the furniture back and danced again on Friday night. You should have been there."

"Except we weren't invited."

"Touché. If it makes you feel better, you were probably asleep already. I work very late, you know."

She and Julia were back on track, having spent most of the weekend together, including a day trip to an art show in Cedar Key on Sunday. They had purposely tabled the idea of sleeping together again until it happened spontaneously and without expectations. Ashley had a feeling that might come in three days at the luxurious Don CeSar on St. Petersburg Beach. Teddie was staying behind to dogsit with Henry, so Julia had decided not to book a room after all. If she joined them for a night on the beach, she could stay over with Ashley instead of driving back late.

"You might have heard…" Robyn dropped her eyes momentarily. "I wasn't very happy with Julia when she told me you guys were seeing each other. I expected her to protect your privacy, not invade it."

"It was always mutual, Robyn."

"I just worried—this is really selfish—I'd hate it if something happened and it got in the way of our friendship."

"I understand, and we don't want that either. But we both feel we need to give this a chance."

Robyn nodded and held up her hand. "Fine. Like I said, it was me being selfish. What I really wanted to tell you has nothing to do with any of that. I did an evaluation this morning for one of my print journalism students I placed at the *Tampa Bay Guardian*. He says Lamar Davidson is working on a profile of you."

"Oh, for God's sake!"

"I think he may have interviewed Valerie…and some people from Missouri. It's probably just a matter of time before he finds out about Julia."

"Why would he care about me? I'm not even controversial."

"Douglas—that's my intern—didn't realize you and I were friends, so he basically spilled his guts on everything Lamar has him working on. The gist of the profile is that you're gay, eccentric and obsessed with privacy."

All of which were basically true, Ashley thought drearily. She said, "He asked Jarvis about an interview a few weeks ago but I blew him off. I figured he would just move on to something more interesting." Someone in the PR department might be able to leverage Lamar's editor into killing this, perhaps in exchange for a few spot ads. It was in TV4's interest to manage these types of stories when they could, as long as they didn't compromise news of genuine journalistic value. This was just tabloid crap.

"I wanted to give you a heads-up, but please tread carefully. I don't want Douglas to get in trouble for talking about it."

Ashley sighed. She'd probably have to call Lamar and give the little bastard his interview after all.

Suzy snipped away on Julia's hair as she chattered. "And you know why there aren't any good potty training jokes? Because they aren't funny. All three of my older kids absolutely loved pooping in the toilet like Mommy and Daddy, but Brandon? No way. He wants his potty chair in the kitchen so he can have a cookie while he does his business."

Julia chuckled at the mental image of an exasperated Suzy pleading with her son, who was sweet, but spoiled totally rotten by his parents and siblings. "Take a little more off the sides, will you? I look like a cocker spaniel."

"Wish I had your wave. Hell, I wish I had your garage apartment too. It would be absolute bliss to go home to nobody but myself."

"You'd go crazy after ten minutes."

They used to trade haircuts once a month but their hectic schedules over the past couple of years had reduced that to the rare occasions when they both had cancellations at the same time. Each knew the other's cowlicks by heart and could render the perfect cut in less than fifteen minutes. Suzy did her own blond highlights at home, using it as an excuse to lock herself inside the bathroom.

"So what's up with you and Ashley Giraud?"

Julia was stunned by the question. She hadn't shared a word about her relationship with Ashley with anyone at the shop, and her first thought was that Teddie had blabbed. She rarely kept secrets from Suzy, but they only talked about their personal lives when they had the chance to speak alone, and they hadn't done that yet where Ashley was concerned.

"Her hair used to be jet-black, but now it looks brown. You're doing one of the naturals, aren't you?"

"Ha!" She couldn't stifle her laugh at realizing Suzy was far more interested in Ashley's hair than her personal life. "Good eye. I moved her over to walnut the very first day she was in here. She's actually a gorgeous brunette."

"She's gorgeous, period. I even like that she's kind of fat. It makes her real."

Julia decided not to take issue with Suzy's characterization of Ashley as fat, especially since she wasn't being critical. Besides, once she divulged her secret, Suzy would be sufficiently mortified by her remark that it wouldn't be necessary to point it out. "I've also been meaning to tell you that she and I are seeing each other."

"Get out of here! You're seeing Ashley Giraud?" Suzy had stopped cutting to stare at her in the mirror, a look of astonishment on her grinning face.

"Shh!" She gestured upward to the girls upstairs. "Why are you looking at me like that? It's not like we're different species."

"Julia Whitethorn, I can't believe you've been holding out on me."

"I wanted to say something but we hardly ever get any time just to talk. It's not like I'm going to go on about dating Ashley Giraud in front of our customers."

"Which means you probably won't let me tell anybody either."

"That's exactly what it means. The world doesn't need another Teddie Teddrick." Everyone knew Teddie's penchant to snitch. "Ashley's a private person."

"Now I know why you've started wearing makeup to work and getting Inez to do your nails all pretty."

"Oh, for freak's sake." Julia wished Suzy hadn't noticed. It was only a matter of time before the sly winks and knowing grins began. Getting that from her co-worker was possibly worse than having her mother comment on her new nocturnal schedule.

"You won't tell her I said she was fat, will you?"

"Do you think I'm insane? And please don't say anything to Inez and Jasmine. I'd like for this to be off the Rhapsody radar."

"I bet you would."

Ashley snuggled against Julia on the couch, having changed from her pink suit into her silk pajamas and robe the moment she walked in the door. The waistband on her skirt had pinched her all day, a reminder that she wasn't spending enough time on the treadmill.

Her bigger problem, at least for now, was Lamar Davidson, and he could be Julia's problem as well. "If I know Lamar, he'll find out who you are, how much your shop took in last year and whether you've paid your taxes on time or not. He might even interview some of the people your father screwed over on his way to prison. If you had any secrets before, you won't have them now."

Julia had come from a meeting with the other office condo owners and was smartly dressed in slacks and an Oxford shirt, though by now she had rolled up her sleeves and taken off her shoes. "Why would Lamar Davidson even care about somebody like me? I'm nobody."

"You aren't nobody now. You're the girlfriend of that eccentric, paranoid lesbian whose father died in prison. Robyn said he called people in Missouri so I guess I can add that little snippet to my official bio now, and probably all the rumors about Cassandra too. She even thinks he talked to Valerie. Won't that be fun?"

"Girlfriend...I can live with that." Julia propped pillows at the end of the couch and drew Ashley backward into her lap in what had become their favorite arrangement, a comfortable embrace where both could gaze at the garden. Tonight a steady drizzle left twinkling raindrops on the plants and windows.

As Ashley's head fell back against Julia's shoulder, it occurred to her why she liked this position so much. The first night they settled this way, it had been a deliberate attempt on Ashley's part to be close without having to look Julia in the eye as she told her shameful secrets. Tonight there was a stronger sentiment. With Julia now sitting taller and wrapping her arms around her from behind, Ashley felt protected but not overpowered.

"What is it they say, Ashley? All publicity is good. If he's going to do the story anyway, maybe you should go ahead and talk to him. That way you get a chance to highlight whatever you think is important."

"That's what I'm thinking too. I figure my best defense is to come forward and pretend not to be eccentric or paranoid about my privacy. And I could always treat the lesbian angle like old news. The problem is that just agreeing to an interview goes against everything I believe about how to stay in control."

"Control is overrated, you know," she said, planting a kiss against Ashley's temple. "Don't forget about our secret weapon. We can turn Teddie loose on him."

"What could she do?"

"Oh, she'd probably put his phone number on Twitter and tell everybody he fed live kittens to his pit bull. He wouldn't be able to use his phone for weeks."

"Hmm…tempting."

"You could always try to be less interesting, but I'm not sure you could pull that off. I find you fascinating." She burrowed into Ashley's hair to place a soft kiss just beneath her ear.

Ashley tipped her head to the side to encourage more exploration. Life had gotten so much simpler since their heart-to-heart at The Reef, when they both had put to rest their insecurities about what the other wanted. Once Julia reaffirmed her willingness to take it slowly, the pressure about sleeping together was off. So was Ashley's effort to orchestrate intimacy through a series of methodical steps—first this hurdle, then the next—which had only fueled her anxiety and made the whole concept of making love about process instead of feelings.

But this neck-nibbling…that was feelings.

"I like when you do that," she said, tickling Julia's forearm. "I put a little drop of Fracas on that spot every morning and think about you trying to find it. Do you even notice it?"

"Notice it?" Julia pressed close and inhaled deeply. "It drives me crazy. The whole reason I do this is to find that little spot."

Ashley luxuriated under the tender assault on her neck, at the same time noticing other parts of her body had begun to respond. The large muscles of her torso contracted in waves as she nestled her hips between Julia's legs.

Julia apparently got the message and allowed her hands to slide inside Ashley's robe to the final layer of silk, never breaking the contact her lips had begun. Finally her fingers breached the seam and wandered across the skin of Ashley's stomach.

This was how Ashley wanted it to happen, unscripted and in

the moment, following only her instincts and desires. Anxiety lurked but was overshadowed by her lust, and she sprang up suddenly, clutching Julia's hand. "We should go to the other room."

They walked silently into the dark bedroom, where she boldly pulled Julia on top of her as she dropped to the bed, needing no more words to express her wants. She closed her eyes as Julia's lips fell upon hers. For all her thoughts about not being ready for sexual intimacy, her body responded instantly by arching upward to press herself against Julia's thigh.

"God, Ashley."

"Please don't say anything," she whispered, touching her fingers to Julia's lips. She hadn't felt this free in over twenty years and couldn't stand it if a trigger from her past broke the spell. All she wanted was to feel Julia's weight upon her and their hot skin melding together. She tugged on Julia's sweater and when it was off, unhooked her bra.

Julia complied with all of her silent requests and went on to remove her slacks, leaving herself clad only in panties. Then she gently tugged open Ashley's robe and released each of the buttons on her top, moaning softly as her warm hand encircled a newly exposed breast.

Fifteen years old and built like Jayne Mansfield. No one will ever believe these are real.

Ashley shuddered and drew Julia tightly to her chest, diverting her thoughts by focusing intently on Julia's body and not her own. She was slender, and Ashley couldn't resist sliding her hands beneath the waistband of her panties to follow the splendid curve of her hip, which she had noticed the first time she saw Julia in a tapered shirt. The skin of her back was cool in the open air, but she seemed oblivious, moving sensuously against Ashley's thigh.

"Can we get under the covers?"

In the dim light she stole a brief look at Julia's breasts, which were small but shapely, with dark areolae surrounding perfect peaks. She knew they were perfect because they had brushed stiffly against her bare skin only moments earlier. That sublime feeling returned the instant they burrowed beneath the blanket and Julia's mouth covered hers in a searing kiss she never wanted to end.

And then Julia's hand was inside the waistband of her pants, cupping her bottom as she pressed her thigh between Ashley's legs. Ashley arched and allowed her clothes to be removed, aching at the void while Julia also removed the last of hers.

When they drew together again, Ashley knew this was it—the very last moment she could call for safety before things between them changed forever. She squeezed her eyes tightly shut as Julia's hand slid through her wetness and circled the taut bundle of nerves. Breathing seemed impossible as she gasped, held it and gasped again. Her hips moved by instinct...side to side, up and down...whatever created just the right friction to send a jolt through her center. When she wrapped one of her legs high around Julia's waist, Julia responded by slipping deep inside her.

You pretend not to want this, but this part of you...it always says yes.

"I love you," Ashley said, forcibly drawing the distinction in her mind that she was making love for the first time in her life.

Julia stroked her in varied rhythms, taking her steadily higher to a point where she expected her climax at every caress.

Why do you deny me this? Why deny yourself? Let it go, Ashley. Give me this one gift for all I've done for you.

And then all at once the tension left her body, dropping her from the precipice of climax to an inanimate heap. For the next several seconds she felt nothing, and then a growing tightness in her chest. "No," she murmured, her voice almost a sob.

"Ashley, what is it? What's wrong?" Julia had stopped her motions to hug her, and was hovering only inches above her face.

A surge of heat hit her like a furnace blast, and she kicked violently at the covers and twisted out of Julia's embrace. Her robe lay crumpled on the floor and she draped it carelessly around her sweat-soaked body.

"Ashley..."

"You have to leave." It was all she could manage as she gulped for breath. The squeezing sensation in her chest worsened and she felt as if she might throw up. "Please go."

Julia stepped into her panties and wrapped herself in Ashley's discarded pajama top. "I can't leave you like this. What's happening?"

Her only escape was to end the threat. She broke free of Julia's hand on her arm and rushed past her into the bathroom, where she slammed and locked the door before sliding to the cold tile floor. "You have to go, Julia. You're making it worse."

Above the din of her own raspy breath, she followed the sound of footsteps back to the bedroom, then past her on the way to the living room. Finally they returned and stopped on the other side of the bathroom door.

"Ashley, I'm dressed now. Please come out."

"I can't." Her jaw trembled. The contractions in her chest had given way to a searing heat that radiated from the center of her shoulder blades. Her breathing had slowed to near normal and the base of her skull ached. It would be over soon.

"I have to know you're okay."

"It's happened before. I'll be fine," she heard herself say weakly. "But I need for you to go."

With tears streaming down her face, she listened to the slowly retreating footsteps and the sound of her front door closing. In the distance, she thought she heard the squeaking of the electronic gate as it rolled across its track.

"I love you," she whispered.

Chapter Twenty-Three

Julia nearly cried with relief at seeing Ashley's car emerge from the gate at a quarter after nine in the morning. In her whole life, she'd never done anything more difficult than leave Ashley behind a locked door, clearly distressed but begging desperately to be abandoned.

Her fears of what might happen had led her to park across from the gate where she could watch the house through the night if necessary. It was thirty minutes after she walked out in the rain that she saw signs of life in the form of lights in the kitchen, and then gradually the house darkened again as Ashley presumably went to bed. Only then had Julia gone home, but she returned at dawn after a sleepless night to reassure herself that Ashley was all right.

Their revealing talks about Ashley's abusive past and the anxieties that still plagued her had done little to prepare Julia for the terrifying scene that had unfolded last night as they made love. When Ashley bent over clutching her chest, her initial instincts had been to call 911. All that stopped her was Ashley's determined insistence that she would be fine if only she were left alone, and the potentially devastating consequences of escalating the drama. She kept telling herself that if Ashley had truly been in physical danger, she would have called the paramedics on her own after Julia left.

It was a new day, a day in which Ashley was returning to work as usual, and no doubt beginning the arduous, painful task of recovery from this most recent trauma. Only now Julia was part of her trauma. She wanted to call but wasn't sure yet what Ashley needed to hear. The lesson from last time was not to wait too long to show Ashley that she understood and would stand by her as she struggled with the aftermath of her memories.

At least Wednesday was a light day at the shop. Her first appointment wasn't until eleven, which meant she had plenty of time for a long hot shower and two or more shots of espresso at Larry's.

Her timing couldn't have been worse, since she arrived home just as Teddie was donning her raingear for the ride to work. "Sure wish I had your sex life."

Julia didn't appreciate the disrespectful insinuation, but biting Teddie's head off would only call attention to her solemn mood, which she needed to keep hidden to ward off questions. "Aren't you late?"

"Doesn't matter. Hardly anybody comes when it rains, unless they get sprayed down with mud somewhere."

"For your sake, I hope that happens a lot."

"By the way, Patsy and I are officially toast. No hard feelings or anything, just a big old red X. Next time you see my tongue hanging out over somebody, will you just go ahead and put me out of my misery? This shit ain't worth it." Though her words were full of her typical swagger, there was genuine sadness in her voice, along with an unspoken plea for sympathy.

Julia chucked her shoulder gently. "Yes, it is. There's somebody out there. It probably won't be easy because it never is, but she'll make you want to tear through all of the crap like wrapping paper to find out what's inside. It'll happen."

"I'll believe it when I see it." Teddie slung a leg over the saddle of her Harley and bounced a couple of times to settle her seat. "I'm happy for you, Jules…with Ashley and all. You've put up with a lot of shit over the years, so I'm glad you don't have to anymore."

As she rumbled out of the driveway, Julia shook her head at the irony. If only there was a limit to what people had to endure...

The entire 4Team was assembled around the large table in the conference room, along with Carl Terzian and the station's legal counsel, Brenda Haywood, a no-nonsense African-American woman, who was there to remind them of their rights and responsibilities as members of a free press. What Carl cared about was the potential for criminal or civil liabilities that might result from their exposé.

Jarvis closed the miniblinds and directed everyone to the screen for the presentation. "Since Tim is our segment producer on this, I'm going to let him walk you through it, but first I want to say how proud I am of everyone on this team. I've already looked at some of the clips—great camera work, BJ—and this story is going to knock our viewers out of their chairs."

Ashley bristled at his reference to the clips—especially since he looked directly at Mallory, who had done voiceover on the explanatory material, along with narration to go with still shots of properties and people linked to the scandal. The real work had been done off-camera on the investigative end in Ashley's interviews with Kevin Finley and Tobias, and in the networks she and Aaron had built to show who was involved.

"Doughnut?" BJ handed her a box and a stack of napkins, which she passed on to Brenda. Two cups of bitter coffee had turned her stomach sour, and the thought of adding greasy dough to the mix made her want to retch.

A persistent headache from hunger and lack of sleep was all that was left from her wild array of symptoms the night before. It was her worst panic attack by far, and there was even a moment where she feared it might be something more serious. Only when she reached the bathroom did she feel the symptoms abate, and she knew then she would be all right, at least physically. The emotional scars from her meltdown felt like third-degree burns inside.

How would she ever be able to face Julia again?

Tim cleared his throat as he took a position at the front of the room near the screen. "Okay, we're going to rock this story on Monday because that's when we have the most eyeballs. We need everything ready to go by Thursday because"—he pointed to Ashley like he was pulling the trigger on a finger gun— "somebody's got a fancy media conference with Katie Couric at the Don CeSar on Friday. All the video's in the can already, except we're going to shoot a few spots at the courthouse on Monday afternoon, and then have Ashley anchor the six o'clock show live on location."

"And if we're lucky, she'll bring us a nice, juicy gotcha interview with our county commissioner," Jarvis added, nodding her way.

She looked up to find Carl smiling at her. Two-faced creep. Around others he made a great show of professional respect and admiration, but the moment he got Jarvis alone, it was "Ashley needs to lose some weight" or "Ashley needs to show more cleavage." He didn't give a rat's butt about the news. What was he even doing in this meeting? Dirtbag.

"For obvious reasons, we need to hold off on shooting these spots until about four thirty because we don't want to alert any of the other stations to the story. I don't have to tell any of you how good it's going to feel to catch everyone else with their pants down…figuratively, of course." Tim leaned across the table to speak directly to her. "And you need to lay low on Monday because anyone who sees you at the courthouse that late in the day is going to know we're cooking a big one. Aaron, start us off, buddy."

The first segment contained the background on whistleblower Kevin Finley. Aaron had cleverly condensed the details about how the property tax database was maintained at the county into a forty-second graphic clip.

Ashley loathed herself.

Here she was on the verge of breaking her most important story in years, and she couldn't focus because her head was still coming down from last night. She had considered calling Julia before coming to work but had no idea what to say. Was it enough to say she was profoundly sorry? That she was humiliated beyond what she thought possible? And that now she knew better than to lure innocent people into her nightmares? Here she was again trying to erase her memories as quickly as she made them.

Or maybe there was nothing to deal with this time. Julia had left her house key on the coffee table, which could very well mean she'd had enough of it anyway. Who wouldn't after getting a look inside the belly of the beast?

The obvious bottom line was that romance just wasn't possible for her. Julia had been her best chance because they actually loved each other, but last night wasn't a misunderstanding they could sweep away after a few jokes at dinner. She had come totally unhinged.

"You all right with that, Ash?" Jarvis was expecting an answer.

On the screen was the news copy she had written yesterday to kick off the story, and Jarvis apparently wanted to change it. She couldn't blindly agree to something just to keep from looking like an idiot. "Tell me again."

"I want to go with breaking on the overlay instead of exclusive."

"Fine, I'll work exclusive into the copy for the voiceovers on all the courthouse background."

"Nah." Jarvis waved his hand dismissively. "Those are already in the can too. Mallory did them yesterday."

The workings and personnel at the courthouse were the most important elements of the story and she wasn't giving them up to a cub reporter without a fight. "It's no big deal. I'll just re-record them this afternoon. We can't very well call it breaking news and show Mallory all over the county doing background on the properties. Viewers know she can't be in five places at once."

Carl nodded earnestly, and she added patronizing to her list.

The gate began rolling as Ashley's headlights lit up the circular driveway, causing Julia to squint momentarily as she leaned on her car. She made no move to shield her face and tried her best to appear nonthreatening. It was presumptuous of her to let herself inside the courtyard after the scene last night. She might have been even bolder had she not forgotten to pick up her key from the coffee table on her way out.

There was no telling how Ashley would react, but anything was better than sitting at home worrying. Her two text messages had been ignored, and she wasn't going to slink off like last time. She understood all the fears and anxieties, and was more committed than ever to helping Ashley chase them away.

As she waited by her car, it occurred to her that Ashley might simply pull into the garage and close the door behind her without ever acknowledging her presence. It would be hard to miss a message like that. She was relieved when Ashley walked out to meet her.

There was no hug this time because Julia was afraid to move and Ashley stopped about eight feet away, her hands buried in the pockets of her raincoat. "Sorry I didn't answer your text. I was surrounded by people all day."

"It's okay," Julia said. There had never been this much tension between them, and Julia realized she very much needed Ashley's reassurance. "I can't imagine what you're feeling today. Probably tired and wrung out, just like I am. I didn't come by for anything in particular, just to see if there was anything I could do."

Ashley shook her head, and her lips tightened as if she were struggling to hold something inside. "There's nothing. I really don't know what to say about last night. I lost it."

"You don't have to explain anything. I understand." Julia had spent the whole evening reading on the Internet about panic attacks, and had nothing but compassion for how much Ashley had suffered. "I'm sorry if I did something to upset you."

"No, it wasn't you. I just went to a really bad place all of a sudden. It's like that." She touched a finger to her eye as if to stop a tear before it could track down her cheek. "I'm sorry for putting you through it."

It was all Julia could do to keep from reaching out, but Ashley was more guarded than she'd ever seen her. "Don't be sorry. That's what I came to tell you. You don't have to worry about what I'm thinking, because all I'm thinking is that I love you. I'll do whatever you need, but this is too important for me to guess about. I'll be right here beside you, or I'll give you a little space. All you have to do is tell me what you want from me."

Ashley's eyes wandered aimlessly, landing everywhere except on Julia, and she began rubbing the center of her chest. "I wasn't really honest with you last night. What happened…it was never that bad before. I thought I could do this but I can't. And I know it scared you too. I can't put you through something like that again. I just think it's best if we—"

"Don't do this." Julia's heart hammered to realize what Ashley was saying. "I know you're upset, but please don't decide something because you think it's what I want or what's good for me. You're what I need."

"I can't be that person for you, Julia." She was crying openly now, and her breathing was shallow and loud, just as it had been last night. "Whether we love each other or not doesn't matter. It doesn't make any of this go away. I thought it would be different, but the only difference is that it feels worse than ever."

"Ashley—"

"Please don't make this hard. Can't you see what it's doing to me?"

There was nothing Julia could say or do as she watched Ashley retreat into her house. She had seen with her own eyes the physical effects of pressing her to fight through her fears, and she never wanted to be the cause of that kind of pain.

But Ashley was wrong. Love mattered.

Chapter Twenty-Four

Thunderous applause broke out in the ballroom as four hundred women came to their feet to applaud Katie Couric's remarks on the status of women in the media. She was positioned front and center on the stage, flanked by *Tampa Tribune* columnist Maria Gutierrez on her left and Ashley on her right. As moderator, Robyn stood to the side at a podium.

All smiles at the obvious success of her panel, Robyn threw open the floor for questions, prompting no fewer than fifty hands to go up throughout the room. One after another, women rose to direct their questions to Couric, the network star.

Ashley didn't mind being ignored, especially in favor of someone with Couric's stature. At least she didn't have to worry about invasive personal questions, or anything that might put her on the spot regarding the investigative story they were set to break on Monday, since the room was filled with reporters from all over Tampa Bay. If it weren't for Robyn's occasional interjection to get input from her and Maria, she could have taken a nap.

Sleep was something she needed badly, having had very little since her disastrous collapse three nights ago, but it wouldn't come peacefully until she set her life right again. Every time she closed her eyes, she saw a movie in her head—not of that ruinous night but of the scene with Julia in her driveway. She had only wanted to save Julia from the misery and hopelessness of trying to have a romantic relationship with her, but instead had gone so far as to accuse her of causing the pain. Needlessly cruel words, uttered only because she felt her resolve begin to crumble.

The moment she had turned away from Julia in the driveway she knew this time was different. Instead of feeling relief from disengaging, she felt a deep sense of loss, so much that she almost ran after her. But Julia didn't deserve to be dragged through this misery, especially since there was no guarantee they could defeat her demons.

"I have a question for Ashley Giraud."

She was startled to hear her name and panned the audience to locate the voice, which belonged to a serious-looking woman with short black hair and glasses.

"This whole conference has been about celebrating women who have made it in a business that's dominated by sixty-year-old white men. We appreciate being recognized for our brains." She paused while many in the audience cheered. "Do you feel your accomplishments have been diminished in any way by the fact that you began your career after winning a beauty pageant?"

"The better question is, do you feel they have?" Her auspicious start as Miss Missouri had been a chip on her shoulder for her entire career. "Are they diminished? No. But are they devalued? Yes, I think so. Half the people in television news look down on you if you aren't attractive. The other half look down on you if you are. Any woman who thinks she can coast through this business on her looks is in for a rude awakening. No matter who you are, there's always going to be someone prettier, younger and smarter with her eye on your chair. All you can do is go out there every single day and earn your job."

Applause erupted again and when it died down, Robyn wrapped up the session by thanking everyone, especially the guest of honor.

Breathing a sigh of relief once the session ended, Ashley traded cordialities with her fellow panelists before Couric's handlers ushered her off the stage to catch a plane back to New York. She was pleased for the chance to appear in such prestigious company.

Robyn was beside herself with excitement. "A bunch of us are gathering in the bar to talk about the conference. It would mean a lot to me if you came in and sat with us for a while."

Deconstructing the conference wasn't something Ashley wanted to do, but there were merits to hanging out in a public area where she could watch for Julia to arrive. Besides, she knew her presence in the cocktail lounge would impress Robyn's academic friends, and she was glad to do it.

Their small group grew as people pulled up chairs to join them. With most of the buzz centered on the thrill of seeing Couric in person, Ashley was able to enjoy relative anonymity. She tapped Robyn on the forearm to get her to lean closer. "I thought Elaine would have joined us by now."

"She just sent me a text. She's been out on the beach all day and wants to order room service. Too bad about Julia, isn't it? I thought she was going to catch a break but she said that dang workshop she wanted was only offered this weekend."

So she had gone to Ft. Lauderdale after all, Ashley realized dismally. She hadn't thought it possible to feel worse than she did, but now she could add guilt for coming between Julia and her friends to her growing pile of transgressions. Why else would she have bailed on a weekend when she had been willing to cancel everything just to be a part of it? This had to stop. "When is she supposed to get back?"

"Sunday afternoon, I think."

Ashley couldn't wait that long. The least she could do was offer an apology over the phone and hope Julia would agree to talk to her once she got back. She began looking for an opportunity to excuse herself so she could go up to her room and call. If Julia was willing, she could be on a plane to south Florida in two hours to deliver her apology in person. Even if romance wasn't possible, she couldn't bear to lose Julia's friendship.

"Somebody tell the bartender to switch it over to TV4. It's time for the news."

Robyn put a hand on Ashley's shoulder and announced to the group, "We don't have to watch the news tonight. We have the star of TV4 sitting right here with us."

The bartender honored their requests and all eyes turned to the jumbo screen, where Mallory Foster stood on the steps of the Hillsborough County Courthouse: *We have breaking news at this hour. TV4 investigators have learned that Commissioner Jack Staley, his administrative assistant and a supervisor in the county tax office may have conspired to lower the property tax bills for dozens of their friends and family. We begin our exclusive report with…*

Ashley knocked over an empty wineglass in her rush to get closer to the television. All the graphics, stills and video played sequentially just as they had laid them out in their meeting on Wednesday, with Mallory's voiceover on every single piece.

I spoke with Commissioner Staley and asked him this. Cut to video. *Investigators will be looking into your communications on the dates in question. Can they expect to find any evidence that you contacted a hacker who goes by the name Obviosity in order to get access to property records?*

This could not be happening.

She rummaged in her purse for her phone, which had been muted all afternoon during the panels. Three missed calls—one from K Finley and two from the station.

"I have to go," she said to Robyn, and played back her voicemails as she walked briskly to the elevator to collect her belongings from her room.

Miss Giraud, it's Kevin Finley. Some guy just called me…a reporter from some paper, and he asked if I knew anything about unauthorized changes to the property tax records. I didn't know what to tell him so I said no comment. Am I going to get in trouble for not talking to him? Call me if you get this message. I'm going to try you at the station.

So that's what happened. The story got out and they had to go with it before someone else broke it on the air. But how?

Ashley, this is Aaron. Call me as soon as you get this. Lamar

Davidson found out about the tax story, and we're going on air with it at six. If you get this message, go straight to the courthouse.

Lamar Davidson! He must have been following her or hacking her phone or something. There was nothing out of bounds for slime like that.

It's Jarvis. Looks like this story's going down today at the courthouse. That little ass wipe Davidson got wind of it and called Finley. I can't hold it, Ash, or we're going to get scooped. Call me when you get this and we'll try to work you in.

She should never have gone out of the office with something this big ready to roll. All that crap about earning her job every day, and she'd just made the biggest mistake of her career.

Everything old is new again, Julia thought as she watched the instructor transform the model's long straight hair into something that looked like a tumbleweed. She had never been a fan of big hair and didn't much want to see this eighties trend take off again.

It was hard to get excited about anything when her head was two hundred miles away at the Don CeSar. Her last-minute decision to enroll in the Ft. Lauderdale workshop had seemed like the right thing to do, both for her and for Ashley. She needed the recertification credits and had already cleared her schedule of appointments for the planned weekend on St. Petersburg Beach. She also needed distraction, something to get her through the next few days while she waited for Ashley to calm her emotions and decide what she wanted. Surely she would realize this was something they could overcome. A little space would do them both good, and they could clear the air on Monday morning when Ashley came into the shop for her monthly style.

Clear the air.

What did that even mean? She had tried to do that on Wednesday but Ashley was more fragile than she'd ever seen her, yet still had the instinct to protect herself by pushing back.

No matter what Ashley had said, Julia knew she wasn't the cause of her pain. She was merely the catalyst and in a day or two, Ashley would come to that realization. That distinction only mattered if she could help Ashley fight her memories, and if the love she had to offer was worth going through hell to get.

Chapter Twenty-Five

Aaron stood with his back against her office door, his head hanging dejectedly. It was hard to tell which one of them was more upset. "It's my fault. I should have kept trying."

"It wouldn't have mattered. I had my phone off. It was just bad luck."

"All that work we did, and then you didn't get to do the story."

Ashley felt the same way, but that wasn't how it worked on a news team. "What matters is that TV4 got the story on the air first, and we got it right. Did you see the papers this morning? It's the biggest story in months."

"Still, I should have called the hotel or something."

She nudged him aside to open the door. "Let's go get this over with. Remember, not a word about our computer friend."

The entire 4Team was on hand all day Saturday at the insistence of the US Attorney's office, which seemed hell-bent on getting its case to a grand jury in time for a Monday morning indictment. Despite their collective resistance to being part of the story, they all had expected this and were proud their investigation was getting the attention it deserved.

Their only gray area, at least according to counsel Brenda Haywood, was Ashley's and Aaron's presence at the meeting with Tobias where she illegally hacked the county database. If she had it to do over, Ashley would have had Tobias skip the demonstration, especially since she had already captured the screenshots of everything she did.

She was glad to see Brenda had taken the seat next to Mallory, who was too inexperienced to answer questions without legal advice. She steered Aaron to a chair next to Jarvis for the same reason and positioned herself closest to Assistant US Attorney Brian Garver, as serious a man as she'd ever met.

Still sporting the buzz cut he'd worn for twenty years in the Marine Corps, Garver had a rude habit of treating everyone like a Parris Island recruit. It was probably effective when it came to intimidating paper-pushers who had done something illegal, but to Ashley it was like trying to catch flies with vinegar. They had constitutional rights to press freedoms and weren't compelled to cooperate at all.

"Let's start with Kevin Finley."

Kevin had come forward almost immediately as the whistleblower after his shady supervisor started pointing fingers everywhere but at himself. On Jarvis's advice, he had retained a lawyer of his own, who offered up the original note from the wastebasket along with the photos he had taken of his search results. He also authorized the release of his interview with Ashley and Jarvis, to which they added nothing.

Brenda fielded most of the questions, with Aaron and Ashley providing details of how they linked the properties through social networking sites. Jarvis interrupted twice to remind Garver they were speaking to him only as a courtesy, and would end this inquisition if he didn't stop his bullying. Ashley found his support both charming and gallant.

After nearly three hours, Garver made it through his list of questions and began to gather his notes. "One last item... how did your station get access to the network administrator's system file? They've got firewalls...passwords."

"Confidential sources, Mr. Garver," Brenda said quickly in a clear effort to shut down his line of inquiry.

"A confidential source who might have broken the law, Ms. Haywood."

"We're done," Jarvis announced, clapping his hands and rubbing them together as he stood. "If you need anything else, file a subpoena."

Ashley followed him into his office and closed the door. "You were terrific."

"He's an ass. Look, I'm glad you came in. I need to talk to you about something." He cleared a chair and gestured for her to sit. "I talked with Carl this morning and...shit, there's no good way to say this. He wants to keep Mallory on the anchor desk while this story plays out."

She was so stunned she could barely speak. "But you told him no."

"She's not you, Ash, but the switchboard lit up like crazy last night. Our viewers identify her with the story, and now you've got a potential confidential source subpoena hanging over your head. We need to be clean on this, or it's going to look like we have an agenda with Staley."

"You're actually pulling me off the anchor desk?"

"Just till the story flattens out. I'll work on Carl tomorrow. Maybe I can get him to back off. You know how much I hate it when he sticks his nose where it doesn't belong."

Ashley walked out in a daze. She had half a mind to march upstairs to Carl's office and call him a lecherous bastard to his face, but it was Saturday. He was at the country club, or the yacht club or a strip club...wherever lecherous bastards congregated.

"...something nonalcoholic...beer if you have it, ginger ale if you don't." Julia wasn't a big fan of bar crowds but the New Moon Bar in Wilton Manors was special. A casual watering hole for the local lesbian community, it was as friendly and warm a place as she'd ever visited. Teddie had found it on the Internet a couple of years ago when she came along for the ride on the last recertification jaunt, and had dropped a week's worth of pay in the tip jar of a cute bartender. Julia didn't know a soul here but that didn't matter. She wasn't here for conversation, but it was impossible not to feel welcome.

Not that she wanted to be welcomed by anyone. She was content just to watch people and vicariously share their fun. From the size of the crowd, it appeared that happy hour started at four o'clock on Saturdays.

The crowd was diverse but no one in the bar compared to Ashley, at least not anyone who caused others to stop what they were doing and stare. There was, however, one woman who appeared to be holding court at a table near the front door. An attractive redhead, she had the rapt attention of the other four women, whether she was talking, listening or laughing along.

"You'd best forget about that one. I found out firsthand she's a heartbreaker." The low, deep voice belonged to a woman named McDowell…at least that was the name on her well-worn camouflage army shirt. She was cute in a rugged sort of way, darkly tanned with brown eyes and short bleached hair. "I'm Kris."

"Julia," she replied flatly, doing her best not to show any interest. "I was just noticing that she reminded me of someone."

"Queenie reminds all of us of someone. Unfortunately it's the woman we can't have."

It was certainly ironic to hear Kris talking about the redhead the same way Julia might have talked about Ashley. Now that she'd been caught staring, she was self-conscious about looking at anyone else, leaving her no choice but to converse. "To the one that got away." She clinked her beer bottle to Kris's mixed drink.

"There's more chairs in the back if you don't mind being outside. Another bar too." Kris stumbled into the wall twice on her way down the hall.

Julia had no idea why she was following this total stranger, who was apparently drunker than her speech had let on. She didn't want company but she nonetheless plunked herself down in a white plastic chair next to the parking lot.

Kris drew a pack of Newports from her breast pocket and

lit one, contorting her face to blow the smoke sideways. "So what's your story? I know you're not from around here because I practically live here and I've never seen you before."

"I'm in town for a cosmetology seminar. The state makes us take courses to renew our license."

"In town from where?"

"Over on the Gulf Coast." Resigned to make small talk, she drew the line at sharing personal information. "What about you? Why do you torture yourself by coming to a place where you have to watch your old girlfriend flirt with everybody?"

"I can't swing a dead cat without hitting an old girlfriend. But I don't drive and this is my neighborhood, so we all just suck it up and peacefully coexist."

Good to know she didn't drive, since she could barely walk. "What kind of work do you do?"

"Just little jobs, mostly. I'm a disabled veteran. What, you thought I got this at a yard sale?" she asked, rubbing her fingers over her nametag. "Staff Sergeant Kristine McDowell, but you can call me what everyone else does—the crazy lady with the nail in her head."

Julia was about to offer up a sardonic salute and decided against it. "A nail?"

"From an IED outside Ramadi." Kris pulled the hair back on her left temple to reveal a five-inch scar that arched over her ear. "Screws up my balance, but apparently it's plugging a hole that keeps my brain from oozing out so I'm stuck with it."

With no small amount of guilt, Julia discarded her disparaging thoughts that Kris was merely drunk and raised her bottle again for a genuine salute. "This probably sounds lame, but thanks for your sacrifice...seriously."

Kris stubbed out her cigarette in a red plastic ashtray, downed her drink and signaled the bartender for another. "You're welcome...seriously. I was proud to do it. At least I ended up with something they could see so they couldn't deny me benefits. The real problems don't show up in x-rays, which means Uncle Sam won't pay to fix you."

"What do you mean by real problems?"

"Different stuff." She glanced from side to side and lowered her voice. "One of our guys got home after three years of dodging roadside bombs and killed himself with his own gun. Two more are in jail for beating up their wives. We're talking paranoia and uncontrollable rage over little shit that isn't even real. All I know is when my jaw starts twitching, I need to get the hell out of there before somebody gets hurt." Kris squeezed the hand of the cocktail waitress who delivered her drink, passing her a ten-dollar bill for a six-dollar tab. "Now you see why I have so many ex-girlfriends."

What she saw was that Kris was putting women at risk every time she went out on a date. Ashley held people at arm's length to protect them from her dramatic mood swings. "Don't you ever worry that you might hurt somebody?"

"I always make it a rule never to go out with the same woman more than a couple of times…three at the most. It's a Catch-22, you know? If I really start to care about somebody—like Queenie—then I don't want her to see that side of me. Hell, I don't even talk about this shit with anybody except with people like you, who I probably won't ever see again after today."

Julia found herself nodding along in agreement, again thinking of her own situation. But she couldn't talk about the difficulties in her relationship with anyone, not even her best friends.

"One of the things I liked about Queenie was she could take care of herself. She doesn't put up with shit from anybody so I always knew she'd walk out if I ever went off on her."

"Seems to me you ought to just tell people what the deal is. If your girlfriend knew what to expect, maybe she'd be sympathetic."

"I don't want sympathy." Kris rolled her eyes with palpable sarcasm. "It's obvious you don't get how scary this is."

"What's obvious is you're playing all these little games with the women you date. It doesn't matter what they want or how it makes them feel. Two or three dates and *bzzzt*! Time's up. And they probably go off wondering what they did wrong and why you never called again." Julia was well aware of the rise in her voice, and also that her frustration was with Ashley and not Kris. "What do you expect when you're basically telling them to get lost?"

"What am I supposed to say? 'I'm fucked in the head and there's a good chance I'll make your life miserable, but since I'm a narcissistic asshole, I'd like it if you stuck around anyway.' Even if somebody's stupid enough to say yes, I'd feel guilty all the time for making her live in a powder keg. And if I ever did hurt her..." She blew out a breath and shook her head, unable to finish the thought.

Until now Julia hadn't fully appreciated that Ashley's reluctance to have a relationship wasn't only because of her fears. Her sense of compassion wouldn't allow her to ask Julia to give up sex. *I can't put you through that*, she had said. But Ashley and Kris both had tried to let someone into their life, which meant they wanted it whether they admitted it or not. "I get that you're scared of what you might do and what she'll think if you lose it. But you keep dating so I know you're not giving up."

At that instant Queenie passed by their table and squeezed Kris's shoulder affectionately before continuing out to the parking lot.

Kris stared after her, and with the corner of her mouth turned up in an appreciative grin she replied, "That's because there just might be a woman out there who's worth it. And if I'm really lucky she won't take no for an answer."

Chapter Twenty-Six

At least Cassandra was having a good laugh…if they allowed laughing in hell.

Ashley wondered if she'd find out firsthand someday. It wasn't as if she had lived a life without wickedness. Who even knew how many people she had stepped over in her single-minded ambition? There was Lori Spearman, for sure. And the woman before her at TV4 who lost her job because Norman Jarvis came in as the news director and brought his hand-picked anchor from the network. To say nothing of all the people she'd made to feel insignificant because she never showed them more than her plastic persona, the one that excused her from treating them like real people.

They could all have a nice laugh now. What goes around comes around.

She tucked her feet beneath her on the wicker love seat and adjusted the crocheted throw around her shoulders. Anywhere else it would have been unseasonably warm for late February but this was normal for Tampa. Balmy weather was just around the corner and before long she'd be coming out here to the patio every evening.

The way her life was going, her evenings might soon be free. She was in the worst possible position going into contract negotiations next month—marginalized from the biggest story of the year, under threat of subpoena, and up against a young, attractive woman who was building audience every day alongside Rod Gilchrist at the anchor desk. Ashley could already envision how it would play out. She'd hand over the mantle in a smiling two-minute signoff encouraging viewers to join her at noon on weekdays, where her guests would break down such fascinating topics as what women think about during sex.

"Just take me out and shoot me," she said aloud.

At least Cassandra wasn't around to taunt her this time. Good news, since Ashley had let her figure go, defiantly telling herself it was everyone else's fault for caring about it. And while the whole world caught the social network wave, she couldn't even manage the pretense of caring how many people "followed" her Tweets or "liked" her on Facebook. She'd gone with smart and serious over bubbly and hip, and until this morning in Jarvis's office, thought TV4 was right there with her. It all added up to Cassandra's ultimate error. She had left the door open for someone else to outflank her and take control.

No matter how many twists and turns of logic she took, she couldn't lay any of this particular failure at Cassandra's feet. If she had covered her butt with the hacker, Jarvis could have used that to convince Carl her experience mattered. And maybe if she hadn't been so vain about being invited to share the stage with Katie Couric, she would have stopped to think that no news anchor worth her salt goes out of pocket on the eve of breaking a big investigative story. None of that was Cassandra's doing.

What Cassandra had done, though, was steal her lifeboat, her parachute, her safety net, reaching once more—from the grave, no less—to make sure nothing was there to cushion the fall. Being with Julia might have been worth losing the anchor desk, just like getting out of Maple Ridge had been worth all the humiliation and wretchedness she had endured to make it happen. Who cared what kind of nonsense you had to put up with at work all day if you had someone who loved you waiting at home? Cassandra had made that impossible.

A faint gust of chilly air stirred the fan palms and Ashley reluctantly drew herself off the love seat to take her pity-fest inside. As she shuffled into her shoes, a swaying stem in her garden caught her eye and she dropped her throw to investigate. It was unmistakably a rosebud, still wrapped in green petals and so tiny she might not have noticed it for days had it not teetered in the breeze. Four tries, and with Julia's help it finally took— and to think she'd almost given up. She ought to have known by now that everything took perseverance, luck and, for better or worse, a hand from someone else.

The digital clock on Julia's dashboard read a quarter past ten when she rolled into Ashley's driveway. It would have been sooner if not for the twenty minutes she'd spent talking her way out of a speeding ticket on Alligator Alley. She doubted the trooper's contention that she'd been doing eighty-five, but secretly conceded it was possible, since she'd been focused solely on getting back to Tampa as soon as she could.

By blowing off tomorrow's session, she had effectively wasted the past two days in Ft. Lauderdale since she only got credit if she completed the course. She couldn't be bothered with four more hours on the looming return of Big Hair. Arguably the most important moment in her life would happen in the next ten minutes.

Whether from nervousness or spending the last five hours on the road, her knees wobbled as she climbed out of her car, and she paced the driveway for a couple of minutes before gathering enough courage to approach the house. Before she could ring the bell, the porch light came on and the door swung open.

Ashley was already dressed for bed in a pale green gown and bathrobe, which she pulled tight around her neck in apparent modesty. Gone was the anguished look of resignation she had worn when they last saw each other, replaced by what Julia thought might actually be a glimmer of relief. Whatever it was, she was holding open the door and unmistakably inviting her in.

Julia had practiced in the car how she would fend off Ashley's doubts and even her outright resistance, but only Kris's words came to mind.

"Ashley, I'm not going to take no for an answer."

With a soft chuckle, Ashley slipped her arms around Julia's waist and rested her head on her shoulder. "I don't even care what the question is. I'm just glad you're here."

"I'm serious. No more of this bouncing around not knowing what we want. I want you, and I'm not going to be scared off or pushed away unless you can look me in the eye and tell me honestly that you don't love me."

"I do love you." Ashley squeezed tighter and nestled her face against Julia's neck. "You just need to know that things can get pretty crazy around here...especially inside my head."

"I know what I'm getting into, but if anything like that ever happens again, I'm going to pick up and go in the other room. You can stay in there and cry and scream by yourself all you want, but when you step out from behind that door, I'm still going to be here."

For someone like Ashley who had suffered real trauma at the hands of a woman who wouldn't hear the word no, her promise needed to strike just the right balance of commitment and respect.

Julia tipped her chin upward to look into her eyes. "I'll never push you to do anything that makes you uncomfortable."

"Unless I need you to?"

The gentle plea was a reminder of the pressure Ashley put on herself to be a complete lover, even if it meant revisiting her fears. "We don't even have to talk about that now, Ashley. There is so much we can share that doesn't carry all that stress. Someday it'll happen, and I can wait for it as long as I'm with you."

She cupped Ashley's face in her hands and delivered a kiss, closing her eyes to savor the warmth of their lips sliding together and the exquisite feel of Ashley's tongue dancing with hers. It wasn't a moment for heated passion, but she never expected to feel Ashley suddenly pull away again.

"What if it never happens? What if I can't do it?"

"It is what it is, sweetheart," she said, cradling her head once again to her shoulder. "If I knew right now that we'd never make love again, it wouldn't change the way I feel."

"Do you hear yourself?" Ashley asked wistfully. "Making love is supposed to be the mountaintop. The whole human race revolves around it."

"Love is the mountaintop, all by itself. If we have to, we'll find other ways to express it." During the long moment of silence that followed, Julia made peace with her words, knowing that simply sharing her life with Ashley was truly what mattered most.

"Look." Ashley pointed to the garden. "We finally have a rosebud."

Chapter Twenty-Seven

In the ladies' room at TV4, Ashley blotted her lipstick—a dark pink shade called Blazing Sangria—and checked to make sure she hadn't smeared it on her teeth. Her hair looked fantastic, thanks to an early morning appointment with her personal stylist. Julia had feathered the sides and fluffed them out a bit with the curling iron…something about big hair being back in vogue. Sergio would have a fit but she didn't care. The new rule was Every Woman for Herself.

She had come to work early to demand a meeting with Carl. Armed to the teeth with viewer data that showed a recent rise in ratings—so much that they threatened even those asinine clowns at Channel 20—she stood ready to refute his every objection. She was tired of his weasely weaseling and thought it was high time to show him how lucky he was to have Ashley Giraud in the anchor chair. By her calculation of advertising rates, she had earned the station millions of dollars in revenues, while picking up prestigious awards for their news team.

And what did Carl have? Sixteen calls to the station on Friday night. She knew because she had gotten Lee Ann at switchboard to pull the phone logs. On any given night they averaged twelve—nine of which came from the same people who called every single night to comment—so it could hardly be argued that four extra calls on a story this big qualified as "lighting up the switchboard." When important news happened, viewers wanted to hear it from people they trusted, and they trusted Ashley Giraud.

Squaring her shoulders, she gave herself a steely look. She was loaded for bear.

As she reached for the door, it suddenly flung open and she found herself face to face with Mallory, who was dressed in a dark brown suit with understated jewelry. It was what a true professional wore when the news was serious, and Ashley had dressed the same in navy blue.

"Gosh, Ashley...I don't know what to say."

"About what?" she asked coolly.

"I just feel so awful about what happened on Friday night. You've been working so hard on this story."

She didn't blame Mallory for seizing the opportunity. Envied her for being a twenty-five-year-old knockout, yes. But not blame. "You shouldn't feel bad, Mallory. You were just doing your job."

"No, I wasn't. I felt like I was doing yours...except not as well." She ran a hand through her perfect hair and lowered her eyes as if genuinely contrite. "I wasn't prepped or anything. If Jarvis hadn't faxed the news copy over, I would've frozen on the spot. I found out later from Aaron that you'd written all of it. I swear I didn't know."

Ashley remembered the day she'd gone into Jarvis's office with the big news that the hacker was Jack Staley's nephew. He had praised her instincts, and she walked out feeling like Helen Thomas. What she wouldn't give to see Jarvis in the big chair instead of Carl. "He saved my butt a time or two. Just keep doing your job and we'll let the chips fall."

They shared an awkward hug and Mallory walked out, apparently forgetting to pee.

Julia pulled off Causeway Boulevard into a parking lot to check her directions. One of these days she would break down and buy herself a smartphone, or maybe a car with a GPS that would scream at her when she made a wrong turn, which was what she'd just done. It would also help if she could read Elaine's handwriting.

Her cell phone rang, and when she saw who was calling she laughed out loud. Sergio Flores. No doubt he was in a snit about Ashley's new hairdo. But she was willing to take her lumps for it. Ashley had left her shop looking like a million dollars. A million-five actually.

"Haaallo," she said, drawing it out to show she already knew she was in trouble.

From his friendly greeting, she could only surmise that he hadn't seen Ashley yet. "I was wondering if you might be able to do us a favor here at TV4. One of our reporters, Mallory Foster, needs a new style. Her hair is long and straight, and we think it makes her face look too thin. Is there a time…this afternoon perhaps…when she could drop by for a whole new look?"

Julia was floored. Even if she had all the time in the world, she wouldn't spend it doing Mallory Foster's hair, not after what Ashley had told her about the uproar at the station. "I'm sorry, Sergio. I'm tied up today."

"I know it's really late notice, but there is a very good chance that whoever makes time for Ms. Foster today is going to get a very nice contract for future services."

Hearing his arrogant tone, it was all she could do to be polite. "I'm sure you'll find someone, Mr. Flores. Most of the mall shops take walk-ins."

She backtracked two blocks and turned south into an unincorporated part of the county. A half-mile later she spotted Elaine's Prius in front of a small brick house, its fenced-in backyard shaded by towering oak trees. When her car door slammed, it set off a chorus of barking dogs in the distance.

Elaine met her on the front porch accompanied by a rugged looking sixty-year-old woman who wore jeans, work boots and a T-shirt that said Greater Tampa Greyhound Rescue. "Thanks for coming, Jules. This is Donna. She has somebody she wants you to meet."

They walked through the kitchen and onto the back porch, where Julia pulled her friend aside. "I haven't agreed to anything. I live in a cereal box, remember?"

"Bijou won't care. She lived her whole life in a crate."

She shouldn't have come. An off-the-cuff remark yesterday about Henry's sweet disposition had led to Elaine's insistence that she adopt a greyhound of her own, which she answered with equal insistence that she wasn't looking for a pet right now. Their compromise was that she would check it out and maybe lend a hand by putting up flyers in her shop. Now she was in for an hour-long guilt trip.

Donna led the way across the yard. "I've got six right now, but I get new ones in about every week. We move them through, though, all up and down the east coast."

"So all these dogs…you find them homes." It was easier dealing with Donna than Elaine, because she didn't know which buttons to push.

"Yeah, but I'm looking for somebody local to take in Bijou." They walked toward a shaded row of pens near the back fence. Three dogs were running free and had joined their parade, and two more came to greet them at the edge of their respective pens. All seemed friendly and rambunctious. "These dogs that go up north have to switch cars four, five, even six times between here and where they're picked up by their new owners. I can't put Bijou through that. She's afraid of new people."

Julia followed her to the last pen, where a gorgeous speckled greyhound—a brindle, Elaine had called it—cowered in the corner. Her right ear was freshly bandaged.

"Most of these dogs end up here after racing a few seasons. Once they start losing they get retired, and if they're lucky, somebody brings them here instead of a pharmaceutical lab… or worse, cramming them into a metal shed with forty other retired dogs right before the air conditioner just happens to give out."

"Amazing how many times you read about that," Elaine grumbled.

"My guess is Bijou didn't take to training because she's just two years old. I suspect they tried a little bit of everything. She's got a bone chip on her back leg where she probably got hit with a stick and a few raw patches on her flank from a cattle prod. They found her at a rest area near Ruskin three days ago."

"What's wrong with her ear?" Julia asked softly.

"Purebred greyhounds get tattooed so you can identify the owner. Whoever put her out cut half her ear off so she couldn't be traced back."

Julia was horrified to think anyone could be so cruel. "No wonder she's afraid."

"She'll let you pet her if you want. She's a real sweetie. She just doesn't know who to trust."

Bijou lowered her head and visibly trembled as Julia slowly approached, but made no attempt to move away. Her smooth coat was cool to the touch from the concrete floor.

"Did somebody hurt you, pretty girl? It's okay now," Julia cooed softly. She was careful to avoid the ear, opting instead to scratch the white tuft at the center of Bijou's chest. "You want to be somebody's baby, don't you? Elaine over there…she's got a nice big house and you could play with Henry."

"I'd take her in a heartbeat if I could, but Henry's afraid of other dogs. Oh, and Robyn would kill me."

Donna roughhoused with the dogs on the outside of the pen. "Most of these animals are socialized with other dogs, and people too. But every now and then we get one that's gotten off to a bad start, like Henry or Bijou. They need something special."

"They deserve it for all the misery those bastards put them through," Elaine added.

Bijou tipped to the side and extended a leg, closing her eyes as Julia stroked her chest.

"I can't promise she won't be a lot of trouble, but I think she's got a lot of love in her," Donna went on. "If you're looking for a dog that you know is going to be fun and easy-going, take your pick from any of these others. Bijou needs somebody special."

Julia could see that, and from the pleading look in Bijou's eyes, she would do just fine.

"God, I look like a drunken raccoon," Ashley lamented to herself, once again from the ladies' room. Black smudges circled her swollen eyes, which at least diverted attention from her puffy red nose and lips. She had finally gotten her tears under control, and once she put her face back in order, that was it. No more crying today.

Back in her office, she found a text message from Julia: *how did it go w/carl?*

There was no way to condense her morning into just a few characters, so she dialed Julia's number and sank low in her chair so she could watch the newsroom without anyone watching her.

Julia answered on the third ring. "Hold on, I'm pulling over."

"Where are you?"

"Long story. You'll never believe what I just did, but I'm more interested in you. What happened in your meeting?"

The newsroom was coming to life with everyone ramping up for the six o'clock show.

"It was probably the worst meeting of my life, but I can't go into it right now. Maybe we can meet for a bite around seven."

"It'll be okay, Ashley...we'll make it okay."

"I know."

"Come to my place for dinner. I have something to show you."

"Will do." Jarvis walked past her window, his face buried in what appeared to be today's wire reports. "I've got to go, hon. Wish me luck."

Just as she stepped into the hallway, Tim and Mallory entered Jarvis's office, no doubt to put the finishing touches on how they planned to cover this afternoon's arraignments from the courthouse. She busied herself at the copy machine until their brief meeting ended, and then scurried into Jarvis's office and closed the door.

"Ash, I'm glad you're here. We were just talking about you." He motioned toward his thinning hair while looking at hers. "You did something different."

"I need to talk to you."

"Yeah, me too. I think we're going to go from the studio tonight instead of on location, and I thought it would be great if you could do the spot feed from the courthouse. Looks like the arraignment is set for about five o'clock."

So he wanted her for cutaways, where she could chat live with Mallory and Rod from the scene. Last week that had been Mallory's job. "You know I'm a team player, Jarvis. I'll do whatever's best for TV4."

"I know that about you. You've always been a pro." He smiled at her sadly. "I know this is tough for you, Ash. You did some of your best work on this story."

"Yeah, it's been quite a ride these last couple of weeks. First I find out Lamar Davidson is asking around back in Missouri about my father. Then the story I've been working on for almost three months leaks out on the one day I happened to be out of town. Next thing I know, somebody else is sitting in my chair."

He came around his desk and squeezed her shoulders in a show of support. "Don't worry about any of that. It's just for a few days, and I'm already working on Carl to get his nose out of the newsroom so we can do our jobs. We'll get this worked out soon."

"And on top of that, I find out my best friend's been stabbing me in the back." She stepped out of his reach and laid a manila folder on the corner of his desk. "I got curious about how many calls it took to qualify as lighting up the switchboard, so I got Lee Ann to pull the phone logs for Friday. I wasn't impressed, I have to say."

"Hmm." He shook his head and went back behind his desk, glancing down as she opened the folder. "They told me it was a lot. Maybe somebody was exaggerating."

"Did you know there's an electronic record of all the calls and faxes that go out? Here's a copy of what you sent Mallory." She spread the papers as if they were playing cards. "These are your handwritten notes on my questions."

"Come on, Ash. This isn't like you. You're part of a news team and we were in a bind. I couldn't expect Mallory to come up with those questions on the spot. She's still wet behind the ears. Is this about her getting credit for your work?"

It was all she could do to keep from storming around his desk to slap that indignant look off his face. "What it's about is the phone logs, Jarvis. Your fax to Mallory went out forty minutes before Kevin Finley's call even came in. But it was only ten minutes after somebody made a star sixty-seven call to Lamar Davidson from your extension." That was the code they had to dial to prevent their station number from showing up in someone's caller ID. Reporters did it so their sources wouldn't dodge their calls, but Jarvis had done so to make an anonymous call.

"I don't know what you're talking about."

"I think you do. You're the one who leaked our story. One of the other tidbits I thought was interesting…Aaron called me an hour and a half before you did. You knew where I was, and a good newsman like you could have figured out that all you had to do was call the hotel and get a message to me. I would have gone straight to the courthouse. But you knew that. You sat on it just to freeze me out."

Jarvis threw up his hands, but the fact that he couldn't look her in the eye told her everything she needed to know.

"All this time I thought you were my champion. Turns out my biggest fan is Carl Terzian. You know, he actually admitted how much he likes seeing my cleavage on the nightly news, but all that business about me being fat? He couldn't care less. Imagine that. His wife loves me and so do all her friends, and that—plus the ratings points I bring him—keeps Carl very happy."

His face had grown beet red, but he tightened his lips defiantly. "Look, it's my job to shake things up every now and then. We have to stay fresh, and looking hip is all part of the game. I don't make the rules about what our audience wants. I only said all that stuff was coming from Carl so it wouldn't hurt your feelings. We're friends, Ashley."

"Oh, spare me. None of this was about me. It was about you currying favor so you might score with a twenty-five-year-old. I've got news for you. Anchor desk or not, Mallory Foster would find you repulsive. There might be women out there who would do something like that for their big break, but the minute it's over, I promise you they'll be in the bathroom puking their guts out."

Defeated, he tossed his pen on the desk and rubbed his face briskly. "Okay, what's it going to take to fix this?"

"One of us leaves TV4 today. Carl wants that to be you."

Chapter Twenty-Eight

The pungent aroma of garlic hit Ashley in the face the moment she opened the back door to the salon. It was spaghetti night, which meant she'd have to cover herself with one of Julia's robes while she ate to keep from dropping dinner on her light gray dress.

Robyn, already barefoot and with her shirttail out, met her with the usual burst of exuberance. "Look who's here. It's the Face of Tampa Bay."

Ashley rolled her eyes as they traded pecks on the cheek, and continued on to give Julia a kiss on the lips. "You guys really need to get a life."

"Why should we when we can live vicariously through yours?" Elaine asked, waving a copy of the *Guardian* from the couch, where she was practically obscured by her very large hound.

"What's with Henry?"

"You should have seen it," Teddie said. She hopped out of the styling chair to give Ashley a quick hug. "He was in the kitchen getting a drink when Elaine started sweet-talking Bijou.

Next thing we know, Mr. Jealous here is climbing all over her. He thinks he's a Chihuahua or something."

The night Ashley had gone to Julia's place for dinner and found a skittish greyhound hiding underneath the kitchen table, it was love at first sight. "And where is my little Bijou?"

Toenails clicked softly on the tile as the brindle emerged from beneath Julia's styling station. For a second, it almost seemed she was looking toward Henry for permission before nuzzling Ashley's outstretched hand.

"Who's got the sweetest kisses?" she cooed, lowering her cheek for a lick. "My baby girl does, that's who."

Julia sighed dramatically. "I always dreamed of winning second place."

Robyn had her own copy of the paper and was reading in the kitchen, where she occasionally stopped to stir the pasta. "You probably don't want to hear this, Ashley, but this is a damn fine profile."

Ashley had finally consented—relented was more like it—to Lamar Davidson's interview after learning Jarvis had pushed it on him only in hopes of undermining her public profile and professional standing. It was to have been another arrow in his quiver to convince Carl they needed to move Mallory to the anchor desk as quickly as possible before they suffered a PR calamity. Instead it had turned into a glowing bio-sketch that tracked her humble beginnings all the way to becoming "arguably Tampa's favorite newscaster, and hands down, the best."

"I love how you put this," Robyn said. "I'm going to steal this quote for my book."

"Call me Ashley," she said, which I immediately took as a sign she was not only gracious, but also unthreatened by the notion of elevating an irreverent word-seller like yours truly to the level of her journalistic peer. "No, I mean in your article. Call me Ashley. Miss Giraud sounds aloof and pretentious, and I don't ever want my viewers to think of me that way. I want to be somebody they feel like they know."

"How come you never told us about your father?" Elaine asked.

"Do I even need to answer that? It's not exactly the kind of thing a person brags about."

"But you told Lamar."

"Jarvis told Lamar. That's how he hooked him into doing this story in the first place, except Jarvis wanted it to be a hit piece."

"That rat bastard," Teddie growled. "Give me his address, Ashley. Bijou and I will drop off a couple of presents."

"You're too late. His new address is in Buffalo, New York. I think next January will be punishment enough."

"Hey, where's my photo credit?" Robyn demanded. "That's a prize-winning picture."

For her forty-second birthday in March, she accomplished something many of us only lie about when she landed a ninety-pound tarpon off Boca Grande, a feat immortalized by her co-workers when they shared a photo with their six o'clock viewers (below right). As with everything, she was characteristically humble. "To say I actually caught him would be generous. I just happened to be holding the rod that held the hook that held the pinfish that he happened to feel like eating." One would think a trophy like this one would adorn the wall inside her Ballast Point home. "He was kind enough to pose, but then he had to run...something about having other lines in the water."

"You're so clever," Julia said, smacking her lips in Ashley's direction.

Elaine nudged Henry from her lap and flipped through the paper. "I'm really proud of you for how you handled the lesbian thing, Ash."

Though loath to discuss her brief, much-publicized affair with KBC news host Valerie Reynolds twelve years ago, Ashley is refreshingly candid about her sexual orientation. "I suppose I realized I was a lesbian about the same age most other girls figured out they weren't. I've never really known anything else so I can't tell you how that makes me different."

On a tour of her garden, which she tends herself, Ashley was especially proud to show off her hybrid tea rose, a striking blend of orange and pink. "It took me five tries to get that color. It's called a Special Occasion, and it was only after my girlfriend added her mojo that it finally took off."

Henry wasn't having any part of being ignored and crumpled the paper as he crawled back into her lap.

Julia poked Teddie, who was back in the chair getting her tips bleached. "Read some more. We're getting to the best part."

The woman in Ashley's life is Julia Whitethorn, owner of Rhapsody, a boutique salon in Old Hyde Park. Loyal TV4 viewers might recognize it as the shop once credited with doing their star anchor's hair. The tagline no longer appears, but Ashley confirms she hasn't switched stylists. "It's customary to run those little ads at the end of a broadcast, but when it's someone you're dating, it starts to look like a conflict of interest. Nobody wanted that so we cut it. I never asked Julia, though. She might have preferred to keep the tagline and date somebody else."

"You wouldn't believe how many of my customers noticed that and asked me if we'd stopped doing your hair."

Ashley broke off a piece of hot garlic bread and fed it to Julia. "Don't worry. No one else is ever touching my hair."

"What's that, Bijou?" Julia chuckled as the dog's good ear went up and she slinked off the couch to investigate. No matter how many times Ashley came through the door from the garage, Bijou always seemed surprised.

"There's my baby girl," Ashley declared, dropping her purse and keys on the kitchen counter to give Bijou a vigorous rubdown.

Julia drew herself up from the couch and stretched. "I used to feel so special because I was the only one you kissed."

"You're the only one who gets tongue," Ashley said, and proved it with a slow, wet kiss.

"You can't see it but my tail's wagging."

"I can feel it though."

Julia wiggled her hips as Ashley's hands wandered her backside. The exchange, like many they shared, was flirtatious but not overly sexual. The playful element seemed to head off Ashley's anxiety.

True to her promise, Julia did her best not to watch for hints that Ashley was growing more comfortable with the idea of making love, though it had proven more difficult than she ever imagined. The signs of their growing intimacy were undeniable, and it wasn't just these familiar touches. They slept together now—all night long and often entwined—though it was Julia who found herself awake at four a.m., sometimes after erotic dreams. Then as Ashley slept, she would relive the moment when she held her soft, beautiful breasts and felt the walls of her warmth.

"Let me get into my PJs. I want to talk with you about something," Ashley said, jarring her from her lustful thoughts.

Julia returned to the couch as Ashley went into her walk-in closet to undress, another routine that had changed now that she stayed over most nights. Token privacy was enough now for Ashley, where she would go behind the door but not close it, allowing Julia the occasional glimpse of her glorious body. And she seemed nonplussed about the fact that Julia never sought privacy when she readied for bed.

Ashley turned off the lights and nestled into her spot on the couch, flicking her fingers so Bijou would come over to lie beside them. "I've been thinking all day about Lamar's article. Every time I turned around, somebody at the station was asking about you—even Carl. They all seemed so happy for me. I don't think it ever occurred to anybody that I might have a personal life."

"I heard about it all day too. Suzy showed the paper to everybody that walked in the shop."

"It feels good." She rolled away from Julia so she could pet Bijou. "I want you to move in with me, but you have to bring this dog too."

"Wow." Julia hadn't seen that coming. "Both of us, huh? I could see you wanting Bijou, but me too?"

"Seriously, Jules. Do you feel like you need space that's all yours, or time apart from me? Because I don't. It bums me out when I'm driving home at night and know you aren't going to be waiting for me. I want you here all the time."

"I never need space away from you." It was all Julia could do not to leap off the couch with joy. Just knowing Ashley was ready for a commitment like this made all the unanswered questions about their future moot. "You realize that once we move in here, you're stuck with both of us?"

"I want to be stuck." Ashley kissed her hand and curled it into her chest. Still looking down at Bijou, she continued, "I don't hear Cassandra's voice in my head anymore, not since the day I confronted Jarvis. It's weird...like I had a chance to finally tell somebody how it felt to be taken by a creepy predator. If I could have said those words to her twenty-five years ago, my whole life might have been different."

"Your whole life *is* different now." She burrowed closer to nuzzle Ashley's neck, inhaling deeply the scent of Fracas. "And so is mine."

"I never thought I'd have this," Ashley said quietly. "Everything I knew about love came from the mind of an infatuated child. You've shown me the beautiful side...and maybe one of these days I'll know what it really means to make love with someone."

For something so grand, Julia would give her all the time she needed. "Everything we do is making love as far as I'm concerned. You don't ever have to worry about that."

"That's the thing, Julia. For the first time in my life, I'm not worrying."

Bella Books, Inc.

Women. Books. Even Better Together.

P.O. Box 10543
Tallahassee, FL 32302

Phone: 800-729-4992
www.bellabooks.com